AWARENESS

BY

TEAGAN BRODY

ISBN: 978-1-946547-10-1
eBook ISBN: 978-1-946547-11-8

ALSO BY TEAGAN BRODY
Awakening
Fugue

For those who realize there is but one meaning and one destiny in life, no matter the size, shape, color or origin of one's physical being and as always,
For Tarod – you make every struggle worth my while.

"Each person is born and will die. It's what one does in between the two that makes a life." – Teagan Brody

"Each person has a purpose. Your duty to yourself and the Universe is to find your purpose and fulfill it." – Joss Tobin

Prologue

Jarba cringed as the dark Jess knelt beside the Samarean Prince. The creature took his hand and cradled it close, staring hard at the unconscious being. Jarba wished there was some way other than allowing the thing near him. Despite the fact that the creature could save the Prince, Jarba cringed at the feel of simply being in its presence. It had been a hybrid before and had then become Jess. But Jarba didn't care if the thing had transitioned. Seeing it touching her beloved Prince drew such a taste of disgust within her that she barely controlled the urge to spit! After several moments, the Jess raised its dark head, its wild, almost-black hair strangely subdued as it said aloud in a strange accent, "Him die."

The disgust that had taken over inside Jarba was now replaced by a fierce anger. This creature, who before had communicated quite well telepathically but who clearly did not understand the spoken Samarean tongue, was the only hope Jarba and her people had and she would not cow in fear to its face. Instead, she barked, "You will save him!"

The Jess tilted its head as it considered the interrogator's words. "You people... lost," it finally said, as if that single word was enough to end the need for the Prince to be saved.

Jarba turned off every emotion but one – anger. The meaning behind each word the creature had uttered was clear. The Samarean were done, according to this being, and Jarba would simply have to accept her fate. Rage bloomed inside the interrogator and took over every part of her as she grabbed hold of the being's upper arm, intent on strong-arming the thing into helping the Prince. Immediately, several strands of hair lashed out, cutting wherever they touched. Jarba practically flew several feet away from the creature, already nursing wounds she feared would now lead to her own demise.

She recalled what the Joss had said the one named Hantsushept had discovered about wounds caused by the dangerous hair of those who had transformed. As the pain from her fresh wounds throbbed, she wondered if this was how everything was to end. Her beloved Prince would die, as would she, and her people would be doomed to an unimaginable fate without ever discovering what had happened to the others.

Cradling her wounded hand and arm, she demanded through gritted teeth, "You must help us!"

The creature's dimly-glowing eyes narrowed, its gaze focusing on the interrogator's wounded arm. "Bring Tobin and I do."

"And if I do not?" Jarba demanded with incredulity.

The hair on the creature's head came alive as the Jess slowly raised its gaze to stare directly into the interrogator's eyes. It shrugged and said carelessly, "Then you and this one die."

The Samarean Interrogator pulled her wounded appendage closer as she focused once more on the ailing Prince. The Joss himself had probably caused all of this. But now he was ill and this vile creature apparently believed it could save him. It was certainly the only one who could save the Prince and possibly Jarba now as well. She knew the Samarean would need both the Prince and whatever information the Joss could give them to make it out of this alive. They could survive without Jarba, but the Prince... the people would need him to get through whatever lay ahead.

With a heavy heart, she knew she was beaten. A little of the fear she had kept tightly locked away now crept up to the surface as she turned to a nearby guard. The guards were to return with the Joss so that the creature could heal both the Prince and its Joss. In a flash, they were off to do her bidding.

"I shall return your Joss," Jarba informed the Jess. "But you must heal the Prince and give us the answers we need."

The enigmatic dark little creature cocked its head. "You not like answer," it softly warned.

Jarba hesitated. The energy coming off the being felt odd to her. All at once, the Samarean interrogator detected care, pity and a smattering of hope surrounding the Jess and it confused her. Her first instinct was to demand an explanation from the being. But before she could get the words out, the guards returned with the unconscious Joss. He was dumped unceremoniously onto the floor directly before the creature. Immediately, it seized upon its mate, its hands and hair caressing and touching the unconscious body.

Jarba felt almost as if she should look away, for the scene she was witnessing was intimate, private, and she felt very out of place. She allowed the moment to stretch only a little before stepping forward and demanding, "Now you will tend to the Prince!"

The Jess raised its weary eyes to the much larger unconscious form lying beside the Joss. Only one of the two could receive the life-giving energies inside her, but how could the Jess choose? As this debate raged within her mind, a slow flow of sub-conscious thoughts and memories trickled in from her Joss. Tobin's body was already pulling on her energies, strengthening and syphoning more energy from her as the seconds ticked by. He was her Joss and she would willingly give all the energy she possessed to help him live. But these were his people. He was half-Samarean. He had come here to help them however he could and, as his Jess, she felt every emotion he did. She knew he would want her to help them, no matter the cost.

Could she do it? That was the ultimate question. To do so would be to stretch her abilities farther than she had ever dared, to keep her Joss alive while also keeping alive a much larger alien Sephor. She honestly did not know if she was capable of such a maneuver. She would need to remain connected with Tobin's mind for the vital information the Samarean needed and for his communication abilities, for he was fluent in their strange tongue. She would simultaneously have to limit the amount of energy his body pulled from hers so that she could redirect enough toward the Samarean Prince's dying form to keep it alive.

This was what Tobin would want.

Steeling herself for the stringent pull she believed his body would make on her energy reserves the moment she restricted it, she consciously made the decision to redirect her energy flow to the strange creature lying beside her Joss. The moment she exerted her will, limiting the supply of energy currently flowing into Tobin while simultaneously opening herself up to the pull of the ailing Sephor, she was engulfed by a fierce rip tide of pain. His body pulled so hard on her energies that she felt as if she might be split in half. Not only had the pull from Tobin's body increased a hundred-fold on her, but now she experienced an insane pull from the alien Sephor male. Transformed or no, a Jess was not meant to sustain a Sephor!

A weak cry escaped her as her dark hair flailed around her, searching for the hungry foe that pulled so greedily upon her energies. Within seconds, the Jess feared this would be the end, for she felt herself weakening beyond her limits. She would soon be rendered unconscious if she didn't stop her energy flow now.

Just then, the pull from Tobin's body decreased and his mind-link with hers strengthened. In a flash, the Jess understood what had happened. Because of his alien half, Tobin was able to pull on the Samarean energies surrounding them to aid in the strengthening of his body. As long as enough of them remained nearby, their weak energy should sustain him until the Jess could take care of the Prince.

Without hesitation, she directed her full energy store toward the ailing alien, allowing it to flow freely into his body. Her hair settled down, wrapping itself around the Joss' limp arm and waist. The next few minutes were tense as the entire assemblage within the small enclosure waited with bated breath. When the Prince's body finally took a deep breath and then peacefully expelled it, the crowd breathed its own sigh of relief. The Prince's health was clearly improving. The Jess had done as she had been instructed.

Jarba's relief was short-lived, however, as she demanded, "Will he survive?"

The Jess did not even bother raising her eyes toward the Interrogator as she honestly said, "I can hold him only for so long. After that, without his mate, he will die."

The creatures increased fluency in the Samarean tongue went by unnoticed as this news hit hard. All within earshot gasped and the stench of fear filled the room.

"Then tell me how to reunite them!" Jarba screeched.

Throwing the demented alien a look of sheer ridicule, the Jess stopped short of telling this Interrogator to go to Hell. Random memories from Tobin's time off-world before he had met her slipped through the **Jess'** mind and her ire with the creature settled. Calmly, she spoke to all those present. "My **Joss** very much wanted you to understand what has happened so that you and your people may take appropriate measures to move forward from here. Only through knowledge of the past, of what has brought you to this point, will you truly understand your current situation and what you will need to do next."

Jarba spared one more glance toward her Prince. His color and breathing were much improved and, as she returned her attention to the darker female creature, she nodded for her to continue.

"Up to this point, Tobin has spoken of the first two Sephor pairs. But to get a full picture of how this affects the Samarean, and indeed was brought about in part by the Samarean, you must learn more about his life... as well as about the lives of a few others of whom he has not yet spoken." As interest appeared on the faces of those surrounding her, the **Jess** began her tale. "I will not bore you with the details of my first encounter with Tobin. Instead, I shall pick up at a point much closer to when our story truly began..."

Chapter 1

A cry sounded far overhead, echoing throughout the canyon. As the ear-piercing screech bounced off the stone walls, Tobin realized it was a bald eagle. The sharp echo soon faded, leaving only a memory of its existence.

The clumsy footsteps of the young female travelling with him were now the only break in the silence that rightfully belonged to the canyon. She was unaccustomed to such terrain and their progress was slow. Tobin had traversed this territory a thousand times over the past two hundred plus years and he knew every twist and turn. This trail was in one of the lesser-known areas of the canyon that humans had not yet discovered. Although he could make the journey in mere hours, he kept his pace slow to assist the girl through the more difficult spots. His keen eyes kept careful watch for hidden dangers.

The specific patterns within the multi-colored striations in the rock face told him it was not far now.

Rieko had never hiked before and Tobin knew she was still nervous about the situation. But at least she was here. It had taken longer than he had anticipated to convince her to accept her fate, but she had finally come around. He only hoped the Receiver would still be waiting at the drop-off point when they got there. Otherwise, what should only have taken a few hours would end up taking a couple of days. The thought of the fight Rieko would put up at having to sleep out under the stars had Tobin quickening his pace.

Rieko was a city girl. She had come from a wealthy Japanese family in Santa Fe and she was *not* the outdoorsy type. She was fairly pretty and had good skin. Her eyes were a brilliant emerald, which was in stark contrast to her shoulder-length jet black hair. Her Asian ancestry was prominent, all except for those eyes.

Tobin didn't care what she looked like. He was concerned only with the genes in her bloodline and whether or not she could safely carry and deliver the scion they had created. Of course, the girl had been devastated when she had learned of the requirements for keeping the child, as well as the consequences if she chose not to follow the rules. But the idea of the rewards awaiting her after the first five years had finally convinced her to abandon her smart phone, her family, her friends, and her posh lifestyle to follow Tobin out into the desert.

She mis-stepped again and he grabbed her just in time to keep her from falling. Tobin silently prayed to whatever force there might be in the Universe that they would make it to the drop-off point soon. If he could just get the girl there, the native tribe would make sure she and the unborn scion were well cared for from then on.

They rounded a bend and finally came in sight of the rendezvous point. Relief washed over Tobin as the shaman and several female natives rushed forward to greet them.

"I thought you said we would be living in a village," Rieko whined, as she looked around at the unrelenting canyon walls. There was nothing but stone and sand as far as the eye could see.

"I told you," Tobin explained. "These people will take you to stay at their village not far from here. I shall return for you in five years to take you to paradise."

The young Asian girl looked sullenly up at him. "I still don't understand why you're not gonna live with us. I mean, it's your baby, too!" She turned pleading green eyes on him, silently begging him not to leave her with these strangers.

But Tobin knew better than to give in when it came to these matters. His function on Earth was to impregnate females and then to deliver the scions, his offspring, to his off-world comrades. Once the scion and its human mother were safely retrieved from the planet, Tobin's role in their lives was over. The human female would be delivered to paradise and the scion would be trained to be returned to the planet where he would perform the functions of a new Star child.

This was what it took to achieve integration – an ongoing stream of Star children to infiltrate the human race.

"Tobin!" Rieko barked. She was accustomed to getting whatever she wanted and he hadn't yet responded to her silent plea.

Tobin shook his head, explaining, "As I said, I cannot remain here with you."

Rieko gaped in shock that he should deny the mother of his child anything.

"I shall return when it is time," he said. "Until then, you must remain hidden." She made to protest, but he cut her off. "Our child will require special attention and these people know how best to attend to him, for I have relied on them before."

This brought her up short. The realization that this strange creature she had fallen in love with had done this with other women before shook her to the core. For a moment, she wondered if she had made a mistake. But then she recalled what Tobin had told her awaited anyone who could provide him with a "scion" – paradise.

He had promised it would be hers and she wanted it.

She turned back toward the strangers who were waiting a few feet away. They were all about the same height as she and each one had long black hair. But their skin was darker than hers and they looked filthy and disheveled to her born-and-bred city-girl's eyes. Tears welled as she returned her gaze to Tobin. He was already preparing to leave her. "Please," she whispered, close to the breaking point. Her round white face streaked with tears.

Tobin merely tipped his hat at the shaman and turned away, leaving without another word. The tribe would take good care of the scion and its mother and Tobin still had a long journey ahead. Daylight was fading and it would be hours before he reached the mouth of the canyon. He would have to camp in the desert tonight and start his return to the East tomorrow.

***

Fading sunlight broke through the thinning cloudbank, shining in a lone thick stream down onto the L.A. River. Tyson watched from the rickety old stoop of his back porch. He liked the way the light sparkled off the newly-fallen rain water swiftly making its way through the cement estuary. It was a bright spot of beauty in an otherwise dirty, dingy world and his Down's-syndrome-afflicted seven-year-old mind grabbed onto it and clung tight, reluctant to lose it for fear of becoming consumed once more by the wasteland that was the only home he had ever known.

The clouds from the fading storm moved in front of the sun again and the little slice of beauty was gone. The sound of Demetrius' lighter striking tore Tyson's mind from its reverie.

"Here," his older brother said as he handed over the little hand-rolled cigarette. "Don't take a lot."

Tyson carefully took the joint, mimicking Demetrius' handling of the thing. He took a little into his mouth, not inhaling yet, and then passed it back. Finally, he inhaled and immediately fell into a painful coughing fit.

"Damn, Ty!" Demetrius scowled as he whacked his younger brother on the back. "I told you not to take too much."

"I di-dn'," Tyson choked out.

As soon as his younger brother's coughing fit subsided, Demetrius cocked a lop-sided grin at him, choking a little himself as he said, "'Assome good stuff, huh?" Tyson nodded and the two fell silent, finishing off the hooch without further comment.

It helped. Tyson wasn't as upset now as he had been earlier. It appeared Demetrius had calmed down, too. The older and much wiser eleven-year-old leaned back to lay against the top step on the stoop and Tyson followed suit. As the two stared up at the thinning clouds above, each was deep in thought until Tyson asked, "D, why'd momma hitchyu while ago?"

It took a second, but then Demetrius said, "She didn' mean to."

Tyson didn't know about that. She had looked pretty upset when she'd slapped his brother earlier. Then she had stormed out of the house after yelling at both of them to "jus' git out!"

"Where you think she went?" Tyson asked next.

Demetrius shrugged. "Dunno," he lied. "But lissen," he said, turning to look his little brother in the eye for emphasis. "We gon' stay outta her way t'night, you hear? We can stay at Miss Johnson's 'til momma's feelin' better tomorrow. Befo' then, we gotta stay away, 'kay?"

Tyson dutifully nodded. He wouldn't disappoint his big brother. But he still didn't understand what could have gotten his mother so upset. The sight of the large dark area still showing through the skin on Demetrius' cheek sent a shiver down Tyson's spine.

He couldn't get the vision or sound of that slap out of his mind. There was obviously no point in trying to get his older brother to talk about it, but that didn't erase the memory of the incident from Tyson's confused mind. The pot had helped him to not be afraid anymore, but he still didn't understand why she had done it.

It was too much to think about for the child and Tyson returned his attention to the clumps of clouds in the deepening twilight. Every now and then there would be a break and he would catch just a glimpse of a star or two in the darkening black canopy of space behind the clouds. Lightning from the fading storm still lit up the cloudbanks every few minutes, but what little thunder he heard came from far off in the distance. He relaxed even more, feeling light as a feather, his body not even a tangible thing anymore. He felt almost like he could just float away up into the sky.

In a cloud break off to the left a star caught Tyson's attention. It appeared to change color and he imagined it was coming closer as he watched. He was filled with a peculiar lethargy as the light grew and it reminded him of the sunlight shining on the rainwater. This light sparkled and glowed with a soft brilliance that mesmerized him with its beauty.

"Ty!" Demetrius shouted, jerking on his arm. Tyson blinked in confusion. "Move!" his brother shouted. Tyson didn't even think about it. He jumped up and turned, already running up the short stairway to the back door. Demetrius was right behind him, his size nine sneakers pounding on the old wooden steps. Then the door was slamming shut behind them as the two brothers made a bee-line toward the hall closet.

Tyson hated that closet because he had seen spiders in it. But he didn't protest as Demetrius practically shoved him into its dark recesses, quickly climbing in behind him and closing the door. "Don' make a sound!" Demetrius ordered in an urgent whisper. "Jus' keep still!"

The two boys tensed up as they heard the screech of the screen door opening. Strange sounds came from the kitchen and the two boys held their breaths, listening. Tyson was glad when Demetrius grabbed his hand and he held onto that hand as tight as he could.

The noises grew closer as if someone was coming down the hallway toward the closet door. The air inside the dark little room felt funny and a strange acrid smell filled Tyson's nostrils. The door suddenly flew open and both brothers screamed in terror.

Demetrius darted forward, forcing his way through the three things blocking the doorway. He never once released Tyson's hand as he ran. "Come on!" Demetrius shouted without looking back. Tyson tripped on the corner of a small metal table, howling in pain at the deep gash it dug into his leg as he fell. His heart thumping wildly in his chest, he managed to right himself a second later with Demetrius' help. His leg hurt and he could feel blood running down it below the knee. But he didn't want whatever those things were to get him, so he kept running.

Demetrius got the front door open in a flash and was racing through it before Tyson could even take a good breath. He yanked on Tyson's arm, urging him on faster toward old Miss Johnson's house. The two brothers raced out onto the front lawn, turning left just outside the front gate.

A heavy metallic sound boomed down onto the land, silencing all else and creating an eerie stillness throughout the neighborhood. Then there was only the sight of the land falling away beneath their feet. Tyson fell forward, his hand slipping from Demetrius' grip, but he still kept going up, up and away from the ground far below. Demetrius was somewhere above and behind him. Tyson could hear him grunting as he struggled against whatever force had hold of them, but the fight was in vain. Whatever it was, it was everywhere and there was no escaping it.

A whoosh of air took hold of them, like a giant sucking in a huge gulp, and both brothers were whisked into what Tyson could only think was some type of flying ship.

Momma! was the first thought that flew through Tyson's mind.

The next thing he knew, he felt himself "touch down" onto a solid surface again and he looked around for Demetrius. Out of the corner of his eye, he caught sight of his older brother, but he didn't turn toward him. Instead, his attention focused with terrified intensity on multiple gray creatures pouring into the room through the only visible opening to where he and his brother stood.

The majority of the creatures weren't quite as tall as Demetrius, but they were all scary looking. The taller ones were a little darker in color and they looked like they could have been really thin, bald men. The smaller ones had giant black eyes in their enormous heads and their skinny little bodies looked too thin to be real. They looked almost like sickening-colored lollipops to Tyson and he would've laughed at the picture that thought created in his head, had he not been so terrified.

One of the taller creatures reached for Tyson and Demetrius screamed as he lunged to defend his younger brother. A swarm of the smaller creatures descended upon the older boy as three of the taller creatures grabbed hold of Tyson, dragging him off into a different part of the ship. Tyson struggled against his strange captors, pulling and pushing, kicking and even hitting them in his attempts to escape. More of the smaller creatures entered the room and they handled him easily. When he was finally plopped down onto a hard metal table, he stilled.

Tyson found he couldn't move at all. Every muscle in his body was locked in a rigid state and all he could do was lie there, staring in terror as the creatures undressed him. He felt pain in his arms and then in his neck. He couldn't turn his head to see what was going on, but it felt like he was being stuck with needles.

He hated needles.

Tears welled in his eyes and his vision blurred. Off in the distance, in some other room, Demetrius was screaming. At first, it sounded like he was still fighting the things. But then the screams changed tone and Tyson knew his brother now screamed in pain.

One of the smaller creatures shoved its giant, bulbous head right into Tyson's line of sight, looking deep into his eyes and Tyson realized something. The thing looking directly back at him was not a living creature! Although it appeared to be living, there was at least some part of it that was a machine, from the looks of it. Tyson could see what appeared to be lights flickering every now and then deep inside the thing's eyes in the center part.

If he hadn't been this close to the thing and looking directly into its eyes, he might not have even seen the lights. Also, its movements were made in such a precise way that Tyson believed it had to be some kind of robot – at least, part robot.

Another agonizing scream from Demetrius from that other nearby room of the ship caught Tyson's attention. The taller creatures as well as the part-robot things working on him all turned at once at this sound and stilled. Demetrius gave one more grunt. As if on cue, the gray things all turned back at once and with skilled precision, they removed everything they had poked into Tyson. Next, one of the taller creatures whipped him off the metal table and slung him unceremoniously into a little room. A piece of clothing landed part way on his body a second later. Then the door to the room closed with a soft swoosh sound and he was alone.

Eventually, his muscles relaxed and Tyson found he was able to move again. He sluggishly reached for the piece of fabric one of the monsters had thought to throw into the room before they had left. It looked like an ugly gray dress. But seeing as how he was currently naked, Tyson decided he would wear it, just in case somebody else came in. The gash on his leg hurt whenever he touched it, but at least it had stopped bleeding.

He sat with his arms carefully wrapped around his

thin little legs and his chin propped on his knees as he shivered, wondering if his momma would be able to find him and Demetrius. Next, he wondered what would happen to them if she couldn't.

***

Tameka Bradley stared down at the dark amber liquid in her glass. The memory of her slapping her oldest son's face played out again before her mind's eye. She shouldn't have done it, especially not today. It was already enough that this day would forever represent the one thing she wanted more than anything to be able to forget. But now she had gone and added to the reasons why it was so awful!

Glass in hand, she slammed back the full contents, hating the burn as it trickled down her throat, but knowing she deserved it. She winced as she swallowed the last drop and then set the glass back down onto the not-so-polished wooden bar top, nudging it forward toward the barkeep.

"Another?" he asked.

Tameka nodded.

Once the tumbler was refilled, he walked off and she was once again left to re-live the past. The slap earlier today and everything that had happened four years ago all played out again in her mind. Tyson had only been three when it had happened, but D had been old enough to remember. He might not have understood what was going on, but he remembered. He had proved that by his comment earlier about how she should leave Tyson and him alone and just go on and get drunk like she always did on this day.

Tameka never drank.

But that wasn't true. She drank once a year on the same date, just like she had on that one night four years ago. Akinaryan had gone crazy that night. That had been the night she had finally had him taken. It had also been the last night she had ever seen him alive, though she hadn't been able to see much that night through her swollen lids.

Ever since then, she had taken care of their two sons. She had paid the bills, put food on the table, kept them clothed and sheltered. When word had reached her that Aki had been killed in a fight at the jail, she had almost felt relieved. But then the guilt had set in and she felt the loss. He had been crazy, but he was their father. Now they had none and she would be damned if she would let another man into their lives!

The liquid burned a little less this time as she slammed it back again. It slowly made its way down to warm her tummy. She slid the glass forward again and the barkeep obligingly returned, filling it once more before walking off.

In her mind, she relived that day. Aki had Demetrius by the arm as he pulled him toward the front door. He had said they were on the way, those men from his tribe, and that they were going to take D off to Africa to keep him safe. *"How can you think of giving our son to complete strangers?"* she had demanded. He had responded by saying his Demetekle, as he had called him, needed protection from those who wanted to steal the secret.

Tameka remembered the old stories Aki had told her about bloodlines and how he and she had been fated to be together, but she didn't care. She wasn't about to let anyone, let alone complete strangers from some other country, come in and take either of her sons away from her. When she had stood in his path to block him from the door, Aki had hit her hard in the eyes. She was no small woman, but his strike had sent her reeling halfway across the room. Fortunately, her elderly neighbor had heard all the yelling and had called the cops. They had shown up not long afterward and Tameka had agreed to press charges – anything to keep him from her precious sons.

The very next day, she had bought a small handgun from a kid in the neighborhood. But no men had come to collect Demetrius. No one had emerged to post bail for Aki. Then he had died in that fight and everything had gone to hell. Tameka had been overwhelmed with guilt and doubt. She had lost her job. She'd had to sell her car to keep the house. Sometimes, they had to go to bed hungry at night, but she did her best. This past Christmas there had been no presents under the old tree she had found in a dumpster near the house, but she had taken the boys out to eat at their favorite fast food restaurant when she had gotten paid a week afterward to make up for it.

She was working three jobs now and things were a little better, with the help of Miss Johnson next door. But today just had to roll around again, bringing with it all the memories and misery it always did. D knew what today did to her. Why he had picked today to smart off to her, she didn't know. But now she felt awful because she'd slapped him.

She slammed back the glass once more, the fiery liquid now a comforting, soothing feeling as it poured down her throat. It settled in her stomach, its fingers of warmth now reaching all over her body and clouding both her vision and her mind enough to ease her tension. She slumped back against the vinyl bar stool as the room started spinning in small little jerks. Her eyes worked to keep up with it, but her mind was off in another time and place, eclipsed by happier times with her beloved sons.

The room suddenly swooped sideways and her fuzzy mind couldn't keep up. She would have fallen off the bar stool had it not been for a quick pair of hands that caught her about the waist.

"Hey, mama," a hi-pitched male voice said. "You lookin' for somebody?"

Tameka finally managed to focus on this newcomer. The image presented to her stupefied mind wasn't what she would have expected for this neighborhood, but she guessed it could be worse. "I think I f-fell," she said, her words only half-slurred.

The greasy-looking white man holding her up chuckled. An odd expression flickered in his eyes and he handed her another drink. The next thing Tameka knew, she was being half-carried down a dark sidewalk by this same man in a part of town unfamiliar to her. He touched her in places he shouldn't and he kissed her as they walked. She pushed at his face and tried to pull away from him, but her balance was still off and her mind was quite fuzzy. A sound up ahead caught her attention then, and she realized there were more men coming toward them. They were all just as white and just as greasy-looking as the man still groping her, and a dart of fear raced down her spine.

"Come on, mama," her escort said. "We just wanna have some fun for a while."

Tameka pushed at him again, now feeling a bit strange. This was more than just the alcohol. It felt almost as if she had taken something and she couldn't understand what was happening. There was a crowd of males surrounding her now and instinct took over. She still had her purse on her and that meant she was armed. As she was manhandled into a nearby alleyway, she worked her purse around to a good angle, hoping no one would notice. Several hands were now groping her and at least one male was behind her, pressing up against her rear end in a lewd and suggestive manner as his hand snaked around and dug up into her crotch. Thank goodness she had changed out of the dress she'd worn to work and into jeans!

But that didn't appear to be much of a deterrent for the pack of rabid men who currently surrounded her. Within seconds, the jeans were jerked off her and that's when the real trouble began. She pushed and kicked, but she was only rewarded with bites on her inner thigh and around her knees. She was also treated to a hard spanking on her buttocks and the backs of her legs while others within the group ripped at her top.

She closed her eyes and focused on what she needed to do. Slowly, but with pinpoint accuracy, she slipped her hand into her bag and wrapped her fingers around the small 9mm. In her mind, she counted to three and then whipped the gun out, shoving it into the gut of the man directly in front of her. She screamed as she pulled the trigger.

"What the...!"

The injured man howled in pain as he limped away. Several others took off and Tameka waved the gun around, shaking fiercely from the ordeal. Just as a sense of relief sank in at the thought that she had scared them all away, something hard hit her on the back of her head and then everything disappeared.

Chapter 2

The young woman laughed as she ran ahead on the lush hiking trail. Tall trees crowded the dense forest and she reveled in the feeling of connecting with nature once more. Her boyfriend, who was still carefully picking his way along the trail far behind her, called for her to wait up. She had no intention of doing any such thing.

For the past three years while she had lived at school back East, he had been there for her. They had met in New Jersey and he had helped her adjust to life in the big city. But now she was finally home and they were in her neck of the woods, so to speak – and she was loving it. She was the expert here, while he was like a fish out of water.

She chuckled softly and picked up her pace to a brisk jog.

The young man following far behind winced as yet another stick or vine or whatever it was scratched him. He wasn't sure about this whole hiking thing one bit. He had lived in New Jersey since birth and wasn't comfortable in these woods. And as for this thing his girlfriend called a trail, well it was nowhere near as smooth as the concrete paths he was used to. That was the only place he had ever hiked.

A little over a week ago, he had come to Anchorage to visit his long-time girlfriend and two days ago she had somehow convinced him to go camping for the weekend.

The young man had seen this as the perfect opportunity to pop the question – kind of an ultimate romantic getaway. But those plans had been tossed out the window when they had arrived to discover another couple already at the campsite and "Beware of Bears" signs up all over the place. The young man had suggested they back-track to the nearest hotel, but his girlfriend had other plans. She convinced him to stay the night, promising he wouldn't regret it come nightfall. Now they were on what she called a healthy late-evening hike before dinner and the young man was doing his damnedest to figure out how to scare off a bear, while also trying to keep up with her.

Suddenly, she screamed from somewhere up ahead and he took off running. His mind filled with visions of her mangled, half-eaten body. His heart raced as he dashed along the path. When he finally caught up to her, she was lying face-down, unmoving on the ground. He raced to her side, fear eclipsing his mind as he reached to turn her over. What on earth could he do if she was seriously injured?

His fears were soon put to rest as she shot a look up at him at his touch. It was then he discovered she appeared to be unharmed.

"What happened?" he asked, annoyed. "Why did you scream?"

"Huh?" the young woman asked as she turned to him again, completely distracted. Then she said, "Oh. I fell, tripped. That's why I yelled. But look at this." She turned back to show him what she had found. There on the ground, barely showing through the dirt, was what looked like a rounded silver plate of some kind buried beneath the trail. She reached out and scraped away the loose dirt around it. It appeared to be larger than a plate – more like some kind of giant metal ball.

The young man frowned as his curiosity was piqued and he moved to a better position so that he, too, could dig. Soon, the couple had uncovered a whole square meter area of the object, though this was by no means the entirety of the thing. They had dug as deep as they could, but the dirt packed around it now was very hard and the couple could no longer remove it with just their bare hands.

They decided to return to the campsite for the night. Daylight was fading and they would have to return in the morning with the little shovel they had brought and whatever else they could find to use to dig up the thing. So far all they knew was that it was a curved silvery-metal object, completely smooth and without a single apparent imperfection.

It was almost full dark by the time they finally reached the campsite. It had taken longer to return than either one had anticipated. By mutual consent they decided to skip dinner altogether. Instead, they laid their exhausted bodies down inside the tent, whispered "Goodnight" to each other around sudden fits of coughing and immediately fell asleep.

Toward late afternoon the next day, a park ranger stopped by to warn the two couples at the campsite that there had been bear sightings in the park not far from the site. When he entered the young couple's tent to check on them, the sight and smell made him lose his lunch.

Hours later, the head of emergency services at the local clinic nearest the park ended the conference call he had been on for the past forty minutes and reached into his desk drawer. He grabbed the bottle of 18-year-old single malt from its resting place at the back of the drawer and took a long swig. It burned as it sliced down his gullet and he winced. The heat hit and then spread throughout his innards as he slouched back in his chair.

He was terrified.

The young couple the park ranger had brought in this afternoon wouldn't make it through the night, and now the ranger was sick. The doctor and his staff had done everything they could to save the kids, but their treatment options had been sorely limited due to the extreme degree of exposure and lack of equipment, meds and training of those working at the clinic. The superficial burns on the couple's extremities had been frightening enough, but the internal damage the doctor had discovered within each truly revealed how dangerous this situation was.

What had done this?

He took another swig from the bottle, pulling on it long and hard. If he never spoke to another government official again, it would be too soon. The NSA and DHS agents who had grilled him for the past forty minutes had been brutal, asking all kinds of questions – some even personal! Now, some DOD specialist was being sent to contain the situation so the story wouldn't leak and cause panic in Anchorage.

A coughing fit hit and he doubled over, finally dragging a handkerchief from his coat pocket. But as he pulled the cloth away to look at it, his hand started shaking. It was already too late for his staff and him. All three of them had worked on the victims and now it was only a matter of hours before they ended up in the same boat as those poor folks.

Another long pull on the bottle finally stopped the shaking in his hands. He would still have to deal with the officials when they showed up, assuming he was still capable of doing that, but it didn't matter. Nothing mattered now. He would have liked to sit back and drink himself into a stupor, but he couldn't quite get the details of this situation out of his head.

What could cause such severe radiation exposure? That was the question the Feds had demanded over and over. The doctor still didn't have an answer. Was it terrorism? Was someone in the area going all Kaczynski and building a bomb? Were they hoping to sneak the bomb *into* the lower 48 from here? Was there even a bomb?

The doctor took one last draw from the half-empty bottle and then put it back in its hiding place. He was definitely starting to feel the effects of the radiation now and his sluggish mind wondered when the DOD spec would arrive.

***

Tobin slowly made his way up the dirt road. His feet and legs were tired, as was the rest of him, but it wasn't far now. After he had dropped off his latest scion and its mother with a local family, he had decided to take this side trip to see Ana. The place where she and little Bianca were staying was so close that he didn't see any harm in dropping by. He just wanted to check in on them. At least, that's the lie he told himself.

A picture of Ana appeared before his mind's eye as he walked and he smiled. She was a tiny little thing, all dark-skinned and elegant. Her brilliant hazel eyes had a twinkle that always made him laugh. And Bianca... well, she was the most beautiful scion he had ever seen and she always had a smile for Tobin, no matter how long it was between his visits.

He frowned at this thought. Bianca had turned five years old this past March. By all rights, he should be making arrangements for Ana's and her journey. In fact, were he honest, he would admit that they were already late. Scions were not meant to live here untutored past the age of five. But Tobin couldn't bear the idea of sending Bianca and her mother to live off-world. He would never see them again once they left.

He shook his head to clear it of such dark thoughts. He didn't want to think about losing those two. His duty was clear and he *would* eventually have to make the travel arrangements. But for now, he wanted one more night with them. As the small village where they lived came into view, Tobin's step quickened and his spirits lifted. He could have this one night with them. Then he would think about contacting the pick-up team.

As usual, Ana was happy to see him when he arrived. He gave her the newspapers he had collected before he had left the States and she pored through them while he spent time playing games with little Bianca. Ana took a break to help her host family prepare the evening's meal, but Tobin knew she would read through every single one of the papers before he left in the morning.

She had left behind so much when she had agreed to leave St. Louis with him and he respected the fact that she would feel the need for news of her home. Tobin was accustomed to being on the road and he had no true home. He couldn't – not with his way of life. But Ana had lived a normal life up until she had met him. She'd had a family, a home, and friends. She had grown up with the internet and cell phones – everything humans took for granted in this age. After she had met Tobin, she had agreed to give up all that to help Bianca.

That was why he listened patiently to her after supper was done and Bianca was in bed. She read several articles aloud to him, sharing her thoughts and opinions on the subjects. For such a young human, Tobin had to admit he believed Ana to have a very level head on her shoulders. She had adjusted to her new way of life with equanimity and poise, doing whatever she could to ensure the health and well-being of their scion above all else.

Ana was more of a conservative thinker and, although she had grown up with the internet and social media, after having been away from it for so long she had come to understand one simple truth about it: the world was not ready for it. That topic was what had led Tobin and her to their current discussion.

"Are you honestly telling me that *aliens* are the ones who first introduced the internet to humans?" Ana asked, half joking and half incredulous. Tobin had a strict policy of honesty with the women who bore his scions. They all knew beforehand that he was only half-human. He didn't think it right to conduct business any other way. To do so would be deceptive, in his mind.

"It was introduced to humans by those who would have you assimilate into the Universal society," he explained. "That is the more accepted viewpoint on how primitive species are to be handled."

Ana turned serious as she realized he wasn't joking. "So, your people want us to assimilate into their culture?"

"Not my people," he replied. "My people are Samarean; they are one of the nine groups of Watchers."

Ana frowned as she thought back over everything he had told her when they first met. She knew he was only half-human and that his "job" here on Earth was to help his off-world relatives integrate into human society by impregnating human females and providing other part-human children, or scions. These scions would then be taken at age five to be taught and raised by the aliens so that they could eventually become leaders among Earth's human population.

But Tobin had never mentioned the name of his off-world relatives, nor had he said anything about them being what he called "Watchers".

"What does that mean?" Ana asked.

Tobin merely shook his head, dismissing her question. "That is a very long discussion," he said, "and I would not waste so much of my time here debating the merit of a belief that, in truth, may be based more on myth and fantasy than facts."

Ana's frown deepened at his response and he changed the subject, saying, "I think instead that we need to discuss Bianca."

Ana's face paled slightly. She had been dreading this moment, but she had figured it was why Tobin was here. She wasn't ready.

"It is past the time that Bianca and you should have been delivered to the Watchers," he softly said, looking anywhere but at her.

Tears sprang to Ana's eyes, but she straightened up and nodded. She would do her duty to ensure their daughter was given the best chance this life could offer her. "What do I need to do to prepare her?"

Tobin did look her in the eye then. He saw the tears pooled there. He saw and felt her tension. To his own surprise, he found himself saying, "You need do nothing. I shall contact my people to ask if Bianca and you may be allowed to remain here on Earth with me."

"But she's already five," Ana said, a little spark of hope springing to life inside her. "Won't you get in trouble for not giving us up?"

"I have produced 137 scions in my lifetime on this planet," he said. "I believe I should be granted the right to keep one – just one." He concentrated for a moment, deep in thought. Surely, his superiors would allow him one scion and its mother for his own?

***

Tyson started and looked up as a door slid open to his right. There had been so many different noises during his long stay in the room that this one shouldn't have startled him. Still, it did.

To his surprise, there was a boy standing in the doorway. He was similar in height, build and coloring to Tyson and he looked to be just a little bit younger. He looked friendly enough, but he was still a stranger. Momma had always told Tyson to never talk to strangers.

The boy slowly stuck his hand out.

Tyson frowned. As he unfolded himself and stood, cautiously approaching the boy, he remembered his momma's instructions. As he drew closer, he looked all around, even down the part of the corridor he could see on the other side of the doorway. There was no one else in sight. He really didn't think he should be rude to the boy. Reluctantly, Tyson took the young man's hand. Silently, the boy led him out of the room and farther down the curved corridor without ever letting go.

The hallway appeared to go on forever and there were so many doors leading off it that Tyson was soon completely lost. He hoped the boy knew where they were going. Finally, they stopped before one of the doors and it smoothly slid open.

Inside, the room was crowded. There was no sound, but there were people everywhere. Some sat around tables looking at each other, while others stood around in groups. There were adults and kids of all ages and everyone appeared to be having a great time just looking at each other. Only one person mattered to Tyson, but he was missing. Tyson didn't see Demetrius anywhere.

The boy pulled on his hand and Tyson followed him on into the room. There was a flurry of activity as all eyes turned to see who had entered. The people gave many smiles and nods as the boy led Tyson farther in toward the back of the room. When they finally cleared the crowd, Tyson was stunned to see that the entire back wall of the room was a window, floor to ceiling and wall to wall. But what appeared outside the window was what really astonished him.

He *was* aboard a spaceship and it was in outer space. Far below was Earth. Tyson had seen this same scene on TV enough times to know that. He stood staring down at the planet in awe. The boy nudged his arm and, when Tyson finally tore his gaze away from his home planet to look at him, the boy smiled and raised his brows, his eyes darting down toward the planet and then back to Tyson. Tyson just nodded and returned his attention to the scenery.

He reached out to touch the glass, except there was no

glass there. A zinging, tingling sensation went up his arm at his first touch of whatever it was that separated the inside of the ship from the vast emptiness of space on the outside of the ship. The boy pulled Tyson's arm back, shaking his head and making a serious face. Then he motioned for Tyson to follow him. Tyson looked back down at Earth for a moment before turning and nodding.

The boy led him over to a table covered with stacks of little square things. The boy picked up one of the square pieces and showed it to Tyson. It had what looked like a piece of paper on the back that was to be peeled off. The boy motioned for Tyson to lift his left arm. After Tyson did so, the boy peeled off the paper from one of the squares and placed the sticky part of the patch inside the sleeve onto Tyson's skin just up under his armpit where it stayed.

The two boys returned to a spot by the window wall, where they sat down on the floor side by side in silence. Tyson kept looking down at Earth, wondering if he could see his house from space. He decided that was crazy. He couldn't see anything except clouds and a few lights and the vague shapes of the land on different parts of the world.

It was odd, just sitting in this room with all these other people and no one talking. The boy sat there staring at Tyson without saying anything. Tyson knew that he should probably be asking some questions, but he didn't know what to ask. Truth was he didn't know what to do here. He didn't mind the quiet. It was just so odd. He decided he had best do what the boy was doing and so he sat and stared right back at the boy, looking him directly in the eyes.

Without warning, the room filled with noise and Tyson looked all around in alarm to discover why everyone had suddenly started talking. The only problem was that no one *was* talking. Nobody in the room appeared to be talking at all. In fact, most of the people's mouths were even closed!

No fear, a boy's voice said in Tyson's mind. He looked at the boy sitting in front of him. The boy was smiling and nodding his head. *I Manuel. What name you?*

Tyson frowned. Could this be real? Without realizing what he was doing, he thought, *I'm Tyson.*

Manuel nodded, still smiling. *You like play?* he silently asked.

Tyson looked around at all the other people in the room. He could hear them all talking now and he wondered if everyone here talked without opening their mouths.

No fear them, Manuel silently told him. *They always talk, but you understand after while. Come. More children there play game.*

He stood and headed toward a small group of kids who looked like they were having a great time with whatever game they were playing. Tyson hopped up and hurried after him. The kids playing the game were all friendly and welcoming and soon Tyson was happily engaged in a rousing war game with the boys pitted against the girls. There were twelve kids playing all together, with the boys being slightly outnumbered. But they didn't care. It was all great fun.

At the end of the game, several of the kids wandered off to start a new game, but some stayed and sat around to talk in a group. Tyson learned that not all of them were from Earth. A few of them, including Manuel, had been born aboard the ship and were waiting to be sent to Earth where they would live for the rest of their lives.

Won't you miss your parents? Tyson silently asked one of the girls.

I have no parent, the girl told him. She looked to be older than him by a few years and he felt so sorry for her that she didn't have any parents. That brought on thoughts of his own momma and of Demetrius.

The girl reached out and put her hand on his. *No worry,* she told him. *You see them again. In fact, you schedule return with us when we go.* She smiled at him, giving his hand a gentle squeeze.

Tyson merely stared back at her, wondering if Demetrius would be going back when he did. He hoped so.

***

Tameka came to in stages. At first, the stabbing pain in her head was all that registered and she did her best to go back to sleep to avoid it. The next thing to hit her consciousness was the fact that she was not at home in her bed. In fact, she wasn't sure she was in a bed at all. Her eyes flew open. The brightness of a nearby street light was blinding and she blinked, finally settling on having her eyes open to mere slits as she looked around at wherever it was she had ended up staying for the night.

She was outside and appeared to be behind some type of business in a run-down part of town. There were multiple filthy dumpsters in the small area and she was leaned up against one. That's when she realized she was half-nude. She still had on her panties, but that was it. She had no socks, no bra. Her shirt and pants were wadded up on the filthy pavement a few feet away, but there was no sign of anything else. It hit her all of a sudden that she didn't see her purse and she looked around frantically as she grabbed hold of the blouse and pants and pulled them on.

What the hell had happened last night?

She remembered being at the bar – her and Aki's favorite bar – and then… nothing.

Had she been robbed? Or worse? There was an unfamiliar soreness all over her body, so she knew *some*thing must have happened. She just couldn't remember. But for now, she was more concerned with what she was going to do. She had no money, no ID, and she had been carrying last night. Her purse was gone. That meant her gun was gone, too.

With no idea where she was, she painfully climbed to her feet and stumbled unsteadily around the building to the front. It turned out to be a short strip mall with an adult video store and another adult store that sold sex toys. There was one final shop on the end that appeared to be some sort of condom shop. Tameka didn't recognize the area, though it was well-lit from the street lights. She also had no idea how she'd gotten there.

She was sore all over, barefoot, cold and lost. And all she wanted to do was to go home. But how could she get there? She decided to head down the street toward what looked like a busier section. Once there, she discovered the exit to a busy Latino dance club. Her head was killing her and she still couldn't recall what had happened last night, but she did manage to bum almost ten dollars off some people exiting the club. It wasn't much, but it would be enough for her to catch a bus.

As luck would have it, there was a bus stop a block away from the club and she took the first bus that appeared, not noticing that it was headed away from the city. She just wanted to sit down and rest for a while. She was so tired; she fell asleep not long after boarding.

Nearly three hours later, Tameka lumbered up the walkway from the driveway of her dilapidated old house to the back door. She had gotten lost and had finally ended up begging once more for enough money for a cab. Now she was exhausted and she just wanted to go inside and sleep a few hours before going next door to get the boys. It was early enough that she knew they would still be asleep. Tameka also knew Sheree Johnson wouldn't mind letting them stay. She walked around to the spot on the back stoop where she normally hid the spare house key. That's when she noticed the back door was partially open.

"What the...?" she stammered, wondering if she shouldn't go ahead and go next door before daring to enter the house. She had taught both boys to never leave the door unlocked or open. With her purse having been taken, she knew someone could have gotten her address from the driver's license she still carried and could now be in there just waiting for her to come home.

A shiver raced down her spine at the thought. She remembered that there had been several break-ins recently at homes of other single women in the neighborhood. That and thinking that whoever had stolen her purse last night may now know where she lived gave her enough cause for concern to back up and turn toward Sheree's house without even entering her own. She would go over there and call the cops. Once they had come to check out everything, she and the boys would come back.

It only took a minute after she had knocked before the elderly Sheree Johnson answered the door. She still had on her robe and nightgown and slippers on her feet.

"Hi, Sheree," Tameka said. "I'm sorry to wake you. Can I use your phone real quick? I lost mine last night and I need to call the cops."

Sheree had opened the door wide to allow her entry before Tameka had even finished speaking. Now she asked, "The po-lice? Wha's wrong?" She closed the door and then led her younger neighbor into her sitting room where she kept her phone.

"I think somebody broke in last night 'cuz the door's open," Tameka said as she dialed. "I just want to make sure everything's okay before me an' the boys go home."

Sheree frowned, looking around before asking, "Where is 'em boys?"

The hand holding the phone dropped a bit as Tameka's heart lurched. "Ain't they here?" she asked.

Sheree shook her head, explaining, "No. I ain't seen 'em since early yesterd'y b'fo the storm hit."

A voice sounded through the phone, "9-1-1, what's your emergency?" Tameka looked down at the hand-held device like it was the strangest thing she had ever seen before she handed the thing off to Sheree and took off running. She had to get home to make sure the boys were okay.

Within seconds, she had passed through the also open *front* door of her house only to stop dead in her tracks. The hall closet door was wide open and a couple of chairs had been knocked over. She took a step forward, but then stopped. There was a small amount of blood on the floor just before her. The metal card table she had told Demetrius to put away before she had left last night was lying on its side and there was blood on one of the sharp corners of it. She reached down and rubbed her finger over it. It was ice cold. Absently, she wiped the blood on her pants leg.

Oh, God! What if Tyson had fallen last night and hit his head on the thing? Terror turned her blood to ice in her veins as she screamed, "Demetrius! Tyson!" She ran to their bedroom, wiping her fingers on her pants as she threw open the door. It was pristine, the same as always, for Tameka would have no mess in her home. She raced forward to tear open the closet door. Clean clothes were neatly hung or folded and neatly stacked on shelves. But the boys weren't there. "Demetrius! Tyson!" she yelled again as she returned to the middle of the room and then slammed down onto the floor to search under each one's bed.

Surely, Demetrius would have called 911 if Tyson had been hurt? But why wasn't there at least a note or something telling her where they had gone?

Tears were flowing freely down her cheeks by now and she was close to hysteria. "Demetrius! Tyson!" she screamed, as she ran out of their room toward her own bedroom. She hoped Demetrius had left her a note in there somewhere. But her worst fears were confirmed as she realized there was no note. Her boys simply were nowhere to be found and she had no idea where to look for them.

Tameka sat on the edge of her bed thinking, which in her current state was not a good thing. Her head felt like it was going to split open and she still had no clue about anything that had happened last night after she had gone to the bar – let alone what might have happened to her children while she'd been out.

The logical part of her mind knew she had to call the cops and then start checking nearby hospitals. But there was another part of her mind that suddenly sprang forward, taking control and bringing forth a fear so strong it gripped her mind like a vise, allowing sanity no quarter.

What if someone *had* broken in last night? Was this her punishment for everything that had happened with Aki? Then an even worse thought occurred and it turned her insides so cold she thought surely she would freeze right through. Had the men he had sent for four years ago finally come and taken them – not just Demetrius, but Tyson, too? Surely someone would have noticed strange African tribesmen going into her house and taking her two sons. The image of dark-skinned men in loin cloths carrying spears as they tromped through her small neighborhood flashed through her mind. Could that really be what happened?

Tameka was so embroiled in her thoughts that she didn't think about the police who would surely be coming soon.

Oh, God! Oh, sweet Jesus, she thought. *Why?* But she had no answers. She knew only that her sons were gone and she was now completely alone. Something inside her snapped at this thought and all she could do was to crawl into a safe, dark space within the confines of her mind. She would stay there – just for a little while. Everything would be okay, if only she could stay hidden away until Demetrius and Tyson came back to her.

One hour and twenty-two minutes after she had arrived in the cab, she was found by two police officers who had responded to the call for two missing juveniles. She was incoherent when they found her, just sitting on the edge of a bed staring at nothing. The next-door neighbor had called in the request for help and the elderly woman was interviewed, since the female in question appeared to be in shock.

Ms. Tameka Bradley was taken to County Hospital for a psych evaluation. Her blood alcohol level was found to be elevated and it appeared she had a common date-rape drug in her system. It was also noted that she had bruises and scrapes on various parts of her anatomy consistent with a person who had been involved in a physical struggle with another individual, possibly even with a strong child or children.

Blood was found on Tameka Bradley's pants, as well as on the floor of the Bradley home. After forensic analysis, it was determined to be that of Tyson Germaine Bradley, the younger of the two missing youths. There were no signs of a break-in and no traces of anyone else having been in the home. The only prints discovered were those of Ms. Bradley and the two boys.

***

Stacy fell through the door as it opened. She didn't care about the keys she had left dangling in the lock, as long as she didn't drop the grocery bags she held in both arms. "Oop," she gushed as she nearly tripped over the door mat. "Matt!" she called.

"Yeah?" her husband of three years asked distractedly from the living room of their small apartment. He didn't bother turning away from the laptop screen to see why she had called him. He was too engrossed in the video footage he was watching online of the most recent debacle at the Baker house in Texas. He and Stacy had been following that case with great interest. They had followed Sarah Baker's blog for the past year, but things had really started heating up when Sarah and her kid disappeared.

"Hey, can I get some help here, please?"

Finally, Matt tore himself away from the images on the screen of burnt houses in Sarah's neighborhood before looking over at her. "What? Oh, yeah. Sure."

Stacy smiled and shoved the three bags out toward him as he approached. Her smile turned into a frown of disgust as he continued on past her to the door, where he removed her keys from the lock and then closed the door.

"There you go," he said. He placed her keys on the kitchen counter and then gave her a quick peck on the cheek as he passed on his way back to the computer. Stacy rolled her eyes in disgust at how idiotic the Y-chromosome-afflicted could be sometimes and then she continued on into the kitchen.

They had a long day ahead of them and she had to get their field snacks ready. Excitement rushed through her at the thought of the day's activities awaiting them. According to all the information she and Matt had discovered last night and again this morning, there appeared to be real video footage of L.A.'s latest encounter. Because Matt had known what to look for, the couple had been the first of the local UFO network groups to make contact with the eyewitnesses of the encounter and that had scored them promises of exclusive interviews and rights to any and all video footage.

There was one witness in particular Stacy wanted to talk to, a Ms. Sheree Johnson. When Stacy had talked with her on the phone late this morning, the lady had indicated there were two kids who had gone missing, possibly during the incident. To get the exclusive on an actual alien abduction case – well, that would do wonders for Stacy and Matt and they both knew it!

Matt finally closed his laptop cover and stood. Stacy

was just finishing packing the snacks in the cooler as he said, "Wish we were in Dallas. That whole Sarah Baker thing is blowing up the internet."

"Well, we're not there," Stacy said. "We've got our own happening right here in La-la land and it's virtually untouched."

Matt smiled and nodded and then asked, "So we about ready?"

"Ready, willing and able," she said as she closed the cooler lid.

It took nearly an hour to get to the derelict neighborhood on the South side of town where the incident had been reported and there were still several police black and whites parked near the end of the street. A few onlookers sat outside on small covered porches as they watched the goings on. Matt and Stacy stuck out like sore thumbs in this neighborhood, but they didn't take any notice. They were here on a mission. They had the names, addresses, and phone numbers of several homeowners nearby and they set to the task of interviewing eyewitnesses.

Several of those people had cell phone video footage of the occurrence, although most of it just looked like flashes of lightning. A couple proved to be worthy of a second look and Matt obtained copies of those so they could be analyzed by "De-bunk Master, Phil", who was a friend of Stacy's who specialized in debunking UFO claims. He was also a film footage guru, able to spot a fake or manipulated piece of footage from a mile away. Stacy and Matt had relied on him many times in the past and he had not yet let them down.

Sheree Johnson was the last eyewitness to be interviewed and Stacy took her time with the elderly lady. This witness had no video footage or anything like that, but she knew more about the two missing boys than anyone else in the neighborhood had known and she was happy to talk about it.

"Po' old Tameka wouldn' hurt 'em boys," she said, shaking her head. "She loves both o' dem mo'n anythang. She even had her husband 'rested a few years ago when she learnt he was gon' take 'em 'way to Africa."

"Why would he have wanted to do that?" Stacy asked.

"Well, 'at's where he come from," Ms. Johnson explained. "But Tameka didn' care. No, ma'am. He even hit her b'fo' she called the police an' had him 'rested." The elderly woman sadly shook her head. "'Course, it was too bad he got killt at t' jailhouse. But I think Tameka an'em boys been much bettuh off widout 'im."

"I see," Stacy said before asking, "So you don't think Ms. Bradley did anything to the boys?"

"No, ma'am."

Stacy leaned forward a bit, zooming in closer on the woman with her phone. "What do you think happened to them, then?"

Ms. Johnson thought hard for a moment before leaning forward herself, as she said, "I can't be sho', since I didn' see it fo' m'self. But I was talkin' wi' my neighbor, Miss Lucretia Butters, 'cross de street an' she told me she heard screams 'at sounded like dem boys right when dat loud noise hit. 'At's about the time dat bright flash of lightnin' hit my front yard, as I recall. Seems to me if dey'd been struck by lightnin', dey'd be sumpin' lef' – don'tchyu think?"

Stacy nodded. "I would think so," she agreed.

Ms. Johnson leaned back in her chair, saying, "So if nobody took 'em, an' dey wutt'n struck by no lightnin'...?" Here she just shook her head, shrugging as if she hadn't a clue what could have happened.

"Do you think they could've run away?" Stacy asked.

Before she had even finished her question, Ms. Johnson was shaking her head. "Dem boys loved they momma," she declared. "Dey wouldn'a lef' her."

Again, Stacy asked, "So what do you *think* happened to the boys?"

After a moment's pause, Ms. Johnson leaned forward one last time and said in a conspiratorial voice so soft it was nearly a whisper, "I 'on't know how it could'a happened – 'specially not right here in Los Angeles – but I think what Lucretia said is true. I think sumpin' done come down from the sky and jus' took dem boys, jus' sucked 'em right up and took 'em off into the night sky – and dat's de blame truth!"

There seemed nothing more to say on the subject and Stacy thanked Ms. Johnson for her testimony and her time as she gathered up her things. She and Matt had a long drive back to their place and it was getting close to rush hour. They had everything they needed, plus some, and Stacy was pleased with all the testimonials and video footage they had gotten. With any luck, they would be able to post their preliminary findings online tonight.

Stacy spent the entire journey home planning out how she would be able to score an interview with the boys' mother, Tameka Bradley. If she could somehow get into wherever the woman was being held and then get her to agree to an exclusive, it would boost the website's exposure galore. Matt thought it was a great idea and he promised to help her contact some people he knew who might be able to help as soon as they were done processing the evidence they had gathered from the neighborhood.

Both of them chatted excitedly all the way home, their heads filled with visions of their little operation blowing the lid off a huge government cover-up that had probably been going on since before the Roswell incident!

Chapter 3

Lluvia made her way up the street toward the burned common area. After the debacle she had seen online from two nights ago, she hadn't thought there would still be any people around the house. But there they were. She'd had to park several blocks away and now she was pissed that she hadn't thought to bring anything other than the high heels she was wearing to work today. It was bad enough she was now subjected to the nasty burnt smell in the neighborhood, but walking half a friggin' mile in her nine-hundred-dollar, too-tight pumps had her seeing red.

As she neared the common ground, she was chagrined to discover that there were cops everywhere, there to stop anyone from getting too close, in addition to being present for crowd control. Apparently, the blog this Sarah Baker chick had been running had more than a few people up in arms – especially now that it had gone viral. Several groups were already talking about suing her for what some had decided were racist and sacrilegious writings and for the deadly fighting that had occurred outside her family's home the other night. Lluvia didn't know if that was even a possibility, but she certainly wouldn't be surprised by such a move, what with all the controversy that night's protests had stirred up.

In the driveway, a flat-foot held out a hand, warning, "You'll have to back off, ma'am. This property is off limits."

Lluvia put on her best pout for the young trooper and used her best southern belle drawl. "But officer, I'm a member of the press and my boss assigned this story to me an hour ago. I just need to get a couple o' interviews from credible witnesses who know what's goin' on here, along with a short video of the scene for the feature. They're gonna air it this evenin', so I really do need to hurry."

The cop looked around, considering his options. "You mean, you're wantin' to interview some officers?" he asked hopefully.

Lluvia relaxed. She was as good as in the house and

she smiled her most appealing smile at the prematurely-balding young man. Within minutes, she had a notebook full of information and amateur video footage of nearly every room in the house. She waved at young baldy after accepting his phone number.

The young man wasn't all that bright. Although he had stuck with her throughout the entire tour of the house, he hadn't noticed when she'd picked up the white strand of hair she had spied blowing along the floor in the master bedroom on the ground floor, nor had he seen her stuff it quickly into her purse. Lluvia had also hidden the fact that she had somehow been cut by the thing when she had put it into her bag.

Now, as she crossed back over to the other side of the street, she wondered what the hell she had gotten herself into. The thing in her purse was actually moving. She could feel it and she had no clue what could be strong enough to move in *her* packed bag. She just hoped she wouldn't catch some kind of disease from whatever the thing was. After all, it couldn't be hair because hair didn't cut or bite people!

She raced back to her car as fast as she could in the heels so she could get rid of it. Once inside, she realized her hand was bleeding. It was a good thing she always kept a pack of tissues handy in the glove compartment and she grabbed one and pressed it against her throbbing wound. The thing still moved in her purse and Lluvia was now worried.

When she had first seen it flitting around on the floor of the house's master bedroom, she had thought it was hair, and had assumed it was simply being blown by the air from the ceiling fan. She had picked it up, thinking it was a piece of forensic evidence she could use to her advantage. The moment she had touched the thing, a shock of energy had raced up her hand and arm. Then, when she'd stuffed the short strand into her purse, she had felt the sting of something slicing into her hand.

Now, as she sat there putting pressure on her wound, she wondered what the heck the thing could be – a snake, maybe, or some type of venomous worm?

Her phone rang suddenly and she jumped, startled.

With her good hand, she answered, "Yeah?"

"You get the story?" her boyfriend asked. He had been the one to send her to the house in the first place. He was a fan of Sarah Baker's and had been trying without success to get into the Baker house since that awful protest-gone-awry two nights ago. This morning, he had come up with the brilliant idea of having Lluvia give it a go, believing she would be more apt to get into the place than he since she was an actual member of the press.

He had been right.

"Yes. I got it, even though I also got hurt doing it," she said, pouting for real this time.

"But you got video, right?" he asked, apparently unconcerned that she had been injured doing it.

"Yes, I got your damned video," she barked. "Now what are you gonna do for me?"

Her boyfriend laughed. "Sweetheart, you name it."

Lluvia smiled. Oh, she could think of several things she would accept as payment.

***

Tyson followed Manuel down another corridor. Several other boys and girls walked along with them and they finally came to a well-lit room occupied by a strange-looking creature with scaly, dark green skin and a similarly-covered green tail. It was clothed in a soft pink gown that appeared to be almost like a second skin as it moved with the wearer. It had no ears sticking out but there were tiny openings on the sides of its hairless head.

Tyson believed the creature to be a female of her species, judging from its chest area, and he was a little intimidated by how odd she looked with her strange green skin and tiny fanged teeth. But then she looked directly at him and he suddenly felt a calming sensation settle over him. When next he looked at her, she was smiling kindly at him in her own strange way and he relaxed.

The room was arranged like a classroom, with tables and chairs aligned so that they faced an outward facing desk at the front of the room. Tyson had started pre-kindergarten school back home on Earth this past year, so this setting was familiar to him and he relaxed even more. He took a seat along with all the others. There were several conversations going on, though no one spoke aloud. But when the lizard-like creature at the front of the room chimed in, the conversations stopped.

Tyson didn't know the words she used, but somehow he understood their meaning. She was apparently their teacher while they were aboard the station and she was charged with teaching them the things they would need to know to survive on Earth. Although Tyson had no idea what types of things those might be, he didn't say anything – aloud or otherwise. He had survived on Earth quite well until he and Demetrius had been taken.

Nevertheless, he listened to what the teacher had to say and he did learn a lot about plants and bugs and how dangerous some people, what the teacher called "humans", could be. They were warnings similar to the ones Tyson's momma and Demetrius were always giving him about people. But Tyson nodded and dutifully answered questions when he was called upon to do so. He also learned that his teacher was what was called a Toti, which was one of the nine species of something called Watchers. He had no clue what that meant, but he kept quiet about it.

When the lesson was done, he followed Manuel back to the room where all the people were and they each put on another of the little patches. Manuel explained that they were called "Geres patches" and that they had to wear a new one each day until it dissolved. Tyson didn't really understand why, but he didn't bother asking about it. He was having fun with his new friend. Until Demetrius came to find him, Tyson figured he would be better off sticking with Manuel.

It was weird. Tyson didn't know how long he had been on the station, but it felt like it had been a long while. Manuel and he went to the class over and over again and the green, lizard-like Toti teacher came each time, teaching them more things about Earth. Tyson found some of it interesting, some of it not. He especially liked the pictures and movies they were shown and he enjoyed the drawing and coloring activities they sometimes did.

One day, they were told to draw whatever they wanted while the teacher worked on a special project. Manuel drew a blue monster. It looked like a blue man with six arms and it had an angry face. He called it a Kordai. Tyson drew a black monster with long green hair that waved around like snakes. When the teacher asked him what his monster was called, he thought long and hard for a moment and then said silently, "It's called a Mahdii."

The Jess halted her tale as several gasps emitted from those seated around the room. She understood that the people were reacting to what the two children had seen. The Samarean knew all too well the history between the Kordai and the Mahdii. But how a couple of hybrids could have experienced such knowledge of the two species before any of the Watchers had discovered what was about to transpire was what concerned them.

The interrogator's voice was barely a whisper as she asked in disbelief, "They saw what was going to happen?" When the Jess nodded, Jarba's eyes widened in anger as she demanded, "And no one thought to do anything about it?"

The Jess spared a glance toward the still-unconscious alien Sephor. All of the things that had happened since that one fateful event, everything that had led them all to this point, the Jess believed, could be traced back to the Watcher who did do something about it.

She turned back to the interrogator and said, "Had not the Watchers done what they did because of what the two children saw, perhaps none may have survived."

Jarba ignored the conversations that sprang up around the room as she thought over the Jess' words. She wondered if the creature was referring to Watchers stationed at the facility where the two hybrids had been held. If so, to which Watchers did it refer?

The soft voiced Jess interrupted her thoughts, asking, "May I continue?"

Jarba nodded and the Jess thought for a moment

before picking up where she had left off.

After her initial shock at what the boys had said, the teacher gave each of the boys a strange look and asked if she could keep both Manuel's and Tyson's drawings. Both boys readily agreed and the class then went on to learn about how humans had been working with the aliens called "Watchers" for a long time. There was even a human man who came into the class to talk with them. He was a soldier in the military and he was part of a group of humans who had been assigned to work on the station with the Watchers. Apparently, there were humans from many different countries on Earth who worked there. The man explained that the Watchers had agreements with several of Earth's governments to monitor and help protect humans.

Tyson found all of this part of the lesson difficult to understand... and boring, so he only half-listened. His mind did focus in afterward on the part where the teacher explained that the station they were on was actually what people on Earth thought of as the moon. She said that was why the same side of the moon always faced Earth, so that the Watchers could always see what was going on down there. The observation deck in the room where they went after each class, the one filled with people where Tyson could look down upon the planet, was on the side that always faced Earth.

When he thought about it, it kind of made him feel comforted to know these Watchers were up here keeping an eye on everything down on Earth. With all the stuff his momma was always talking about going on in the world, it felt good knowing the Watchers were so close that they could help if people needed them to.

When the latest class they were in ended, Tyson followed Manuel down the long curving corridor again along with all the other kids from the class. This time when they stopped, they were not at the crowded room where they usually put on a new "Geres patch". Instead they entered a giant room that housed several small ships. There were multiple different types of aliens working in this room. Some were on and in the crafts, some were up on scaffolds doing what looked like construction work. There were many creatures off in one section sitting in a group using what looked like virtual computer screens. Tyson had seen similar things on movies. Although these appeared more complicated or advanced, he realized that was what they must be.

The group continued on and so Tyson followed along as one of the aliens in this room led them to one of the busier areas there, where a ship stood that had a ramp leading up into it. Several people and aliens entered and exited the craft, as if prepping it for a journey.

That is ship take us to Earth.

Tyson looked at Manuel. *Are you gonna come live with me and D and my momma?* he silently asked.

Manuel chuckled, shaking his head. *No. I already have place live. Host family waiting for me.*

Tyson sighed. He liked Manuel and he wished he could keep him as a friend.

We always friends.

Tyson smiled over at Manuel, glad his friend felt the same as he.

A tall, commanding-looking alien with dark blue eyes and black hair corralled them all together and then led the whole group up into the ship. He got everyone settled in their seats in one large section of the ship and then he went into another section. Tyson looked around for Demetrius, but his brother was nowhere in sight.

***

Demetrius cringed as yet another creature with a needle came at him. He already had so many needles stuck in him he didn't know where else he could be stuck. But the creature found a spot and in went the long needle. An involuntary cry escaped Demetrius at the pain, but he could not move.

It had been this way from the beginning. Once the aliens had finally gotten him onto the table, they had done something to him to make all his muscles freeze. All Demetrius had been able to do after that was scream. At first, he had screamed in anger. Then in frustration and desperation. Finally, his screams had turned to cries of terror.

Over and over, the creatures had poked and prodded. They had removed so much blood he had trouble remaining conscious. But every time he awoke from having passed out again, his first thought was that he had to find some way to break free so he could go find Tyson.

Oh, how he wished his mom was here! She would tell these fuckin' aliens a thing or two! She would kill 'em all!

Another needle was inserted and Demetrius gasped at the pain, his mind returning to the horror of his situation.

Why? Why were these things doing this to him? Were they torturing Tyson, too? He wouldn't understand what was going on and Demetrius hoped his younger brother would forgive him for not protecting him. Momma was always saying it was Demetrius' job to protect Tyson. After all, Tyson was different and he didn't know any better.

Demetrius always did his best to stand up for Tyson. Like when the other kids in the neighborhood made fun of Tyson because of how he looked or how he talked, Demetrius always fought them off. Now there were these aliens. Demetrius wondered if they were making fun of Tyson, too. He hadn't heard or seen Tyson since the creatures had taken him into a different room just after they had been brought on board the ship, so he didn't even know where Tyson was. But he had to find a way to get out of this room and go find his brother.

If only his mom could help.

Another alien approached. This one reached above him and moved a big machine down toward Demetrius' face. Demetrius tried to move his head as the machine kept coming closer and closer, but he couldn't move a muscle. He stared in horror as a needle came out of the center of the thing toward his eye. He couldn't even blink as the needle touched his eyeball. Then he heard a pop. More pain than he had ever thought possible wracked his brain and he screamed in agony until everything went black as he lost consciousness again.

Chapter 4

Diego carried Lluvia's limp form into the emergency room, yelling, "We need a doctor!"

Blood flowed from every opening on Lluvia's body and the trail stretched from the parking lot into the sterile ER.

Within seconds, a whole team of doctors and nurses had whisked her away from Diego and he was left sitting outside a set of double doors leading down the corridor where they had all disappeared with his girlfriend. Lluvia was the best girlfriend he had ever had. She was beautiful, smart, and she had a job – a *real* job even!

Now, some mysterious illness had taken hold and was threatening her life.

As he sat there over the next few hours, all he could think about was the thing Lluvia had brought home from the Baker house. She had shown it to him the moment she had gotten back from there. He had thought it was cool. Even when she had shown him the tiny cut she had gotten from the thing, he hadn't thought much about it. But when it had continued bleeding, and then her nose had started bleeding, he had become worried.

They hadn't been able to stop it, either. It had become progressively worse and worse. Then her eyes and ears had started bleeding.

Diego hated hospitals. He wanted nothing to do with the government or any type of officials, but this time he had had no choice. When she collapsed right in front of him, lying there unconscious on the floor of his mom's kitchen bleeding all over the place, he had realized there was no alternative but to take her to the ER.

This all *had* to have come from the cut Lluvia had gotten when she had stuffed the weird white thing into her purse. There was no doubt in his mind. The thing was he didn't know what to do about it. If he gave the thing to the doctors, it would be gone for good and they would bury the story.

No.

What had Lluvia told him when they had first gotten together? She had given him the name of some New York reporter she had said she knew and she had instructed him to contact the guy if anything ever happened to her.

Well, something had definitely happened to her!

Diego sat for another hour, watching the clock, wondering what the hell was taking so long. When one of the doctors who had been working on her when they had wheeled her away hours ago finally emerged from the double doors, Diego jumped up, his eyes full of hope.

One look at the doctor's face was all it took to realize it was over. Lluvia was... gone. He listened as the doc said what they always said. She had lost too much blood, they had done their best, that sometimes these things just happened – all the usual bullshit they told people when they failed to save somebody.

In a daze, he answered all the questions he was asked about Lluvia and then he drove himself home in his mom's old station wagon. Lluvia didn't have any family that Diego knew of. She didn't live with him, so the two of them really had nothing legally binding as far as bills and everything went. Technically, he wasn't responsible for any of the normal stuff a husband or relative would have to take care of when something like this happened.

He had no memory of the drive home to his mom's house. But he soon found himself standing in his room in his still-bloodied clothing, staring down at the still-moving white object he had placed in an old fish bowl before everything had happened. It had grown since Lluvia had first brought it home, he noticed. He wondered what it really was.

As he stood there staring at the thing, he held in one hand the piece of paper Lluvia had given him containing the name and contact information of the reporter she knew. His other hand held a knife he had grabbed from the kitchen before coming upstairs to his room.

The plan was to cut the evil thing to see if he could kill it. If it was moving, that meant it was alive, right? He didn't care. He was going to kill it the way it had killed Lluvia.

He carefully placed the knife blade down into the fish bowl, the sharp point hovering just above the thing. Then he quickly stabbed at the evil piece of white material. It cut in half, yet it still moved and moved, flipping this way and that inside the fish bowl. Although now it flipped a lot faster and more violently, striking out at the knife's blade. Each time it hit, there was the tinkling sound of metal on metal.

Diego removed the knife and then carefully picked up the fish bowl so he could examine the white objects from below. Oddly enough, the things did appear to have razor sharp edges along the ends of each section. As they flipped around within the bowl, it sounded like metal hitting glass.

This was too much for him to deal with. He put the fish bowl back onto the table and put a book on top of it to contain it. He then went in search of something he could put the thing in to mail it. He was done. He would send the thing to the reporter Lluvia had told him about and be done with it. He had a phone number and he would call the man and get this thing out of his life!

As he sat on the floor rummaging through the bottom cabinet in his mom's kitchen for a plastic bowl with a lid, he used his mom's land line to call the number Lluvia had given him. After several rings, he got what he assumed was the reporter's voicemail.

A computerized female voice said, "The person you have dialed is unable to answer at this time. Please leave your message after the tone."

The short beep sounded and he said, "H-Hello. This is…" Diego then paused. What could he say? *Hey, person I've never met. You don't know me and what I'm about to tell you is insane, but I've got this thing that killed my girlfriend and I want to send it to you. Would you mind giving me your address?* And besides that, how could he leave his name? Anybody could be listening to this call… the NSA, DHS, FBI – the list of possible acronyms went on and on.

He realized he was still recording and he cleared his throat before saying, "I'm, uh, a friend of Lluvia Rivera's… She, um, gave me this number once and told me to call if anything ever happened to her. Uh, I uh…," he paused again, shaking as emotion finally overwhelmed him. It took a minute before he was able to calm down enough to speak. In a tear-filled voice, he continued, "Lluvia's dead. I'm sorry to put it out there like that, all blunt and just in your face. But I don't know how else to say it."

He struggled for a moment to breathe, before saying, "Look, this is connected to the Sarah Baker case. If you've heard of that, then you know how important it is. Lluvia died trying to help and I know what killed her."

Diego paused when he found a large plastic bowl with a screw-on plastic lid that would work perfectly. This was it. He had found what he needed to be able to get the evil white things out of his life. An eerie calm settled over him and he pulled the wireless phone back to the ready, saying, "If you're interested in getting this damned thing, call me back at this number."

He pushed the end button and stood, holding the phone, the bowl and its matching lid. It was clear what he needed to do: transfer the evil worm things from the fish bowl into this bowl, seal it and then wait for the reporter to call. Then… what? Lluvia was gone, dead. He still had all her notes and the few bits of video and pics he could use to get the story out. But she was fucking dead!

As emotion started rising within him again, he shook his head and told himself, "One thing at a time, man. One thing at a time."

Back in his bedroom, he put the phone, the plastic bowl and lid on the desk top and removed the book from on top of the fish bowl. *Tink, tink, tink,* went the two strands as they wiggled within the glass fish bowl. It appeared almost as if they knew something was up, because they began moving faster and faster in their little prison.

Diego stared at the strands; his top lip curled up in hatred of the things. He would happily have burned them, thrown them in the microwave – anything he could to kill them. But doing that would only betray Lluvia's request. No. He would get them to the reporter she trusted. Diego had to believe that man, whoever he was, would then take care of this whole thing.

He carefully picked up the fish bowl and positioned it above the plastic bowl. In one quick motion, he flipped the fish bowl over and fitted it almost perfectly over the top of the plastic bowl. The two hair strands whipped around inside the plastic bowl like angry snakes, writhing and twisting this way and that. As quickly as he could, Diego removed the fish bowl and slapped the screw-top lid onto the plastic bowl. He pinched himself doing it, but the lid was on. He screwed it onto the bowl as tight as it would go.

It was done. The plastic was fairly thick and durable, which meant the strands couldn't puncture through it and escape. The bowl was small and light enough that he could ship it without any trouble, too. Now all he had to do was wait for the reporter to call.

As if on cue, the phone rang.

"Hello?" Diego answered, eager to get this over with.

For a moment, there was no response. Then a male voice asked, "Who is this?"

Diego paused before saying, "Bob Smith. Who are you?"

"Are you the one who left the voicemail about Lluvia Rivera?"

Hearing her name hurt and Diego closed his eyes up tight to keep the pain away. A second later, he was back in control. "Yes."

A pause. "Was she involved with Sarah Baker?" the man asked.

"No," Diego explained. "I asked her to snoop around the Baker house after the big meltdown over there the other night." He paused and then said, "It's my fault she's dead. If I hadn't asked her to go in there... if I hadn't made her..."

"Hey. Calm down," the voice on the other end of the line said. "How did you know Lluvia?"

When he was able to speak calmly again, Diego said, "She was my girlfriend."

"And so *you* knew Sarah Baker?"

"No, but I follow her online. I have a pretty popular conspiracy junkie vlog on a channel online and I thought

Lluvia would be able to get into the house, since she's with the press and all. Then she could get video and other stuff I could use online to talk about Sarah's case. I mean, there are a lot of people interested in this case and I just wanted to get as much information as possible." He slowly shook his head, tears threatening again as he continued, "And I sent her into that – that hell hole, with no protection!"

As Diego broke down again, the man asked, "So what happened to her in there? You said in your voicemail you knew what killed her. What was it?"

Sniffling, Diego explained, "She found a strand of hair – or what she thought was hair, while she was in there. Strange enough, it cut her when she picked it up. But she brought it back with her anyway, thinking I could use it somehow. When she got back here, we tried to stop the bleeding, but nothing worked. It just kept getting worse. And then she started bleeding from everywhere. I-I took her to the emergency room. I thought they would be able to help. I mean, what the fuck, man? She had a cut – a cut! From a fucking strand of hair!"

"Do you have the hair strand?" The man's voice was so neutral and calm that it helped bring Diego back under control.

"Yeah. I took a knife and tried to kill it, but I think I only pissed it off. I cut it in half, but it's still movin' and it's still pissed."

"Do you have it contained? I mean, are you safe from this thing?"

"Yeah. I was able to get it into a sealed container."

"That's good. Ah, listen. Can you overnight it to me? I'll pay the shipping costs."

"Yeah." Relief flooded through Diego as he wrote down the address the man gave him. "What name do I put for the recipient?"

Without missing a beat, the man said, "Bob Smith."

***

After serving her required ticket at the psychiatric wing of County Hospital, during which time she had been allowed visits only from her court-appointed legal representative and medical staff, Ms. Tameka Bradley was moved to a holding cell within the local correctional facility to await her first hearing. The general consensus was that Ms. Bradley had murdered both her children and dumped the bodies somewhere. However, thus far there was no trace of the boys. Forensics had gone over the house and all of the collected evidence, but had turned up nothing.

Tameka Bradley had still not said a single word.

***

"What's that?" the man called, whipping off the safety goggles he had been wearing for the past few hours as he looked up at the figure standing on the rim of the dig site.

"Secretary's on the horn for you, sir," the young private repeated.

"Thanks," the man said, annoyed that the kid had called him "sir". He worked for a living, goddamn it! He made his way out of the pit and then over to the tent at the top of the dig site. There was a large group of scientists milling about inside the tent, but the man ignored them all. Instead, he went directly to an open laptop where an image of an older, gray-haired man was displayed on the monitor. The man put on the headphones connected to the computer as he took the seat before it. "Mister Secretary," he said in greeting.

"We've got a situation," was all the older man said in return.

"Sir?"

"You're needed in Dallas," the elder man informed him. "Pack up. Your flight leaves in one hour from Anchorage."

"We're at a critical phase here, sir. We've already lost three to radiation poisoning and we're still not sure what the hell this thing is."

"It'll have to wait," the gray-haired man stated. "We can't risk this getting out to the public."

"So, what's in Dallas? Another device?" the man asked.

"You'll be briefed on the plane," was all the Secretary said.

The man nodded as the screen faded to black and then he sat there for a few minutes thinking. This site was now property of the U.S. government and would probably remain so for the rest of eternity because of the device a couple of hikers had discovered here. Those two were dead now, along with a few others who had come in contact with them. And now he was needed in Dallas? What the hell was going on?

Picking himself up off the chair, he made his way to a nearby tent and quickly packed his gear. He would do as he was told. If he was needed in Dallas, then off to Dallas he would go.

A tall young man with dark hair and ice-blue colored eyes entered the tent. "You are leaving?" he demanded in disbelief.

"Yep," he said.

Yaniv Nisrahali studied him suspiciously for a moment. He wasn't accustomed to working with Americans, but he had thought he could at least trust this one. The dark-skinned American man had earned Nisrahali's respect early on with how he had handled himself on what was turning out to be a very dangerous project. Now, however, Yaniv wasn't so sure he had placed his trust wisely.

"When will you be back?" he asked, his Israeli accent thick but understandable.

"Don't know," was all the American man said, as he continued packing his gear.

The two of them had been thrown together on this project just after Yaniv's partner had been lost at the site in Southeast Asia. Although neither one of them had been comfortable with having to work with a partner they knew nothing about, they had formed an uneasy alliance with each other. Eventually, each had earned the other's respect for their work ethic. But everything must eventually come to an end…

***

The police cruiser pulled to a halt without a sound and

the two officers inside cautiously emerged. This was the right place, but it appeared they had missed the party. Dispatch had indicated multiple reports had been received of noise disturbances at this location, but now the place felt like a ghost town. The senior patrolman frowned, concern heightening his sense of caution. The younger patrolman silently signaled that he was going to move around the back of the building to check for anyone hiding behind there. Senior nodded and continued forward along the front.

This part of the beachfront was popular at all times of the year, which made it all the spookier to find it this deserted. Senior checked the doors to the first shop. It was locked tight and there were no lights on inside. The next two yielded the same results. At the fourth shop door, the knob turned without a hitch and the door swung open wide.

A shiver ran down Senior's spine and he drew his sidearm, gripping it at the ready in front of him with both hands. "LAPD," he called out into the darkened shop as he slowly stepped inside. He thought he heard an echo of laughter. He licked his lips and moved forward into the dark interior, his heartrate increasing ever so slightly.

More laughter sounded and Senior pivoted around in a flash. The sound had come from just beside him, but there was no one there. Senior wondered if he was just spooked. He edged his way over to the nearest wall and started feeling along it with his hand for a light switch. Another round of laughter, this time from several individuals – all male and all right behind him. Senior whipped around, his piece pointed toward the direction from which the laughter had come.

A light appeared in the shop door and the younger patrolman called, "Grimes, you in there?"

"Yeah!" Grimes replied, only just managing to keep the tremble out of his voice. Someone was dickin' around with him in this place and he was glad the junior officer had come in with the flashlight. Now they would get to the bottom of this.

"Grimes! Are you here, man?" Junior called again, advancing into the shop. Laughter sounded again, but this time it sounded closer to Junior's position.

"Grimes… are you here?" a high-pitched male voice softly mocked.

The younger man whipped around, clearly shaken, gripping the gun in his hand with stiff fingers. "Grimes! Was that you?"

Grimes called out again, "I'm here."

Junior appeared not to hear him.

"Get him, Iblis," a whiney male voice called and Junior jerked around, his piece firing at the would-be attacker. It merely blew through a window along the outer wall and out into the night air, for there was no one in the shop that the young patrolman could see. He was shaking all over now and he had no idea where his senior partner was. But whatever was going on in this place, he wasn't about to wait around a second longer by himself! He high-tailed it out the front door back out onto the boardwalk. Laughter sounded again all around within the darkened shop interior.

Grimes was more pissed now than spooked, even though he hadn't seen anyone within the shop's interior while the kid's flashlight had been on. But he also had enough years of experience to know that the best thing here was going to be to call for back-up. He had counted at least four different voices laughing that last time and they hadn't all been high-pitched. Several of them had sounded like their owners were larger males and Grimes, who was all of 5'9", had no wish to get into a physical match with a deranged body-builder all juiced up on 'roids – if not something worse!

He slowly made his way toward the shop's entrance, intent on getting out to call for back-up. Before he had taken two steps, a deeper male voice softly brushed just by Grimes' left ear, asking, "Leaving so soon, Ronnie?"

For the first time in his life, Ronald Grimes, 42 years old, after 19 years on the force, saw his life flash before his eyes. In that moment, that split-second moment of such terror he was certain every last hair on his body would turn white as snow, Grimes realized he had but one option – to run!

Wild, raucous laughter followed him all the way out onto the boardwalk. No matter how fast Grimes ran, the laughter followed close behind him. Junior was standing with one foot inside the driver's side of the cruiser and one foot out, with a terrified but relieved look on his face as he yelled, "Grimes! Where you been, man?"

Grimes didn't stop to explain as he made a bee-line toward the passenger side of the cruiser. But before he could even reach the car, there was a bright flash and a loud "BOOM" that sounded on the beach, shaking the ground and knocking Grimes to the ground. He quickly picked himself up and looked over toward the beach, wondering what on earth could have happened.

The night was quiet and still. Even the waves that earlier had splashed spray several feet high as they had crashed onto the shore were now silent ripples, appearing still. The entire ocean looked like one giant piece of smooth glass reflecting a perfect picture of the velvet black night sky above it.

A noise like a cough sounded from a few yards away, bringing both officers' attention to the spot where the bright flash of light had presumably touched down. Standing there alone on the beach on what looked like a round sheet of glass was a short, dark figure in what looked to be some sort of mini-dress.

"Can you help me find my momma?" a young male voice called.

Grimes frowned, wondering if this kid was in on whatever joke was being played here. But when he looked around, there was no one else on the beach. The evil laughter that had plagued him and his partner was gone. He hadn't heard it since the light flashed. Maybe the light had frightened away the perps and this kid was really lost.

The older officer made his way over to the figure on the beach, noting that the surrounding sand was all blown out from the glassy center and there was a depression like a slight crater where the kid in the dress stood. It turned out to be a skinny, odd-looking child, an African American male – probably about five or six years old. He was wearing some kind of shiny cloth sack, it looked like. Grimes reached out to touch the cloth. It felt almost like silk and he shook his head, wondering what on earth possessed people to spend money on such useless extravagances. Imagine – putting a silk dress on a little boy!

"You lost, son?" he asked the kid.

The kid looked up at him with eyes that were slightly askew. *Can you help me find my momma?* asked the same young male voice again.

Grimes ripped his hand back away from the boy, his breath locked tight in his chest. The kid had spoken without even opening his mouth! Either that, or Grimes had finally lost it!

Grimes took a step away from the kid, finally remembering to breathe as he called over his shoulder for his partner to come to him. He kept his eyes on the boy the entire time, not trusting anything at this point. When the younger patrolman arrived, Grimes could tell he was still shaken from their earlier bout with the pranksters. But he didn't care. The incident in the shop had been spooky enough, but this was beyond what Grimes could handle.

"Stay here with the kid while I go call this in," he instructed his partner. He didn't wait for a response. Using the transmitter on his shoulder, he reported back to dispatch and called for back-up to the scene as he crossed the beach to the spot in the parking lot where the cruiser waited. He was instructed to take the kid over to County Hospital where he was to hand the child over to protective services.

Grimes wanted to argue, for he didn't want to go anywhere near that freak again. But there was no logical reason he could think of to give dispatch as to why he and his partner couldn't transport the lost child. Before settling into the driver's seat, he waved and called to his partner, "Bring the kid! We're takin' him over to County!" It was only when he heard his partner's voice over the walkie asking him to repeat his instructions that Grimes realized the waves were now crashing against the beach again. He stared out at the roiling ocean in wonder as his partner and the strange young boy approached the cruiser.

The ride over to County Hospital was quiet and uneventful. When a nurse asked if the child had spoken since the officers had found him, Grimes merely shook his head. Who would have believed him otherwise?

Chapter 5

Lieutenant Treyvon Manning read the report. Pretty gruesome way to die – some foreign organism decimating one's insides. Whatever this thing was, it was nasty. As he reread the report, he studied the photo of the young journalist. Her name was Lluvia Rivera and she had been beautiful at one point. The piece of meat he'd seen when he had first arrived at the M.E.'s office in Dallas this evening, however, had looked nothing like her picture. It had looked like it had been melted from the inside out. The medical examiner didn't know what to make of it.

A line in the written report caught Manning's eye and he sat up straighter.

It seemed Ms. Rivera had been brought to the hospital by a boyfriend, a certain Diego Montoya. *Where is this Diego Montoya?* he wondered.

As he went in search of the M.E., the black phone he had been forced to carry for the project rang.

"Manning," he answered tersely.

"Do we have containment?" asked the voice on the other end.

"Mister Secretary," Manning said, "I'm not even sure what this bug is. But whatever it is, it hates people."

"How many have been infected so far?"

"Unknown, sir. Thus far, we only have the one body, but there was a young man involved. I'm searching him out, as we speak."

"Von," the Secretary said, his voice deadly serious, "I cannot tell you how vital it is that we discover the root of this thing."

"Understood, sir."

The line clicked and Manning pocketed the despised phone as he continued along the hallway toward the M.E.'s office. He would happily have tossed the thing into the garbage. Unlike most people, he preferred to keep himself out of reach and off the grid as much as possible. The only reason he had agreed to carry the damned thing was because the Secretary had asked him to do so as a personal favor so they could keep in touch, updating each other with new developments whenever necessary.

Manning despised technology. He much preferred things old-school. A good face-to-face conversation with someone was infinitely more informative than a phone call or a text or email, in his opinion. He could actually get a feel for the other person that way. Online, he couldn't tell if a person was lying or not.

He believed people relied too heavily on technology. He also believed the time was fast approaching when all the conveniences everyone had grown so accustomed to would be rendered useless. All it would take was one electromagnetic pulse and it would all be over.

What were they going to do then?

As he reached the M.E.'s office, his thoughts returned to the case. The man wasn't there. One of his assistants said she thought he had gone to the restroom, but that he had been gone for some time now.

Manning wordlessly back-tracked down the hall to the restrooms. Inside, he discovered the M.E., a short, balding Indian man, lying unconscious on the floor of one of the stalls. He jimmied open the door to the stall and leaned in to check the carotid for a pulse. He halted just before touching the man, as he noticed a tiny drop of milky pink liquid emerging slowly from the corner of one of the man's eyes. Within seconds, there were minute amounts of milky blood emerging from all over the man's body until his skin virtually poured blood.

Manning jumped back before any of the blood could touch him. Whatever this thing was, it spread quickly – and it was a brutal killer.

For the first time, he was happy to have the cell phone as he called for a containment crew to come to the scene. He already had his crew in town taking care of the young reporter's things at her place, so it wasn't long before members of his team showed up.

Manning had had just enough time to watch as the flesh on the M.E.'s body was eaten away by whatever bug this thing was inside him. It was a horrible way to go. Never had Manning encountered anything like this, even after his time working with USAMRID, the CDC and the WHO!

The containment team took over the scene and Manning left them to it. He would get the boyfriend's contact info on his own. Ten minutes later, he was on his way. The woman at admissions had been only too happy to supply the kid's contact information after just a little flirting from him. What he found when he got to the boy's home was really no surprise. The kid and an older woman, presumably his mother, were both dead. As soon as the containment crew was able to get there, everyone suited up in protective gear and Manning informed them in no uncertain terms he wanted the place searched with a fine-toothed comb.

"What the hell is this thing, boss?" asked one of his more experienced team members as the crew first took in the bloody scene.

Manning wished he had an answer. Instead, he said, "I don't know. Just take every precaution before touching anything." He sighed heavily as he stared at the two bodies. It had been a little more than 72 hours since the young reporter had died at the hospital. Now, the kid who had been with her in her final moments was dead, along with his mother. It was going to be tough to examine the bodies, what with the milky pink liquid still streaming from their insides. Most of the flesh on each corpse had been eaten away from the inside and there wasn't much left that could be used for identification other than teeth. Even those appeared to be being eaten away by the bug.

"I want cell phones and computers checked for any communications with others. We're stopping this thing right here, right now, people."

An hour later, one of the techies of the group called, "I've got something!"

Manning and several team members gathered around where the tech was sitting with a laptop he had hacked into. "It looks like a package was picked up the day everything happened," he said. "It was overnighted to the U.K. to a Bob Smith."

"Phone records?" Manning asked.

"Nothin', boss."

"All right. Check with the carrier to see if anyone there has been affected. Then get the London team over to that address ASAP to check out this generic Bob Smith to see if he got the damned package." Manning turned and headed for the door.

"Where are you goin', boss?" one of the team members asked.

"To London. Bob Smith, my ass!" he stated as he walked out.

An hour later, he was back on board an airplane, heading for London this time. With the entire team of emergency room staff who'd worked on Ms. Rivera now dead or dying, Manning only hoped he could make it to the U.K. in time to stop anyone else from catching this thing.

***

Nikolai Sharapov adjusted his grip on his bag as he dug his vibrating cell phone from within his back pants pocket. This was no simple task as he made his way as quickly as possible without running down the moving walkway between terminals. He finally managed to pull the flat chunk of metal out of his pocket and then nearly tripped over another person's bag as he performed the maneuver on the lighted screen to allow him to be able to pick up the line.

"Damn it!" he barked into the phone as he righted himself.

"Well, it's great to hear from you, too," his boss' heavy New England accent growled from the other end of the line.

"Sorry, Frank," Nick quickly apologized.

"Humph," was all Frank said.

"What can I do for you?" Nick asked, picking up his pace once again along the moving walkway.

"Your story's late," Frank said. Frank always said that. It was always late. Nick Sharapov was perhaps the best reporter in New York, and certainly the best one he had on staff and Frank knew it. So did Nick. That was why Nick never bothered with things like deadlines.

Well, that and the fact that his parents had left him a boat-load of money when they had passed away a few years ago. Nick didn't have to work, but he loved it and he was great at it. Frank also knew that and that was why he kept Nick on his staff at the paper.

"I know, I know," Nick said as he finally disembarked from the moving walkway only to turn a corner to discover yet another one he would have to take. "Look, Frank," he said, exasperated. "The story's gonna be a bit later than usual, but I'll get it to you just as soon as possible. I've got another lead that just came in and I really need to check it out before I finish this thing. Could blow the whole thing wide open, if what I just found out is true."

Nick had more contacts worldwide than most people had as friends on those idiotic social networking sites everyone was so addicted to these days. Frank knew if Nick said he had a good lead, then he had best give him some time and space to check it out. "Where are you?" he asked.

"DFW," Nick said. He heard the last call for his flight and broke into a run. This damned lead had only just come in an hour ago and, as luck would have it, it was rush hour. Nick had been all the way on the North side of Dallas when he had gotten the call. He had taken one taxi and a helicopter to get to the airport on time and, now that he was this close, he was *not* going to miss his plane.

"Listen, Frank," he said. "I've gotta go."

"Here, I hope," Frank immediately interjected.

"Nice try, but nope. I'm headed to Sydney," Nick said as he handed his ticket and passport to the agent at the International Departures gate.

"Australia?" Frank demanded. "I thought you said this thing was happening down in Dallas."

"It was and I checked out everything here," Nick explained, "and, guess what, there was already a net around the whole thing by the time I got here. But now a lead has come in on a new development and I have to go to Australia to check it out." The agent handed his items back, all checked and approved, and he sprinted for the gate. "There's been another disappearance, this time down under, and it looks like the same M.O. as the one here. I'm hoping I can get there before anyone else. If I can, I'm gonna check it out and see where it can take us."

The airline employees were just closing the plane's doors as he rushed up to them waving his ticket, wildly motioning for them to hold up. The closest one to him checked out his credentials, ticket, and boarding pass and waved him on through. "Look, Frank, I'll call you as soon as I know anything," he said, rushing down the aisle toward the back of the completely full plane.

He hung up without waiting for an answer and smiled politely at the flight attendant who was heading in the opposite direction up the aisle toward him. She noticed his carry-on and said, "I'm afraid there's only one seat left, sir, and all the overhead compartments are packed. You'll have to give your bag to me and then take your seat. It's the last row back on the left, middle seat."

Nick nodded and passed on through to the last row of seats at the back of the airplane. He had barely had time to pack for this trip in the first place after he had received word about the thing Diego Montoya had sent him in the mail, so he had only the one bag. He wasn't concerned overmuch with that. Whatever he might need in Australia, he would just buy once he got there.

He found the one empty seat at the back of the plane. It was between a large-breasted blond who looked to be an American about eighteen, barely legal, and a stodgy, round British-looking businessman who looked as if he was *not* looking forward to the long flight. Nick usually flew first class, so this was not his ideal, either. But if he had to sit scrunched up next to someone, he would prefer it to be someone of about the teenager's height and build.

He gave her a crooked smile as he waited politely for old stodgy to stand and move to give him access to the middle seat. Once seated, he turned away from the aisle.

"Hi, I'm Nick," he said to the blond, completely ignoring the businessman in the aisle seat.

"Hi," she said with a high-pitched cheerleader voice,

"I'm Buffy."

"Of course, you are," Nick said with a smile.

***

Iblis watched from a crouched position behind the trash dumpster as the light faded back up into the sky. His upper lip curled in disgust. The creatures' craft slowly moved on in the dark night back up into the stratosphere.

A dart of anger shot through him and he stood, already turning toward the other end of the alleyway. The Designers and creatures like them were free to roam about the Universe while he was stuck on this rock. He couldn't even return to his own home because of the one who was waiting there to pounce the moment he crossed the barrier. He hated this side and he hated his side. It wasn't fair and he was sick of it! It was time he took matters into his own hands instead of allowing others to rule his world.

"Where are *you* going?" the Shaitan Satariel asked. He was still shaken by the threat posed by the recently-departed ship and he was in no hurry to leave the safe haven of his hiding spot behind the dumpster.

Iblis flashed a wicked lopsided grin toward his friend. "To pick a fight," he said.

***

"Come on," Stacy whispered as she stealthily turned the corner. Matt followed close behind. The pastel pink scrubs she wore were a little tight, but at least they helped it look like she worked at the hospital. Her sister, Samantha, was not going to be happy when she found out Stacy had borrowed the scrubs. When she found out *why* Stacy had taken them, she would be livid. Hopefully, Stacy's story would have gone viral by the time Samantha did find out so she would forgive her only sibling.

Stacy stopped in her tracks. Matt silently moved in close behind her. Ten yards down the corridor was the pediatric floor nurse's station. There were two nurses stationed there going about their nightly routines. Neither one noticed the two people lurking in the darkened hallway.

"How are we gonna get past them?" Matt asked in a whisper.

A plan sprang into Stacy's mind. Her sister had only just been hired on to work in the ER here and hadn't yet had enough time to get to know any of the nurses in the building. Stacy just hoped these two hadn't yet met Samantha. She motioned for Matt to stay back as she adopted an air of confidence and moved forward toward the nurse's station.

The nurse closest to her looked up at her approach.

"Hi, there," Stacy said, smiling. "I'm Samantha Buffington. I work downstairs in the ER. I heard a boy had been brought in tonight before I came in for my shift. His name's Tyson Bradley?"

The nurse nodded, smiling back, and said, "Yes. The boy was admitted. Are you a friend of the family?"

Stacy sighed in not-so-mock relief, saying, "Yes. His grandmother, Sheree Johnson, is disabled and she can't make it in here to visit him, so I told her I would check in on him for her. Would that be okay?"

"Well, he's asleep right now and visiting hours are over for the night," the nurse said, frowning as she thought out the situation. Then she smiled back up at Stacy and said, "But I guess it wouldn't hurt if you just look in on him a minute." She stood and came around to the outside of the desk. "Follow me and I'll take you to him."

The nurse headed down the same corridor where Matt was and Stacy cringed on the inside as she followed the woman, hoping with all her heart Matt had the good sense to hide before the woman spotted him. She needn't have worried though, for he was nowhere in sight and the nurse continued on down the hallway to the boy's room.

***

Tyson woke with a start. He was lying in a strange room and he was all alone. He could hear rain pounding against the window just off to the right and there was a trace of light showing there from the streets below. But other than that, there were no sounds or other sources of light in the room. He sat up a little and realized he was in a hospital room. At least, he thought it was a hospital room. He hadn't been in a hospital since he had been a baby, so he couldn't be sure. But it looked like the ones he had seen on television.

He frowned as he thought back to what could have happened for him to end up in a hospital room. Was he back on Earth? He could recall nothing beyond his time with the kids on board the spaceship. He had played the game with them and then he had talked with the one girl. After that, he had no idea what had happened.

He sat up fully on the bed, lifting his arms to examine them. The sticky thing Manuel had put on him wasn't there anymore and Tyson wondered what had happened to it. He sat thinking for a moment, trying to remember what could have happened. He didn't feel hurt or sick. He moved his legs. They seemed fine. He looked around the darkened room, wondering how he had gotten there.

Looking over the edge of the bed, he realized it was up pretty high. It would be a long fall to the hard floor below if he didn't do it right and Tyson was more than a little afraid of heights. He sat back again, deciding it would be best to wait for someone to come to him rather than him going to look for someone. Maybe whoever came into the room next would be able to tell him what had happened. He hoped it would be his momma or Demetrius.

Just then, the door opened and two white women in hospital clothes walked in. The first noticed he was sitting up in bed and she flipped on the light switch, sending a bright fluorescent gleam throughout the room. Tyson quickly shut his eyes against the blinding light before slowly opening them again to mere slits and blinking.

"Hey, sweetheart," the first woman softly said. "You're supposed to be asleep."

As Tyson looked at her, he heard her thoughts. She was truly concerned about him and he believed her smile to be genuine. He hesitantly smiled back at her. The second woman who had entered the room wasn't so easy to read and he frowned, tilting his head a bit as he studied her. She had a nice smile and she appeared to be friendly, but there was something kind of secretive about her. He couldn't hear her thoughts and that bothered him.

Who are you? he silently asked, but he received no response.

"I bet you're happy to see her, huh?" the first lady asked as she plumped the pillow behind him. "Samantha here has come to check on you for your grandmother. Although I know your grandmother wanted to come here to check on you, herself."

Tyson's frown deepened.

The silent lady stepped forward and took hold of his hand. Her eyes were very serious, as if she was trying desperately to communicate some secret to him. Aloud, she said, "I told Grandma Johnson I would look in on you when I got here tonight."

Tyson had no idea who she was talking about. He didn't have a grandmother, as far as he knew. He caught the name "Johnson" though and he wondered if she meant old lady Johnson from next door. He pulled his hand back and the lady let it go. Tyson didn't know what kind of game this woman was playing, but something told him he needed to play along.

"Wh-Where's momma and Demetrius?" he asked aloud in a timid voice. It seemed like it had been a long time since last he had spoken aloud and his voice sounded strange to his own ears.

The woman who had first entered the room looked down at her watch and said, "I've got to get my reports done before I start my rounds." As she looked at the one named Samantha, she asked, "Will you be okay in here with him if I leave you for a little while?"

The Samantha lady assured her, "Oh, yeah. You go right ahead. Ty and I will be fine. I'm just gonna talk to him for a few minutes."

The other lady appeared relieved and she left.

Tyson waited for the door to close completely before turning on the stranger named Samantha. "Okay. Who are you and where is my brother?" he demanded, keeping his voice low.

The woman gave a sigh of relief as she said, "Oh,

good. Listen. My name is not Samantha. That's my sister. I'm Stacy and I'm here to help you."

Just then, the door opened and a tall white man walked in. Tyson tensed for a moment until Stacy smiled at the man.

"I was wondering when I'd see you again," she told the man.

"I had to wait for Nurse Ratchet to leave before I could get in here," he said. He looked at Tyson and a strange expression flew over his face.

Stacy turned to the boy, saying, "Tyson, this is my husband, Matt. Matt, this is Tyson."

Matt nodded, saying, "Hiya, Tyson."

Tyson just nodded back. The man was looking at him so funny it made Tyson want to hide behind Stacy, but he didn't. Instead, he watched as Matt produced some clothes from inside his backpack and handed them to Tyson.

"These will probably be too big for you, sport," he said. "But it was the best we could do on such short notice."

Tyson took the clothes and then tensed as Matt reached for him. He quickly realized he had nothing to worry about as the man simply picked him up and then helped him to stand on the cold floor. "Thanks," Tyson told him before going into the bathroom. After closing the door, he used the restroom and then put on the clothes they had brought. Matt had been right. The T-shirt, sweatshirt and jeans were way too big. The socks, too. But the tennis shoes fit almost perfectly. He left the discarded hospital gown on the floor of the bathroom. He had no idea what had happened to the ugly dress thing the aliens had given him to wear.

"I thought those old jeans of mine would be too big," Stacy said resignedly when Tyson re-entered the room. She quickly produced a belt and looped it around his waist, buckling it as tight as it would go. The pants were still loose, but at least they would stay up without him holding them and she nodded in satisfaction.

"We ready?" Matt asked. Stacy and Tyson nodded. "All right. Let me make sure the coast is clear." Matt slowly opened the door enough to stick his head through. He looked both ways and then opened it wider, signaling for the others to follow. All three of them made it out into the deserted hallway and then moved as quickly and quietly as they could toward the elevator. The wait there seemed interminable and Tyson's heartbeat was pounding so loud inside his chest he was sure someone was going to hear it and they were all going to get caught. But then the bell on the elevator dinged and the doors slid open.

After reaching the ground floor, no one stopped the trio as they left the building. He was just a regular kid wearing baggy clothes leaving a hospital in the middle of the night with two adults. That's what people saw when they looked at him. Tyson knew this because he could hear their thoughts. He didn't know how he could hear them, but he could. All Matt was thinking about was how to get them out of the hospital and into the car he had parked just outside without getting caught. However, Tyson still got no readings from the Stacy lady's mind.

They made it to an SUV and Matt opened the door for Tyson. It was tall and the boy looked to the taller man for help. Without a word, Matt picked him up and gently placed him onto the back seat, carefully buckling and fitting the seat belt around Tyson before shutting the door. Stacy climbed into the front passenger side and then Matt slid behind the wheel. They were gone within seconds and Tyson turned in his seat to watch the hospital fade into the distance as they drove away.

Matt turned left at a stoplight and Stacy said, "We can't go to Sam's."

"Why not?" Matt asked as he turned on his signal and pulled over to park in the only open space he could find on the side of the road. It was still nighttime and the streets were crowded. "That was the plan."

"I know," she said. "But I had to use her name to find out what room he was in. So, we can't go there."

Matt shook his head in despair. "Stace, that means we can't go to anyone's place we know. They'll know exactly who we are. Hell, we might already have our own satellite tracking us by now!"

"I know!" Stacy barked at him. "It was the only thing I could think of."

Matt sighed in frustration. "Let me think a minute. I'm sure I'll figure out something."

Tyson wondered what they meant. "We can go to my house," he offered. "My momma'll be waitin' for me anyway."

Matt and Stacy turned to look at him, both of them wearing strange expressions. From Matt's mind, Tyson learned a great deal of what had been happening while he had been up in space. Tears sprang to his eyes as he learned of the things people had been saying about his momma for the past few weeks, of the things they thought she had done. It appeared that his momma had been sent to jail for killing Demetrius and him. Only thing was – she hadn't done it!

Tyson turned his head away.

Stacy turned more fully toward him, reaching for him. "Tyson?" she asked out of genuine concern.

He turned back to her, swallowing hard and saying, "My momma didn't kill me or D."

Stacy looked in shock at Matt. Neither one knew how the boy had discovered his mother had been accused of murdering his brother and him.

"We know, sport," Matt finally said as he turned to face Tyson. "And we're gonna make sure she's okay, but we've gotta find Demetrius first."

Tyson's face crumbled again and he shook his head. "You c-can't," he choked out.

"Why not, Tyson?" Stacy asked.

"Because he's still up there," he whispered.

"Still up where, Tyson?" Matt softly asked, barely breathing.

Tyson looked at both of them, his expression serious. "Up in space," he said.

Chapter 6

Demetrius slowly roused back into full consciousness. He still lay atop the hard metal table, and tubes still ran from his body to machines stationed all around the table. He still felt the hum of the ship's vibrations. He had no idea how long he had been out this time, but at least there were none of those scary-looking aliens around poking and prodding him. They had hurt him so much the last time he couldn't bear the thought of them doing the same to Tyson.

Just the thought of his younger brother enduring the same had him trying to move, testing his strength. He had to get up, had to go find Ty. Then he had to figure out a way off the ship. He couldn't let them do this to Ty.

A sound off to his left alerted him suddenly that he was no longer alone in the room. He tensed as visions of the scary tall gray aliens coming at him with more needles crowded into his mind. Worse yet, what if it was the even scarier small gray aliens? Those were the worst because they hurt him without even caring. At least the tall ones appeared to try not to hurt him.

But the image that presented itself to him when the newcomer finally reached his field of vision was not that of either type of gray aliens. Instead, it was a much taller and greener alien. It had scaly skin and no ears, almost like a lizard. Its eyes were blue and its teeth were more like tiny fangs with sharp points at the end. It looked like it was a female, judging by its boobs and the clothes it wore.

A calming sense of peace descended upon Demetrius' mind and he relaxed. The creature flipped some kind of switch and Demetrius immediately felt the control of his muscles return. He calmly watched as the creature reached and began removing the multitude of needles the other aliens had stuck into him all over his body. She did it so gently that he barely felt any pain. It took only a couple of minutes before he was completely free of the tubes and wires and then the creature motioned for him to sit up.

Miraculously, he discovered he was able to pull

himself up on the table. His body was incredibly weak, but he finally managed to roll over. He practically fell off the table, but the creature caught him to keep him from falling and getting too banged up. She helped him stand and supported him as he walked a few steps until his legs stopped shaking.

He was naked, but she had some sort of dress thing for him. She helped him pull it over his head. She then motioned for him to follow her and Demetrius did his best to keep up. They left the room and silently made their way down a great curved corridor. There were many doors along the long corridor and Demetrius was afraid the whole time that someone was going to come out into the hallway and see him. Still, he followed the lizard-like creature.

When she came to a stop before one of the doorways, she turned to him and motioned for him to follow her. But Demetrius still needed to find Tyson. Was his brother behind this door? The creature returned her attention to the door and it slid open. As she moved through into the room beyond, Demetrius pulled up behind her, bending to see inside the room.

Tyson was not inside, that he could see. But there were noises coming from somewhere deep within the room they entered and the female creature silently motioned for Demetrius to move along the back wall toward a darker part of the room. He stayed behind her as she moved quickly through the room, keeping close to the outer wall and moving ever closer toward the darker recesses. The noise of the same door they had used opening behind them sounded and the creature pushed Demetrius ahead of her and through another doorway, quickly closing that door between them so that he suddenly found himself alone in a dark room.

He took a step along the wall, wondering if there was a light switch or something he could find to use for light. Without warning, the entire room suddenly lit up from some type of motion detection and Demetrius could see. This room was huge and it appeared to go on forever. He heard more noises from off to the left and he quickly hid behind some stacked round containers. He was alone now and more than a little afraid. Instead of allowing the fear to take hold, he looked around and spotted some sort of metal tool. He grabbed it to use as a weapon should any of the aliens spot him and attack.

There was a grinding noise coming from just in front of him, like some kind of machine was operating. Demetrius moved to see if he could get a glimpse of what it was. Through an opening between the stacks of the containers he had hidden behind, he could see through a window in another doorway along the back wall of the room. In that other room, he caught sight of a multitude of some brown-colored alien creatures as they worked to load bits and pieces of things into a huge vat. He saw all manner of items being thrown into the vat and he wondered if that was trash.

Another door off to his left opened and Demetrius quickly moved away from it, hiding behind whatever containers or other obstacles he could find. He kept moving to get away from the creatures that entered the room until eventually he came to a different part of the ship where it was much darker. Here, there was another room and he moved into it, keeping low and to the edge of the room to avoid accidentally setting off the lights. He was about to sit down to rest against the wall, when even more aliens came through the doorway and into the room. The lights flared to life and Demetrius rushed toward the back of this new room.

He came to an open corridor and ran into it. This one was much smaller than the other and he quickly picked a door to try. It opened onto a dark room. Demetrius scooched into it and squatted just on the other side along the wall, waiting for it to slide closed again. It did and he slumped against the wall. The room was pitch black and he appeared to be alone. He sat down on the cold floor, stretching his legs out as he laid his head back against the wall. He had no idea how he was going to find Ty in this huge maze of a place. He was so tired and he had no clue where to go.

A new vibration flared to life and it shook the floor and the wall. After his initial fear at the new noise and vibration, he relaxed back against the wall again. It was just some other machine working. The low hum and the vibrations were like a soothing balm to his frazzled nerves and within seconds, Demetrius was sound asleep on the floor beside the wall. The rumbling vibration of the smaller ship he had inadvertently boarded leaving the hangar had lulled his exhausted body to sleep.

***

Nick Sharapov disembarked from the plane and moved on through customs with the rest of the passengers at the Sydney International Airport. He was never so glad to get off a flight in his entire life as he was to exit this one. The young Buffy had talked his ear off the entire way from Dallas to Sydney and Nick had had enough! If he never met another blond bimbo cheerleader type, it would be too soon. As if that hadn't been enough, the old stodge sitting on the other side of him had been one of the most flatulent people Nick had ever had the misfortune of encountering and Nick now sucked in a huge breath of clean air, grateful to finally breathe something other than gas!

Fortunately for Nick, the man had bolted like the proverbial bat out of Hell toward the front of the plane the minute the captain switched off the seatbelt sign. As for the cheerleader, the ditzy young woman had brought along a whole shop's worth of luggage and Nick had last spotted her with several of the bags lying open inside one of the inspection rooms in the customs area. He didn't think she would be getting released anytime soon, so there was no danger he would have to spend any more time with her before his next flight was due to leave.

The customs agent handed him back his passport and Nick grabbed his single bag and headed off in the direction of the gate indicated on his connecting flight ticket voucher. He still had another hour to wait before that flight was due to leave, but that didn't mean he couldn't get some work done during that time. His contact in Australia had instructed Nick to call the moment he landed in Sydney and that was just what Nick planned to do.

This case struck him as being kind of strange. Normally, serial killers tended to stick to one particular area, someplace close to home where they felt comfortable. This globetrotting theory bothered Nick in the extreme, even though he had at first scoffed at the idea that this disappearance in Australia could have anything to do with the Baker case in Texas. But after hearing what his source in Australia had to say about what she heard had been found at the scene of the crime, Nick had quickly decided this new case was worth checking into. He had booked his flight to Australia while packing his bag in the hotel room where he had been staying in Dallas.

Now, as he sidled up to the counter at one of the few pubs that offered relief from the ultra-bright whiteness that filled most of the airport, he dug out his satellite phone. He ordered a pint of their darkest lager and then made the call to his source. He sipped the lukewarm lager as he waited for an answer. Beer didn't taste good with ice cubes in it, but he sure wished he had some.

The airport was plenty busy, but there were still many open seats around him and he felt quite comfortable making the call. Nick was simply happy to be somewhere cool. It might be winter in the outback, but they still needed air conditioning in their buildings. Unfortunately, the Aussies didn't always consider that a necessity.

Nick knew it would be cooler outside at night, so he guessed he should be relieved he was visiting now instead of during the summer months. The outback got so hot then that it was almost unbearable to the non-native tourists. Nick had visited Australia many times as a child, but had long ago decided he would never visit again during the summer months. He recalled being stuck there during such hot times that he had thought he would die.

"Yeah?" a sharp female voice asked in answer to the ring, bringing Nick out of his reverie.

"Kiley?" Nick asked. "It's Nick."

Immediately, the voice on the other end of the line turned smooth as silk and dripped with feline flirtation, as she said, "Nicky, darling, I was hoping it was you. Where are you? I'll come right over and pick you up."

"Ah, that's not necessary," he said. "I've just landed

at Sydney Airport, but I'll be heading out for Alice Springs in less than an hour. I just needed to go over some of the fine points of the information you gave me earlier so that I can contact the inspector on the case once I arrive there."

"You mean, you're not going to stop by and see me before?" she pouted over the phone line. Nick could just imagine her Botox-filled lips doing their best to frown and he almost smiled. Kiley Plimpton and he went back a long way, even before his parents died, and Nick knew if he gave her a minute, she would take a week. She was just that good at sucking away time.

"I'm afraid I don't have time for socializing on this trip, love," he informed her smoothly. "This is strictly work."

"Oh, pooh," she complained. "And I got all excited about your coming to Australia to see me. Surely there's some way you could manage to fit me in?"

"Not this time, sweetheart," he explained. "It's strictly a fact-finding mission. My editor's already champing at the bit for this story and if I don't get it to him soon, he's gonna have my head."

"Ah, the plight of the working man," she sighed. "Well, I guess if you can't do it, then you just can't."

"Right," he agreed, relieved that she had relented so quickly. "Now, tell me again about this friend of yours. Her name was Lisa...?"

"Murdoch," she finished for him. "Lisa Murdoch. She and I went to school together here in Sydney. She's the daughter of a half-caste, but her mum always wanted the very best for her, so she made sure her daughter was accepted at all the finest schools. We took our A-levels together. She was brilliant. Went on into Fashion and Merchandising. She always said her dream was to own her own shop here in Sydney. She's good at what she does, too."

"Uh-huh, and how old is she?" Nick asked as he wrote in the little notepad he always carried around with him.

"Twenty-six, same as me," she answered. "Oh, Nicky, you just *have* to help them find her. Where will I get my clothes if anything happens to her?"

"Uh, I'll do my best," he said, wondering how anyone could be so self-centered that she would think only of clothing when her friend had gone missing and might be in danger. This was supposed to be her good friend, right? Yet all she appeared to be upset about was the fact that the person who designed all the great outfits she wore was not available to do it anymore, not that the girl might be hurt, or worse. Nick just didn't get it.

"Hold on a sec, Nicky. There's someone at the door."

Nick held the line as he went back over the information she had given him, both now and before he had left Dallas. The whole bit about the evidence the locals had supposedly found was what disturbed him. From what Kiley said, it appeared to match perfectly with what Nick had been told was found at the Baker household in Dallas and that was what linked these two cases together. If what Kiley had said was true. Her description was so close to the thing the kid from Dallas had said he would send to Nick in London, though, that Nick could see no way it could be just a coincidence. The two cases had to be linked.

"Okay," Kiley said as she came back on the line. "It was just my lunch being delivered. Now, where were we?"

"You said she was interested in the Sarah Baker case back in the states?" he asked, hoping to connect the dots even further.

"Oh, yes," she agreed. "I remember her telling me all about that woman's blog, or something or other that she had been following on the internet. A few weeks ago, I just happened to catch a headline out on the internet while I was shopping for some new shoes. It was about this American woman named Sarah Baker and her blog and I immediately forwarded the link to the story to Lisa because I knew she would be interested in it. I know she got the link because she emailed me back thanking me for sending it.

"Lisa said the woman's writings were causing quite the stir and that people all over the world were trying to track her down, but that's the last I heard from her. Then at the beginning of this week, I realized I had nothing to wear to this party I'm attending next weekend and I thought I would call Lisa to see if she might have any ideas. But when I called, an inspector picked up and informed me she had gone missing. I did a little finessing and found out what little information I could, and that's when I called you."

Nick's flight was suddenly called. "Can you send me that link you sent to her about the American's blog?" he asked as he finished writing and then folded up his notepad and gathered his things.

"Of course," she said. "You want me to send it to your work email address or your personal one?"

She was fishing for his personal email address and Nick never gave that one out. "The work one would be great," he said. "Listen, my plane is boarding now, so I'm gonna have to get going. Thank you so much for the information, though. I definitely owe you one, sweetheart."

"I'll hold you to that, Nicky, darling," she said.

Nick ended the call and quickly gulped down the remaining half-glass of tepid lager. Damned Australians! Why couldn't they drink cold beer like Americans did?

He made his way over to the gate and boarded the smaller twin engine along with his fellow passengers. There were several businessmen, though none as stodgy-looking as the flatulent Brit from the last flight, but mostly there were families with two or three kids each who boarded with him. *Great*, he thought. *Just what I need, a bunch of screaming brats all the way to Alice Springs!*

Finding his seat, he stuffed his bag under it and plopped down. At least he was next to the window so he could avoid conversation. The flight wasn't scheduled to be that long, but Nick wasn't overly fond of kids, and *any* time spent with more than one of them was way too much time in his opinion.

As it turned out, the flight out to Alice Springs wasn't that bad. The kids on the plane were all well-behaved and Nick never once heard a single one of them whine or complain. Before long, they were making their descent into the little airport there and Nick was soon standing outside it, staring at rows of solar panels as he waited for a car from the rental company.

He wasn't finished with his journey, as the woman, Lisa Murdoch, lived in a small town called Barrow Creek. That town was still quite a distance from Alice Springs. Nick would have to drive the rest of the way on his own, unless he wanted to take one of the tour buses up that way. He had seen several of the families with kids boarding one of the buses parked just outside the airport, and decided a rental car was definitely a better choice.

Nick didn't hold out much belief in the parenting skills of many in this day and age and he figured his luck with how well-behaved those kids had been on the plane would run out if he boarded a tour bus with them. Nope, a rental car would be just fine by him. He also had no idea how to drive on the wrong side of the car, or the road for that matter, since he always used public transportation when he was in London and he always had a hired driver whenever he had been in Australia before. But he was sure he would be able to figure out driving here!

The next to the last car the rental company had was some sort of SUV. The make was one Nick had never heard of before and it looked like it was from World War I. Other than that, there was just a one-seater, and that was being generous. It was actually a European model, but it looked as if it would fall apart if anyone over 50 lbs. sat in it. Nick asked which had air conditioning and decided that way. The old one-seater European model it was.

He stowed his single bag in the spider-web laden trunk of the vehicle and then carefully folded himself down into the deep bucket seat. He spent nearly a half hour adjusting everything that could possibly be adjusted just so he would be able to drive the rickety old jalopy. By the time he actually pulled out of the parking lot, the sun was heading down toward the horizon. Nick didn't want to be stuck out in the middle of nowhere in the Outback. That, he knew, was dangerous for a foreigner. After all, Australia not only housed the most venomous and deadly wild animals on the planet, but some of the deadliest humans as well.

***

Matt winced again as they hit another deep rut in the dirt track they were on. The SUV lurched dangerously to the right before jerking upright again as it dug its way out. They had been driving all night and the sun had just peeked over the horizon, its blinding early morning rays doing nothing to help Matt see where to drive to avoid the ruts in the road.

"Is that it?" Stacy asked, breaking Matt's concentration as she pointed to what looked like a run-down shack situated on the side of a mountain about a mile up the road.

"Yeah," Matt said in relief. "That's Lonnie's place." Lonnie Whittaker had been Matt's best friend in college. He had made a mint a few years back with some popular online apps. Afterward, he had publicly denounced social media and retired, preferring to live out the rest of his life in privacy. He had been living out in the boonies in northern Arizona since then. Matt hadn't seen him in years, but they had written to each other every so often through snail mail. That meant no one would be likely to make a connection between the two. And that also meant Lonnie was their best hope of staying safe – at least, Matt hoped that's what it meant. He swerved just in time to avoid another car-eating rut in the road and then went back to concentrating on reaching their intended destination.

The house Lonnie had often referred to as the "shack" turned out to be a virtual mansion dug into the side of a mountain. It was much larger on the inside than it looked to be from the outside, as over half of the place had been built into the mountain itself. Lonnie welcomed Matt as if he was a long lost relative and soon Matt, Stacy and Tyson were enjoying a hot meal and great company. Lonnie offered them the use of the shack for as long as they wished. He assured them there was plenty of room for everyone.

Matt and Stacy told Lonnie as little about the situation as they could get away with so he wouldn't be held liable should anyone track them to the shack. Surprisingly, even though he had publicly sworn off technology, he had Wi-Fi and a satellite phone, which he offered to them should they need it. But after just an hour or so, the three on the run from

L.A. fell into their guest beds and were out.

It was early evening when Matt and Stacy finally got up. They had a lot to do and time was running short. Neither one had meant to sleep so long, but after the night they had had they figured they needed the rest. Tyson was still asleep and the two adults were glad. What lay ahead would not be simple and he was going need all the rest he could get.

But, first things first. Matt and Stacy dug out their laptops to start looking for anything they could find online that might lead to the place where Tyson's mom was being held. If what Tyson had said about his brother was true, there would be no way to find him. But they could find his mom. Once they did that, they could at least prove that she hadn't killed Tyson, and that should buy her freedom. At least, that was their hope.

"So, you guys really think you can help this kid find his mom?" Lonnie asked. They were all sitting in the great living room in front of the darkened fireplace with a television mounted above it. They had told Lonnie they came across Tyson in a grocery store parking lot and that he was looking for his mom. They discussed the possibility of taking the whole thing online, of documenting everything so the whole world would be able to help. The television was on and the sound was muted while they discussed things.

"We have to," Stacy said. "Maybe if we put the whole thing online, we'll get more exposure for him and he'll be reunited with her all the sooner."

Matt thought it over from every angle. Something about Stacy's idea didn't sit well with him.

"I don't see why you didn't just take him to the cops," Lonnie said.

"We couldn't," Matt and Stacy said simultaneously.

Lonnie didn't ask why, but the couple could tell his curiosity about the boy had just grown by leaps and bounds.

"Look," Matt said. "I know this sounds crazy and I can't give you a better explanation other than to say this boy needs our help. He's in trouble, but we can't call the cops. He needs his mom and, honestly, she needs him, too. As far as the internet idea, I think that's a no-go. I mean, the minute we put anything out there it'll be tracked, which would lead whoever's looking straight to us."

"Yeah," Stacy said, her shoulders slumping. The situation appeared hopeless.

"Well, do you at least know who the mom is?" Lonnie asked.

"Yeah," Matt explained. "But she's kind of been in the public eye over the last couple of months and not in a good way, so she's not exactly easy to get to. I mean, if we could get in touch with our usual contacts, there would be no problem. It's just, we kind of…" His words trailed off as Lonnie's attention was suddenly focused on video footage from a news piece airing on the large flat-screen television above the fireplace.

Matt and Stacy turned to watch. There on the screen was a larger-than-life photo of Tyson and his brother, Demetrius. Beneath it read the caption, Suspected Murder Victim Found Alive, Then Kidnapped. Next, a snippet of video footage of Stacy and Matt at the hospital was shown. Their faces were plainly visible in the footage that showed them escorting young Tyson out of the hospital in the middle of the night.

Lonnie turned questioning eyes toward the couple.

Matt looked at Stacy. She was clearly scared, he could tell. But Lonnie had been his best friend for so long, Matt had no other choice but to believe the man wouldn't betray him now. He leaned forward, elbows on his knees, looked Lonnie directly in the eyes, and said, "Look, man. What I'm about to tell you is gonna sound insane. But you have to believe it's the truth."

Lonnie frowned a little, but said nothing.

Matt told him the entire story, with Stacy jumping in every so often to fill in missing bits and pieces. They covered the abduction, the evidence, the trial, and then the revelation that Tyson was still alive. "I'm tellin' you, man, when I heard that they had found that kid two days ago on the police scanner, I couldn't believe it," Matt gushed. "I mean, it was like fate validating everything I had worked my entire adult life to prove. And then, when I met the kid and he told us his brother was still up in space... Well, what would *you* think?"

Lonnie thought in silence for a minute. Then he asked, "So you... really believe this kid was... abducted – by aliens?"

His expression clearly indicated he thought they were both insane, but that was it in a nutshell.

"Yeah," Matt softly told him. Crestfallen because he could see they were getting nowhere fast, he stood. "I do."

Stacy stood and snaked her arm around Matt's waist, saying, "I do, too. And I think if you were to talk to Tyson, you might just become a believer, yourself."

Lonnie sighed, shaking his head a little as he too stood. "Look," he said. "I love you, man. But I gotta tell you, this is kind of a little too far out there for me. I mean, you pulled some crazy shit in school and all, but this... I mean, kidnapping – I just... I just can't."

Matt nodded. He understood. Hell, had he been anyone else, he wouldn't have believed him, either. He nodded again. "I understand. We'll be gone in just a few minutes." As he went to turn away, he paused. Looking back at his friend, he said, "He's a pretty great kid, you know? And all he wants is to get back with his mom. But she's been thrown in jail because the cops think she killed him and his brother." He paused, swallowing a huge lump of emotion before saying, "I've never met her. But I know if that were me, I'd want someone to stand up for me, to do what's right and to help my kid and me get back together. Wouldn't you?"

Lonnie looked around at his giant, luxurious palace in the mountains. He was all alone and had been ever since he had retired from his old life. Now, his best friend in the world was asking for his trust.

A sound off to the right and up brought everyone's attention to movement at the top of the stairs. There stood the object of their conversation. A single child.

What's goin' on?

As Lonnie stared at the boy, he suddenly realized he had heard the boy speak. The kid's mouth was closed, but

Lonnie could actually hear the boy talking! In a flash, his whole life changed. He knew everything his friend had told him was true. This kid – this idea – it was all freaking true!

Without a word or even a thought of doubt, Lonnie headed toward his bedroom.

"Where are you going?" Matt asked.

"Gimme ten minutes," Lonnie said over his shoulder. He was going with them to find Tyson's mom. He had the resources they needed and his money would ensure they would be protected should they somehow pop up on the grid.

Lonnie also had contacts, some in high places. After packing and getting everything ready to go, he reached out to a couple of people and discovered that Tameka Bradley had recently been transferred from a women's correctional facility to some super-max detention facility in Las Cruces, New Mexico. There was no explanation as to why she had been transferred, nor any information about when she was to be tried, but that didn't matter. Nothing mattered now that the kid was here.

The group made arrangements to head out for Las Cruces the next morning. Within just two hours, Lonnie had an entire storage unit worth of provisions delivered to the shack for the trip. He also stuffed a backpack full of money from his safe into a tricked-out SUV he had acquired when he retired. All this time and he had only ever driven the thing to town and back two times. Well, he was going to drive it now.

Chapter 7

Von Manning sighed in frustration again as he waited for his flight to be called. He was tired. The team in London hadn't found the infamous Bob Smith, but they had found the corpse of what they now knew to be a virologist named Judith Wickham who lived alone at the address to which the late Diego Montoya had mailed the package from Dallas. Manning had no idea how the kid and this virologist in London were connected, nor why she would have used the name "Bob Smith". But what mattered was that they had recovered the package.

It was strange, but the package contained what looked like two single hair strands inside a plastic bowl. Nothing more. One would think a virologist would have known better than to casually handle whatever the things were. However, it appeared she had opened the package without a thought to the danger lurking inside. Judging from the security video the team had found within her flat, she had been bitten or cut when she first opened the lid to the plastic bowl. The video showed her quickly slapping the lid back down onto the bowl before she walked out of view of the camera into the kitchen.

The time stamp on the video put that at just 19 hours ago. As the video progressed, everyone watching fought the urge to vomit. The London team were every bit as seasoned and hardened as the Dallas team. But still, watching a person's flesh practically melt from the inside out had each one feeling a distinct case of nerves.

Manning had finally ordered, "Turn it off."

Questioning the neighbors and Ms. Wickham's co-workers had turned up no leads and the scene had been cleaned within 24 hours. Manning sighed again as he waited.

He had wanted to return to Dallas immediately to pursue the original lead on the hair strands, if that was what they were. But again, the Secretary had contacted him with instructions to get to a small town just outside Reno, Nevada. Another device had been located and it was imperative he be on scene for the next few days while the crews there attempted to remove it. Thus far, they had had no success at extraction of any of the three devices they had discovered, and several of the construction team members had been sickened by radiation poisoning themselves.

One team member had died – in the beginning. That was when Manning had been brought in to work with Yaniv Nisrahali. Nisrahali had been on the team from the beginning and it was his own brother who had originally spear-headed the project. The brother was the one who had died. So Nisrahali, who had still been in Southeastern Asia working at the site there at the time his brother died, had briefed the American on the project when the Secretary brought Manning on board.

But now there was more at stake than just the lives of the team members. Although the team hadn't yet been able to activate any of the devices or even to open them up to discover what they were designed for or just what kind of damage they could do, the metal devices were proving to be dangerous enough just from the radiation each emitted. In fact, the scientists working on the project so far hadn't been able to get close enough even to detect any kind of buttons, knobs or anything that would allow them to activate or open the things.

They were just giant, seamless round balls of some unknown metal. Each one was solid and emitted a huge amount of radiation. There were lights all over the devices that showed through from the inside and some of the lights blinked, so there was definitely *something* going on inside them.

The problem was, no one knew where the things had come from, nor what they were doing on Earth. Scientists couldn't take samples of the devices themselves. But the earth around the devices where each had been found had been tested using the most advanced technologies known to mankind and, as far as anyone could tell, they appeared to have been here for around 64 million years.

Manning sighed again as he thought of the bodies he had left in Dallas and now this new one in London. Was there a connection between the bug he was chasing and the

devices? He didn't know. As far as he knew, no device had
yet been found in the U.K. What he did know was that the
Secretary wanted all of this kept as quiet as possible and
Manning was the one who had been assigned to ensure that
happened.

The idea of a technology or weapon such as this bug
getting into the hands of a rogue government or terrorist
organization scared the living daylights out of him and he
would do whatever he could to keep that from happening.
And the same went for the devices they had found. But
Manning wasn't sure he wanted his *own* government having
such deadly weapons in its possession, either.

He didn't know what he was going to do. He simply
knew he couldn't allow the knowledge of either the bug or
the devices to get out to the public or there would be mass
hysteria overnight. He would have to get matters having to
do with the newly-discovered device taken care of back in the
States before he could get back on the bug hunt. The team in
Dallas would continue working things from that angle and he
was more than confident the London team would continue on
with the necessary research here. He knew without a doubt
that both teams would do whatever it took to ensure there
were no leaks to the press. They knew, as did Manning, that
that was the only way to be certain the public was safe.

The voice of a female newscaster on the television
screens inside a nearby pub within the airport caught his
attention. She had a nice voice and he glanced over to see
what she looked like. It was an American news feed and the
journalist, who was a brunette, was detailing a report of the
continued search for two young African American boys from
Los Angeles who had disappeared several weeks ago.
Pictures of the boys' mother flashed across the screen as the
anchor revealed the woman had tested far above the legal
alcohol limit and had been positive for drugs in her system
when officers arrived on the scene after her neighbor had
called to report the woman's sons missing.

He sighed again as he wondered if perhaps this new
bug was nature's way of getting rid of all the crazies in the
world. That woman might not have done anything terrible to

her sons and, yes, they may very well have been kidnapped. But Von knew reports like this ended all too often with the parent being charged with killing the kids – often in some horrific manner.

The call for his flight finally sounded over the P.A. system and he grabbed his small carry-on. He was only too happy to leave London's Heathrow Airport.

***

Tameka Bradley awoke in stages. Lately, she had taken to sleeping as much as she could because her dreams were better than her reality. Not by much, but they were still usually better than what awaited her when she awoke.

But tonight was different. There was someone new in her cell. Normally, only the guards visited her there. Tonight, there was a man dressed in a suit. He was a tall white man and even in her groggy state Tameka got the sense that he was dangerous. His oily dark hair was long and he had it pulled back into a rounded ponytail at the base of his skull. His hands were smooth-looking and well-manicured, which made her believe he had never done a day's hard work in his life. His clothes were a little rumpled, but Tameka knew from the cut and the fabric that they were expensive.

She finally sat up on the thin mattress of her little cot, swinging her legs over the side to rest her bare feet on the cold cell floor as she stared up at him. She hadn't said a word all this time, just that once the day she had discovered D and Tyson had been taken, and she had no plans to start talking now. Whatever this man wanted, he was tough-shit-outta-luck, as far as she was concerned. All she wanted was to be left alone so she could go back to sleep and forget about everything that had happened. Then she could dream of better times when she was still with her two boys and of the day when she would be with them again.

A guard stepped into the room and asked, "Is she the last one, sir?"

The tall man looked her up and down, pursing his lips, before saying, "Yeah. I'm leaving in ten minutes. Have her ready and waiting with the others by then." With that, the tall man left and the guard moved in to prepare Tameka to be taken from her cell.

Tameka didn't know what was going on, but she didn't protest. She had realized not long after the boys disappeared that she really was all alone in this world and that nothing mattered anymore. She had lost everything she ever held dear to her heart and there was nothing left for her but to live out the rest of her days on this miserable planet until God chose to end her suffering by finally taking her. Until then, she would do whatever she was told without putting up a fuss. But she didn't have to talk to anyone to do that. And she wasn't going to.

The guard attached cuffs to her hands and feet before leading her out of her cell and down to a different part of the holding facility. There were five other prisoners waiting in the room to which she was taken. Each of them wore the same type of shackles as she. Each appeared to be just as clueless about the situation as she, as well. Tameka quietly sat where she was instructed to sit.

Another guard entered the room and nodded to the three who were waiting with the prisoners and then all six female prisoners were led outside and loaded into an unmarked van. They were secured to the seats with yet another set of cuffs and special seatbelts. The tall man in the suit took a seat in the front passenger side and closed his door. A guard slid behind the wheel and turned over the key. The engine roared to life and they were off.

Not long after they had left the jail, one of the prisoners in the first row of seats asked where they were being taken. Without a word, the man in the suit turned and shoved a small hand-held Taser into the woman's chest. He held it there until the prisoner vomited all over herself. Then he removed the thing from the woman's chest and turned back toward the road ahead.

Not one other word was spoken for the rest of the journey.

A little more than 24 hours after the start of the trip, full twilight was setting in when the van carrying the group of female prisoners finally pulled to a halt at a checkpoint outside the gated entryway of a darkened concrete building. The majority of the prisoners remained asleep, as they had been for the past few hours – all save one.

Tameka Bradley was wide awake. She had started the journey feeling a little sluggish from having been awakened in the middle of the night. She had no idea where she and the others were being transferred, nor why, and had thought the journey would be a short one. But the farther away from the holding facility the van had gone, the more concerned she became. When the van crossed the state line and merely continued on in its original East-southeast heading, Tameka knew something was definitely wrong.

She had done whatever she could to ensure her eyes closed for no more than a few minutes at a time. There was no way she was going to ask about what was going on – not with Taser man running the show. But she wasn't about to be led off by God-knew-whom for God-knew-what. The idea that these people could be taking the women to be sold had even flashed through her mind and she had forced herself to calm down.

She knew human trafficking was very real and that prisoners like her with no family would certainly never be missed should that be the case. But she had to believe the Lord would help her out of this mess, no matter what was going on here. She just had to do her part and keep focused. And she had to have faith.

The van was finally allowed to pass through the gate and was soon traveling around a huge underground parking structure beneath the concrete building. Taser man pointed to a spot and the driver parked there. The six women were then unhooked and unbound and led in a single line up some steps and into the building's underbelly.

As all but the guard who had driven the van piled into a huge elevator, Taser man inserted a tiny key into the button control panel and pushed an unmarked button. A tiny metal door slid open just in front of Taser man's chest and he held up his wrist in front of it. An electronic voice asked for identification and Taser man said, "4291." By this time, all six women were inside and the doors slid closed.

Tameka was surprised when she felt the contraption immediately start its descent. From the sound of all the dings emitted by the elevator's floor counter, they may very well have been descending all the way down to Hell. She swallowed a lump of nervous fear as she reminded herself to have faith in God.

The elevator finally came to a halt and the doors opened. The group was led out into an undecorated round room that appeared to be completely made of silver. Even the floor was covered in silver and she could almost make out her reflection in the dim light filling the room.

Taser man suddenly stopped and turned, ordering, "Spread out and form a line."

No one spoke as each woman lined up beside the next one.

When all six regarded him expectantly, Taser man ordered, "Now remove all clothing."

A couple of the women looked from side to side to see if any of their companions were willing to contest the order. But as the other four were already undressing, they too began to remove their clothing. The room was freezing, but all six were soon standing compliantly in a line, completely nude with each doing whatever she could to cover her private parts.

"Now," Taser man said as he went to the far end of the line. "You have all been found guilty of whatever it was you did wrong in the eyes of the law." He reached the end and turned, walking back along the front of the line as he continued. "You had your chance and you blew it. Some of you have had multiple chances, have even had all kinds of help from others in attempts to get you on the straight and narrow path..., but you still wouldn't behave."

He had reached the other end of the line by now and he reached out and ran his index finger down the arm of the woman standing there. She was a large-boned amazon of a woman that most men would probably shy away from – especially since she sported multiple tattoos and scars from previous battles. She was tough and she immediately jerked away from him and gritted through tightly-clenched teeth, "Don't you touch me! I have rights and I want my lawyer!"

The look of utter glee that took over his face then was more frightening than anything any of the women had ever seen and all six of them, even the amazon, shrank back in unison from the man, sensing some unknown danger that lurked just beneath his surface. With whip-like speed, he pulled a shining rope from something on his wrist and had it wrapped around the throat of the woman who'd spoken before she could even move. The shiny rope dug deep into her neck as she struggled for air. Her mouth gaped open and her hands clawed at the metal rope digging into the soft flesh of her neck as blood poured from the wound all around. The other five women screamed and moved as far away as they could against the round wall.

Taser man spared the cowering group an angry glare as he demanded, "Who said you could break the line?"

The fearful women were visibly shaken, but they slowly returned to stand in their original places with tears streaming down their faces as they watched his muscles flex as he held the struggling amazon woman until, with a final jerk, she stopped struggling. Her tongue hung half out of her mouth and her eyes looked as if they were about ready to pop right out their sockets. It was a ghastly sight, but the women couldn't avoid looking at her as Taser man dragged her corpse along with him back down the length of the line.

"You see," he calmly said. "You no longer exist. You are nothing and there is no one coming to rescue you." He turned and took the bloody rope from its position deep within the dead woman's neck. He removed what looked like a watch from his wrist. It looked to Tameka like the watch was attached to the bloody rope, but she couldn't tell for sure. The man bundled up the rope and watch and, taking out a pristine handkerchief from his pants pocket, wrapped the whole thing together inside the white cloth and finally returned it to his pants pocket.

Addressing the women again, he said, "So go ahead and pray to whatever gods you choose, because today is the end. No matter how horrible you thought your lives were up to now, ah..." Here he paused and asked no one in particular, "How's that old saying go?" It appeared he found the answer and he smiled as he finally drawled with an evil sneer, "You ain't seen nothin' yet."

He chuckled at some private joke as he reached a high-quality-leather-clad foot out to kick at the head of the corpse. He looked back up at the line of women and nodded. Smiling a great smile, he rounded the line and re-entered the elevator. The doors smoothly slid closed and the women were suddenly left alone in the room with the corpse of the tough amazon woman.

No one moved. The room was silent, except for the sound of each woman's shaky breaths. Taser man's last words still hung heavy in the frigid air as the women began looking around, first at each other and then the room. There did not appear to be any way into or out of the room except through the elevator and it appeared the key was required to open it at this level. Taser man had the key.

Tameka shivered and moved to collect her clothing from where she had dropped it earlier. Just as she bent to pick it up, a soft sliding noise sounded off to her left and she rose, turning as an opening appeared along one wall. High-pitched screams suddenly filled the air as Taser man's warning was suddenly understood.

Chapter 8

The car rental attendant had informed him the road to Barrow Creek was a good one, but Nick knew one had to take words like "good" with a grain of salt in the outback. Nearly an hour after he had arrived in Alice Springs, he finally set off. The car jerked violently in the beginning until Nick realized it was necessary to shift into reverse first each time he needed to change gears. Other than that, Nick encountered no further difficulties with the vehicle. He had to stop three times to refill the gas tank, but he had plenty of fuel in plastic containers and he finally coasted into town around nine o'clock at night local time.

"Where the hell am I?" he asked of no one in particular as he drove through the small town.

The place was very tight-knit, with most of the buildings grouped as close to each other as possible. It reminded Nick of an old West town from those spaghetti westerns he had grown up watching. It appeared not too many people actually lived in town, but that it was more just a meeting place where all of them could come together.

There was one pub and one motel, one bank, one grocer, and one petrol station, along with just a few tiny shops on a short strip. It appeared Barrow Creek was more of a place on the way *to* someplace else rather than one's final destination and Nick wondered if he, himself, wouldn't have done whatever he could to escape such a lonesome place. It would explain a lot in this case. The missing girl may well have just run off to find a better life for herself instead of having been kidnapped.

Nick mentally checked himself as he approached the address Kiley had given him for the kidnap victim, Miss Murdoch.

Don't go jumping the gun, Nick, he said silently to himself.

He had come here to review as much of the evidence as possible. If she had left without foul play, then he would go home and turn in the piece he had already written on the

Sarah Baker case in Dallas. But if there did turn out to be a connection between this case and that one, he would be damned sure to follow through with the evidence until he had the whole story before he would submit one word to Frank.

As he walked up to the front door of the little ground-level flat where Ms. Murdoch had lived, his camera bag in hand, he noticed there were lights on inside. Two muffled, deep voices could be heard through the door and Nick wondered if he might need to return some other time. Just then, the front door opened and a whip-thin uniformed officer of the law stepped out.

He paused when he caught sight of Nick standing outside the flat. After a quick examination of the newcomer, the officer turned back to poke his head just inside the door and barked, "Inspector, I believe your Yank is here." With that, the man rushed walked quickly on past Nick away from the building without another word.

Nick raised his brows and said under his breath, "O-kay."

"Sharp-off?" A booming voice called from somewhere deep within the little flat.

"Hello?" Nick called as he made his way back through to the small bedroom of the single flat.

There, a very tall, very large, and very hairy man stood in the middle of the room. "Sharp-off? Am I sayin' that right?" the man asked.

Nick stretched out a hand and said, "It's Sharapov. But you can call me Nick."

"Right," the man said as he shook Nick's hand. "Gorman's the name. I'm Senior Sergeant assigned to this case." He turned and picked up a packet of photos from an open desk drawer. "I've been instructed to cooperate with you however you need."

Nick allowed his bag to drop to the floor as he took in everything in the room. "I appreciate that, sir," he said.

Gorman turned from the desk to regard Nick with interest. "You must have some pull with someone pretty high up to get that kind of clearance on a case like this," he said. When Nick merely shrugged, he asked, "So, what's so important about a half-caste Aboriginal girl goin' missin' that's got a New York City journalist flyin' all the way to the outback in such a hurry?"

Nick ignored the question, still looking around the room. Everything appeared to be in its place. "No signs of a break-in or a struggle?" he asked, instead of answering.

"Nah," Gorman replied, looking around the immaculate room himself. "The place is clean. Everything's in order. The girl's prints are everywhere, but no one else's."

"Nothing's been found?" Nick asked.

"Well, nothin' really conclusive," the inspector said evasively.

"Nothing at all?" Nick pointedly asked. "No DNA? No... hair strands?"

Gorman instantly stilled, going completely white with shock. "Fuck all! How did you...?"

Nick nodded and said, "There's the answer to why I'm here."

Gorman shook his head, explaining, "It's the damnedest thing I ever saw. You said it's hair?" When Nick nodded, he shook his head again and said, "I never saw any kind of hair like that. We thought it was some kind of snake or worm or something."

"Someone touched it?"

Gorman nodded.

"And?"

Gorman's eyes bulged, and he said, "The damned thing bit him, or something, and he's dead now!"

"Did anyone else touch it?" Nick urgently asked.

"No! I wouldn't allow it!"

"You got your people working on it?" Nick asked next.

Gorman nodded. "Sent it off to Sydney this afternoon," he said as a shiver raced down his spine. "I couldn't wait to get that thing out of the office. Didn't much feel like returning to this place, either, after we found that thing, I tell you. Had to threaten my officers just to get 'em back out here."

Nick pulled out his camera and note pad from his bag

and started filling a film roll while stopping every now and then to jot down a few observations. "Have any of your officers taken ill since you found it?"

Gorman frowned. "Haven't heard of any. Should I be worried?"

"No, no," Nick quickly responded. He had to get off this subject fast. "Any idea who saw the girl last?" he asked as he worked.

"We got a couple of station hands who say there were two tribesmen who performed some type of ritual ceremony with the girl the last night she was seen," Gorman said.

"I'd like to talk with them, please," Nick requested.

"With all of 'em?" Gorman asked.

"If that's possible," Nick affirmed.

Gorman scratched his great hairy head, his bushy eyebrows raised nearly all the way up to his hairline. "I can get you the two station hands easy enough," he said. "The two tribesmen though, they'll be a bit more difficult to track down, I imagine."

Nick stood up straight, reaching his full height of 6'6" and looking expectantly at the other man.

Gorman stared right back, considering his own height was still a couple inches higher than that, but then he sighed and shook his head again, rubbing the back of his neck in frustration. "I'll-I'll see what I can arrange," he said. "It's gonna take some doin', though. Word's got out that she's missin' and since then, we haven't had too many natives around town."

Nick nodded. "Whatever you can do, I'll appreciate it," he said.

Gorman sighed as if the weight of the world was suddenly resting atop his shoulders. "One of my officers is from one of the local tribes native to this region. I'll see what he can do as far as diggin' up the two boys."

Nick nodded again. "I'll be at the motel when you've got something," he informed the inspector as he packed his gear back in his bag.

"Right," Gorman said, back to his gruff composure again. "I'd avoid the steak, if I were you. And er, check the towels and the bed clothes for spiders before usin' 'em. Had a ton of bites there this past year."

"Thanks," Nick said.

***

Tyson sat in the rear seat of the SUV as Lonnie drove down the road. The nice lady named Stacy sat next to him and her husband, Matt, sat in the front passenger seat. The three of them talked the whole time, leaving Tyson plenty of time to think. They had said they were going to some place called Las Cruces in New Mexico. That's where they said his mom was now.

Tyson didn't understand why she would've moved from their house in L.A., especially not while Demetrius and Tyson were still missing. But maybe the police had made her leave after they let her out of jail? Tyson hoped that was it, but he still didn't understand. Of course, there wasn't a lot he had understood since his mom had hit Demetrius the other day. All he did know for certain was that those mean gray aliens still had Demetrius, and Tyson wanted desperately to go rescue him. These people appeared to believe his story and they were willing to help, so he was going with them.

He turned to study each of them in turn. Stacy had a very gentle way about her and she reminded him of old Ms. Johnson next door, except Stacy wasn't old and she was white. She believed his story about the aliens and he believed she really wanted to help. Her thoughts were still blocked to him and Tyson didn't like not being able to hear what was in her mind. He tried calling out to her now, but the only response he got was that she turned to smile over at him.

Tyson gave a small smile back and then he turned his attention to Matt, Stacy's husband. He seemed like a real fun guy and all he ever thought about was aliens – well, aliens and Stacy. His thoughts were like giant screaming eighteen-wheeler trucks along the road and Tyson couldn't *not* hear them, even if he tried. Matt was head over heels in love with Stacy and he didn't care who knew it. Tyson tried calling out to Matt, but Matt never even twitched a muscle. He just kept on pointing at the map on the GPS screen on the dashboard as he discussed alternate routes and things they needed to watch out for on the way.

Tyson next turned his attention to Lonnie. Lonnie had come as a complete surprise to Tyson when he first encountered him. The guy was tall and had the whitest skin Tyson had ever seen on a white dude. He had short dark hair, but it was his eyes that were so surprising. They were the bluest eyes Tyson had ever seen.

Also, he could pick up on some of Lonnie's thoughts, but not all of them. And he knew Lonnie could hear *his* thoughts whenever Tyson chose to communicate with him that way because he would respond every time Tyson spoke silently to him. What really amazed Tyson was that Lonnie could talk to him silently, too, as if he was knowingly speaking with Tyson with his mind. For the moment, Tyson just studied Lonnie. He didn't want to disrupt the man's concentration while he drove. But there was something about the man that worried Tyson.

There was within Lonnie a great sadness that eclipsed every thought and emotion Tyson caught from him. It was so profound that Tyson didn't like opening himself up to it. It made him want to cry each time he felt it and he had to block out everything whenever it encroached upon his mind.

That might explain why, after having been on the road for several hours, Tyson only just then realized where they needed to be going and that it wasn't where they were currently headed. Somehow, from somewhere deep in his mind, Tyson knew they needed to go to a place in Mexico near a town called El Sueco. That was where they would find Demetrius. That was where they had to go.

"E-Excuse me," he softly said, interrupting Matt's constant flow of chatter. Lonnie's attention immediately switched to Tyson, as those bluer-than-blue eyes flashed in the rearview mirror. Tyson felt the man's concern as if the guy had placed a hand on his shoulder.

"What's wrong, Tyson?" Stacy asked. She did place her hand on his shoulder.

"I know where my brother is," he told her.

Wide-eyed and eager, both she and Matt turned to him with rapt attention. "You do?" they both asked simultaneously.

Tyson nodded and gave them the name of the town.

"But how do you know?" Stacy asked.

As Tyson thought hard on the answer, Lonnie studied his reflection in the mirror. It took just five seconds before he turned to Matt and asked, "Can you find El Sueco on the GPS?" A minute later, the coordinates having been updated on the navigation system, the crew were headed toward their new destination. Not one of them knew what to expect in this new place, but all four of them had high hopes.

***

Tobin stoked the campfire. The flames caught on the unburned wood he added and flared to life again. It was a crisp, clear night and a blanket of stars covered the sky. This far away from civilization meant the sky was as big as the ocean and the crisp, cold night air made it all the clearer. His two charges were sound asleep in the tent behind him and he leaned back to gaze upward. All he had to do now was wait.

He had transmitted his signal earlier before setting up camp, so it had already had time to reach those he sought. But past experience had taught him it could take more than 24 hours to get a ship down here.

A strange sense of doubt nagged at his mind at the thought of his superiors not allowing him to keep this scion and its mother. After all, he had never asked for such a thing before. Indeed, he had never even heard of a Star child being allowed to keep a scion or bearer. It wasn't what they were here to do and Tobin wondered suddenly why he should be feeling this way now, after all these years. After all, he had been on this planet far longer than any human and this was his job. So why did he now feel this undeniable need to break with tradition to keep this particular scion and its bearer?

He remembered the training he had received long ago during his time off-world. He was to locate genetically-compatible humans and produce viable scions with them.

Once the scion matured four or five years, Tobin was to transmit the signal so the scion and its bearer could be taken off-world. The scion would be trained the same as Tobin had been and then be returned to the planet to carry on as a Star child. The scion's bearer would be escorted to her new home where, Tobin had been told, it was such a paradise no bearer ever wished to leave.

Was what he wanted to do so wrong? Would he be denying them a better future by keeping them with him on Earth? Could this thing he wanted, which felt so right to him, actually be a bad thing?

As he thought of the two resting peacefully in the tent, that same strange sensation overwhelmed him. He cared for this scion, for certain. But it was Ana who drew him so. He had never taken the time to get to know any of the humans he had dealt with on Earth. That was not his function. As a Star child, one thing was expected of him and he did it to the best of his ability. Sure, he was getting older now. But he still had some years left in him, thanks to the non-human part of his genetic make-up, and he could envision himself keeping active in the field for at least a hundred years more. If he suddenly decided not to do what he had been sent here to do, there was no telling what might happen to him.

A memory of one of his instructors while he had been off-world unexpectedly popped into his mind. She was what was known as a Toti. The Toti were another of the nine species of Watchers – strange, lizard-like creatures with scaly green skin. This particular one from his flashback had taught the class of future Star children about an old folk tale her species had about some creatures called the Mahdii. In the story, the Mahdii were a species of creatures long extinct in the Universe, but who had once ruled everything.

The Toti instructor had said the Mahdii had been the longest-ruling species ever. Although they had been a warrior race, they had always been merciful and peace-loving in their rule and they had encouraged what were called relationships between individuals. The current rulers of the Universe were a species known as the Kordai and they were anything but peace-loving and merciful. They encouraged conformity and submission and nothing else.

The old Toti instructor had taught the class the story of how the Mahdii Royals had discovered the secret of the Universe and that only then had they given up their rule to the Kordai at the end of the Great War. No one in Tobin's class had understood what the old instructor had meant nor why she would have taught the class this particular lesson, since it was presumably just an ancient story passed down through thousands of generations of her ancestral line.

However, as Tobin thought again of the two precious creatures sleeping so soundly in the tent behind him, he wondered if perhaps there hadn't been more to her reasoning for teaching the class that particular lesson. Tobin had only ever thought he had one job, to discover compatible humans and produce viable scions. But was it possible his benefactors had been trying to teach him something else? Was he meant to do something else here?

Tobin shook his head and chuckled. That was crazy! He had done his job for more than two centuries and, yes, he *should* continue doing it for as long as his body lasted. When it finally stopped functioning, a signal would automatically transmit up to those stationed in orbit around the planet and someone would be sent to collect the body. There would be nothing left of him on the planet. He would simply cease to exist and life here would go on.

The scions he had helped produce would continue on here with no knowledge of or even any desire for knowledge of who or what he was. That was life. It was how it had always been and would always be. Tobin was cognizant of this and he had always accepted it as fact.

But as a picture of Bianca and Ana flashed before his mind's eye, he admitted that he wanted more. He wanted to spend what time he had left on this planet raising Bianca to full maturity with Ana. He wanted to experience the things human fathers experienced as their children grew. He wanted to take the time with Ana to get to know her – to learn everything about her. And he wanted her to come to know him.

His heart was pounding inside his chest and he realized he had felt this way far longer than he had previously thought, but that he had simply denied the feeling. Now a part of him wanted to revel in it. Several days ago when he arrived at the small Mexican village where they had been living for the past five years, Tobin had felt his usual relief at seeing them again. They had been happy to see him and welcomed him with open arms, as they always did.

Five years ago, when he first sought out Ana in St. Louis, he had explained the whole process to her. She had accepted everything and agreed to help him. Their trial run had been met with success and they produced Bianca, a beautiful female scion. Female scions were actually rare for Tobin and he had been overjoyed at her birth.

Throughout the years, he stopped in to check on Ana and Bianca every now and then when he had been in Mexico delivering other scions and their bearers to his benefactors. The child had progressed beautifully and she now had the most beautiful blue eyes of any he had ever seen. But Ana had become the best part of his life. She always offered him the brightest smile and the warmest sense of welcome whenever he visited.

Tobin felt more than just responsible for the two. He had never understood what the word "Love" meant, but now he felt as if that might be what he was experiencing, that he loved them both. He vaguely recalled his own bearer – or mother, as humans called them. The few memories he retained of her were no more than still photographs within his mind's eye. But the photos always brought on a sense of warmth and peace and safety. Because of this, he knew she had loved him during the five years he had spent with her.

She was long gone and would live forever in paradise.

His thoughts returned to Ana and Bianca. If he was honest with himself, he would admit that he also felt something akin to fear for both of them should his people deny his request for them to stay with him on Earth. He had never experienced a feeling of fear for anyone. He was always cautious, but he had feared no one and nothing during his time on Earth, caring only for his work. But this feeling of care and responsibility for Ana and Bianca had nagged at his mind for the past few years and now he couldn't get it out of his head.

He sighed in resignation and he adjusted his body to a more comfortable position against the rock behind him. He had a job to do, he knew, but was that really what he *should* do? The question nagged at his mind. He focused on the stars above. The fire was burning quite well now and there would be no need tonight for another log. He would sleep out under the stars like he always did. In the morning, they would strike camp and then head to the rendezvous point to await the arrival of the pick-up crew. Hopefully, Tobin's request for clemency for Ana and Bianca would be met with approval and there would be nothing more to think about.

Still, a niggling little fear of what might happen if his plea was rejected remained at the back of his mind.

Chapter 9

Nick was truly thankful for the inspector's earlier words of advice regarding the towels and bedclothes, as he stomped on two of the ugliest spiders he had ever seen in the tiny bathroom at the end of the hallway in the little motel. The spiders had fallen from the towel he had picked up from where they had been hanging on a peg on the wall next to the shower. Nick had remembered the inspector's warning just before he had undressed and shook out the towel and there they were.

"Great," he said to himself after the two were finally mere pools of goo on the stained once-white tile bathroom floor. "I think I'll skip the shower tonight."

He made his way back down the hallway to his room and spent the remainder of the night in bed with the light on, itching every few seconds and checking each time to make sure he didn't have a spider on him. By the time the sun rose the next morning, Nick was so tired he was ready to jump out of his skin. He had barely any sleep for the past 48 hours and it didn't appear he would be getting any before his return to the States, either.

He nearly jumped out of his skin when someone knocked on the door and practically raced to answer it.

"Good morning!" Gorman boomed with a huge smile on his face. He carried a brown paper bag and a tall steaming cup of what Nick hoped was very strong coffee.

Nick said nothing, but quickly grabbed the steaming cup and sipped. It was coffee and it was *very* strong. After a couple of mouthfuls, he bent around Gorman to peek inside the brown bag. Four giant muffins, each one steaming and smelling better than muffins had a right to beamed right back out at him, and Nick quickly snatched a couple of them out of the bag, giving Gorman a quick wink and a nod, grunting, "Thanks."

Gorman chuckled. "You look like hell," he said. "Didn't get much sleep?"

"Are you kidding?" Nick asked incredulously. "I

probably would've been wrapped in webbing and sucked dry by now if I had slept."

Gorman guffawed. "Caught sight of 'em yourself, did you?"

"Too right, I did!" Nick shivered visibly at the mere thought of the spiders he had killed in the bathroom crawling all over his body.

"Well," Gorman said, sobering suddenly, "we got some information back on that, er, hair strand we found in the girl's flat."

Nick didn't even look over at the man as he replied, saying, "Yeah? Let me guess, it's nothing they've ever seen before."

"Not only that," Gorman confirmed, "it's not human or any other species known to man. They can't figure out even how the damned thing's still movin' about. But they did say it's bloody dangerous." He paused to stare intently at Nick for a second before quietly asking, "What the hell are we dealing with here, Nick?"

Nick paused in his feast and regarded the giant man seriously, then said, "I wish I knew, my friend. I wish I knew."

Gorman nodded, accepting the man's answer. "Well," he said, moving on, "I told them to take extra precautions with it, since you seemed to think it can make people sick as well as kill them. Oh, and I've got an appointment set for you to meet with the two station hands this afternoon out on the property where they work. I've come to take you out there since it's a ways off."

"What about the two Aborigines?" Nick asked.

"I've got my man working on it," Gorman stated. "I told you there's been very few natives in town since news of the girl's disappearance got out. But if they can be found, my man will find 'em. He's a top-notch tracker, that one, and his kind still trust him, even though he associates with the whites so much."

"Good," Nick said, finishing off a third muffin. He peeked into the brown bag at the lone remaining muffin.

"Go on," Gorman said. "I've already eaten this mornin'."

Nick wasn't about to argue and he quickly wolfed down the fourth giant muffin from the bag.

As soon as he was done, Gorman said, "Good. Let's get goin', then."

Nick nodded and grabbed his camera bag.

It took a couple of hours' driving deep into the bush to get to the station where the two men worked. *This must be the part of the map the Aussies list as "Nothing" on their tourism website*, Nick thought.

When they arrived, Gorman quickly introduced him to Erskine Banks and Iain Thompson. They were the two men who had witnessed the two Aborigines performing some sort of ritual with Lisa Murdoch the night she had disappeared.

"I'd like to hear any information you can recall about that night, if I could," Nick said after the introductions and pleasantries were over.

Iain was the one who answered. "Me an' Erskine here were on the truck with them two tribal boys that night, when they just up an' suddenly jumped off an' went runnin' after this beaut we'd all been lookin' at on the side o' the road. It was like they knew her, or somethin'."

"And so what did the girl do?" Nick asked as he wrote in his little note pad.

"Nothin'," Iain said, shrugging. "She just stood there while the two o' them set to work performin' some kind o' ceremony. When we got off the truck, Erskine an' me went over to see what was goin' on, but the two natives said all they were doin' was helpin' the girl out wi' somethin'. I didn't ask with what an' the girl looked fine, so we all just went on back to the pub. The two natives, too."

"Where did the girl go?" Nick asked.

"Dunno," Iain shrugged, again. "Didn't pay any attention once the two natives came with us back to the pub. They both proved themselves out here to everyone on the station. They're hard workers an' they've done a good job all season long. It's been sheer hell without 'em since they up an' disappeared. That's why we're hopin' you can get this all settled quickly so the two o' them can get back to work soon. It's hard to find such good laborers these days an' we need 'em back."

"Right," Nick said. "Anything else you can recall?"

"Nah," Iain replied. "Erskine?"

Erskine thought for a moment before shaking his head and saying, "I think Iain's covered everything. I just remember the two native boys leavin' the pub a little later that night. They looked kind of strange, the way they were walkin', but I figured they were just pissed, that's all."

"Right," Nick said again, nodding to the two of them. "Well, if you think of anything else, you make sure to give me a call, will you?" He handed both of them his business card and turned to leave.

"Sir," Iain said, stopping Nick and Gorman in their tracks. "I wasn't kiddin' when I said those two were good men. I mean, I know they might've been the last two to be seen with the girl, but I have a hard time believin' they had anythin' to do with her disappearance."

Nick nodded once more.

"We'll do what we can to help them when they're found," Gorman assured the man.

***

"Did they send any kind of message telling you it was okay?" Ana asked Tobin.

They had been going over and over this all day long... ever since this morning when the pick-up team's ship had just up and disappeared without waiting for Tobin to meet with them to even discuss the possibility of Ana and Bianca staying on Earth with him.

"No," he explained again. "I told you. I would have to have had an opportunity to meet with them to discover why they left, but I must contact them again." As her face screwed up with concern and worry, he reached over and cupped her cheek reassuringly. "Do not worry. We shall work out everything and you and Bianca will be allowed to remain here with me."

Ana finally nodded and pulled away. Glancing up at

the early-evening sky, she silently thanked every new star she saw that she was still standing on solid earth. She couldn't say that aloud, but she was more than fine with not having been taken up into space with whatever aliens had been aboard that nearly-invisible ship! Up to this morning, she realized she had not really believed Tobin's story about the aliens, which he called "Watchers." She had willingly overlooked this one bit of craziness in the man she had come to love.

But this morning when he pointed out the ship both as it had approached Earth and then again as it had departed shortly thereafter, Ana had been dumbfounded. They had made an early start of it this morning to get to the rendezvous point he said he used before. But they had not yet reached it when he spotted the ship's approach. Had he not shown her how and where to look, she never would have noticed it. It had simply been that well-camouflaged against the blue sky. The only way to see it, he had explained, was to use one's peripheral vision.

Tobin had explained that the entire outer lining of the ship was coated in a special polymer designed to mimic the surroundings from whatever viewpoint one saw it in order to create the illusion of invisibility – and he had been right. The most she had seen of the thing when looking directly at it was a slight warping in the air around the ship where he directed her to look. Other than that, it had been silent and invisible to the naked eye, as far as she could tell.

Now, as she returned to the small tent she shared last night with Bianca, Ana felt a little uneasy. If those ships were invisible and undetectable even in broad daylight, who could tell if they were around at night – or anytime, for that matter? What if there were aliens watching all the time, everywhere there were people? What if aliens were watching her and Tobin and Bianca right now?

She shook her head. Bianca was sound asleep and didn't stir as Ana pulled the top part of the sleeping bag up to cover her daughter's arms. She was glad their child was none the wiser to the thoughts currently plaguing her mother's mind. Ana would not wish such fear upon her sweet Bianca.

Although now that she thought about it, the fact that Tobin had told the truth meant that he *was* part alien, at least, and *that* meant *Bianca* was part alien.

It didn't matter, of course. Ana would love Bianca even if she grew a third arm or sprouted tentacles. No matter what, Bianca was her daughter and she loved her dearly. She also loved Tobin and would continue to love him, no matter what. But the fact that what he had told her was true... well, that just changed everything! Everything Ana had ever learned, all of history – everything was different now.

She laid down next to their daughter, taking care not to disturb her. It was too early for her to go to sleep, but she needed some time to think. She hoped Tobin would understand and that he would just let her be for a little while.

So aliens were real and Tobin was half-alien. That meant Bianca was a quarter, right? Or maybe she was only a quarter human? Ana couldn't remember enough from the one genetics class she had taken in college to know which was correct. What she did know for certain was that the whole world was in for a serious wake-up call and she was glad she had been given a preliminary heads up – *and* that she had Tobin here with her to protect Bianca and her should anything happen, like an invasion.

Ana made a face at how ridiculous that thought was. Tobin had told her the Watchers had been here since the dawn of time, so it wasn't likely there would be any kind of invasion. But he had also told her that no Star child to his knowledge had ever asked to keep his child and its mother. What if the aliens left this morning because they had known Tobin was planning to ask to do just that? What if they had somehow discovered that that was what he wanted and they were now working on a plan to come and take Bianca away by force?

Her heart thumped wildly within her chest and she turned to closely cradle their daughter within her arms. She would fight every Watcher tooth and nail to keep Bianca safe. She had no idea how she could possibly win against aliens, but Ana vowed then and there that she would do whatever it took to keep Bianca here on Earth.

In her mind, she heard Tobin's voice asking, *What is that? A boy?* She knew she was just imagining things and she shook her head. It started hurting at that point, she guessed from the stresses of the day. They didn't have any aspirin, which was the strongest thing she ever took for anything. If she ignored it, perhaps it would just go away on its own.

To take her mind off the pain, she wondered if Tobin wanted a boy, instead of the girl they already had. Maybe he would like to have a son *in addition* to their daughter? Ana would be fine with that. She had always loved kids and Bianca was the best child imaginable. Ana could only believe that having a son with Tobin would be just as wonderful. But where and how would they live? Now that he had decided not to give up Bianca and her, would they be allowed to live on Earth together as a family?

Tobin's voice outside interrupted her thoughts. At first, she thought he was speaking to her or maybe even just to himself. But then she heard another voice, softer and at a higher pitch. Ana frowned as she extricated herself from around her daughter's soundly-sleeping form and crawled out of the tent to go see who their company was.

***

Von Manning reached Sydney in time to discover that there had already been two deaths in a forensics lab used by the local authorities. Apparently, there had been another "hair" discovered at the home of a young woman in a small town somewhere out in the middle of the country, far to the North-West of Sydney. The woman had been reported as missing and the "hair" had been found at her place, same as in the Baker case in Dallas.

Whatever was going on, Manning wanted it stopped! This was crazy!

As he packed his bag that night in his small hotel room, he wondered where the women were disappearing to, or if they were being abducted. That made as much sense as anything, at the moment. The only difficulty was that Manning wasn't the type to just take things on faith. He wanted proof. He wanted to understand the nuts and bolts of what had happened and then he wanted it shown to him again so he could truly understand the process and figure out a way to stop it from ever happening again.

The containment crew he used in Dallas had just been returning home to the D.C. area when he finally caught up with them. They hadn't complained when he told them they were suddenly needed in Australia, though, and soon all arrangements had been made. All Manning had to do was to sit on things until they got there and took over. Then, he would be back on his way to wherever Nisrahali and the team were currently working. They had been in the Arizona desert before he jetted off to Australia, but who knew where they would be by the time he got out of Sydney.

He just hoped he could get a handle on this bug before it became public knowledge and a full-fledged panic occurred. Too many terrorist organizations were looking for things like this new bug to help get themselves noticed. When the public found out about such occurrences, those terrorist groups did, too, and that wasn't good for anyone.

Manning sighed. He hated waiting. He plopped down onto the bed and flipped through the stations on the flat-screen mounted to the wall opposite the bed. Finally, he found an American news broadcast station and settled for that. It was, of course, the same old pack of lies that were fed to the public each day by those in control and he found himself only half listening to the reporter's jibber-jabber.

What could be the link between Sarah Baker's disappearance, along with her family members, and this new girl's disappearance half a world away? The idea that it was one psycho who had taken them all just didn't sit right with him and he wanted to know exactly what had happened. It was like an itch he couldn't scratch, the not knowing. Also, where did the vile hair strands come into it? What were they and where did they come from?

Von sighed in frustration, reaching for the remote control to switch off the television, when his attention suddenly caught on a new story the man on the screen had switched to. It was about the two boys from L.A. who had gone missing. It appeared all evidence pointed toward the boys' mother and she had been arrested and taken into custody for their murder, even though no bodies had yet been found.

A previously-recorded clip of the woman being taken in handcuffs from a police vehicle into a hospital played out on the screen. Then the news piece switched to a prominent state prosecutor who announced that his team had uncovered evidence the woman had a history showing evidence of domestic violence and that she had been linked with a man from some obscure part of Africa. This, of course, had led to speculation that she may have been radicalized and that she had possibly sent her sons off to some camp, as well, so they could be trained as terrorists and could then re-enter the U.S.

Manning switched off the television. He was tired.

Seeing stories like that made him wonder if everything was worth it. The world was so fucked up that he just didn't know the answer anymore.

Chapter 10

On the drive back to town from the station where the two work hands had been, Gorman got a call from his native officer. He had found the two tribesmen and arranged a meeting with them and Nick for later in the afternoon. Apparently, there had been a week-long ceremony going on and the tribal elders had forbidden their sons to return to the city until it was over. Now that it had ended, however, the two young men would be allowed to return.

Again, Nick was glad Gorman had volunteered to drive him around, as later that afternoon they proceeded out into an area even more remote than the station had been. When they finally rolled to a stop, Nick looked around. There was nothing around, just brush. No one was there and there were no outstanding landmarks that Nick could detect, either. He was about to ask Gorman why they'd stopped when he suddenly caught sight of some movement off to the far right of the road.

"Ah," Gorman said. "Here they are."

Two very dark-skinned slender black men with crazy, short-cropped hair atop their heads approached the vehicle. They were both shirtless and barefoot, wearing tight-fitting jeans held together at the top with wide leather belts. The thing that made them so very striking, however, was the light blue color of their eyes. Both of them had brilliant light blue eyes and it made a striking contrast against their dark skin.

Nick opened his door and stepped out of the utility vehicle to greet the two. They both merely nodded upon being introduced to him.

"Nick here needs to know exactly what happened the night you two were seen with the missing girl, ah, Lisa Murdoch. You know the one I mean?"

Both young men nodded, but remained silent.

"We've come to believe that was the night she disappeared," Gorman continued, "and we're just looking for whatever information you might have, in case it would help us to locate her."

The two young men stared at Nick for a moment, then said something to each other in a language Nick didn't recognize.

"What was that?" Gorman asked.

The shorter of the two responded, explaining, "The girl was bein' bothered by some Murngin. We just helped to block 'em from her. It was our Father who allowed the powerful one to take her over to the Dream World."

Nick had no clue what the heck a Murngin might be.

"Are you sayin' you know who took the girl?" Gorman asked, interrupting Nick's thoughts.

"And where?" Nick quickly threw in.

"Nah, mate," the shorter of the two responded. "You'd have to talk with my Father for that kind o' thing. I just remember the thing comin' to beg for us to undo the wall we'd built around the girl so he could have access to her again."

Nick frowned in utter confusion.

"What are you talkin' about?" Gorman exclaimed. This was making no sense to him and it clearly showed on his expression.

"You need to talk to m'dad," the young man simply said.

"So, can you take us to him?" Nick asked derisively.

After a short consultation with the taller young man in that other language, the shorter one said, "Come back tonight an' we'll see what we can arrange." With that, the two walked off back into the brush and were almost instantly gone from view.

Again, there was nothing to be seen and Nick wondered if he was in some bizarre alternate dimension where nothing was as it seemed.

"Well," Gorman said as he yanked open the door on the driver's side of the vehicle. "We'll head on over to Dongara Station for some tucker, right? Then, we'll come back by here 'fore the night's too far gone. What d'you say?"

"Dongara?" Nick asked.

Gorman nodded. "Best tucker a man can get out here.

Not bad view, neither."

Turned out the view was a saucy red-headed sheila named Nicola Weigert who was the current station owner's only daughter. It appeared the owner was away with his wife on a business trip in Melbourne for the week and his 28-year-old only child had been left in charge of running the station while he was gone. Gorman and she apparently had a thing for each other, judging by the longing looks passing between the two. Nick felt distinctly like a third wheel all throughout the meal.

But the food was excellent! This Nicola could've been a professional chef in New York City with her culinary skills and Nick told her so. She merely blushed and brushed off the compliment as she wished them a good evening and a safe journey back into town.

***

Nine hours later, Manning sat on the plane studying the files Yaniv Nisrahali had sent him regarding the team's latest find. Although the plane did not carry a full load and he was practically alone in the first-class section, a part of him felt almost paranoid that someone would sneak up behind him to discover the secrets revealed on his tiny laptop, regardless of the privacy screen. The things his team had uncovered in yet another part of the world were far too dangerous and he knew when it got out, the world was going to be in utter chaos.

This time, Nisrahali and the others were in Colombia, South America, in some jungle or other. Yet another of the devices had been discovered by some migrant kids. Because of the scope of this project and its urgency, Manning and his team had been called in. Now, however, it appeared more issues had crept up in the case and Nisrahali had sent a new file to him with a briefing of what he was about to walk into once he reached Colombia.

Apparently, according to the latest information, the team had discovered semi-fresh humanoid body parts at the new site. This could mean that either someone else was trying to undermine this operation or that they had finally stumbled onto something *really* big in the investigation. No matter what the test results on the body parts revealed, Manning knew he and his team would have to tread carefully from now on.

As he pored over the pictures and descriptions contained within the electronic files, his mind kept flashing back to those individuals who had already died after having come in contact with the strange "hair" found in Dallas, London and Sydney. Their deaths had thus far been kept quiet, although he was certain there had been plenty of threats made in order to keep certain individuals within the media from putting it out to the general public. He didn't know which departments or who within the government was doing the threatening, but he knew it was happening.

He wondered if the owner of the mysterious body parts had died by coming into contact with the strange hair. Manning could certainly see how it could become an epidemic. After all, the stuff appeared to be indestructible and who *knew* where it was coming from? For all any of them knew, the strange hair things could be all over the world already. It certainly appeared that way.

There was no mention in the brief of the hair, so he had to assume no evidence of it had been found thus far at the scene. What did that mean as far as the fact that body parts had been found on-scene?

He switched off the computer and heaved a deep sigh, letting his head fall back to rest against the comfortable headrest of the first-class seat, his eyes closing immediately. He was too tired. Not only that, he felt as if his whole world was being turned inside out and upside down.

What the Hell were the hair things? Where did they come from and why the Hell were they now showing up all over the place? Something was going on here and Manning, for one, needed to get to the bottom of it. If only he could discover something more about the strange strands of hair...

Three hours into the long flight, Von Manning finally fell completely and utterly asleep, his body finally demanding that he get some much-needed rest.

Chapter 11

"How long have the two of you been seeing each other?" Nick asked as the police vehicle headed away from Dongara station. It was long dark by now and there were a million stars out. Nick marveled at the sight up in the heavens and he wondered how anyone out in this godforsaken part of the world could ever find the heart to sleep at night knowing they would miss seeing such a wondrous show.

"Me and Nicola?" Gorman asked. At Nick's nod, the giant man blushed a little in the dim light from the dashboard and gruffed, "Ahem, ah, well, we haven't, ah, well, I mean, we're not officially, um, strictly speakin', that is…"

"Look," Nick interrupted. "Be her man or don't. Stop all this mamby-pamby bullshit and man-up."

Gorman blinked a few times in astonishment. Who the hell did this yank think he was, anyway?

Nick shrugged after a moment and said, "Whatever, man. I just don't think it's fair to the girl to keep stringin' her along like that simply because you don't have the balls to stand up in front of everybody and tell them she's your woman. If you're not willing to at least do that, you need to let her go so she can go find a real man."

"Bloody hell!" Gorman growled, slamming on the brakes. Neither one of them was wearing a seatbelt so they both had to push against the dashboard in order to keep from flying through the windshield. Gorman turned to face Nick as soon as the vehicle stopped. "Listen, Mister high-an'-mighty-New York journalist," he barked furiously. "I don't know how things work back in America. But here in the outback, we keep our business to ourselves and we keep ourselves to our own bloomin' business! So, you just stay the hell out o' mine, you understand?"

Nick pursed his lips and silently regarded the much larger older man for a moment before nodding and saying, "Sure, I'll stay out of it. I just thought I'd lend a little helping advice, seein' as how you seem to be having so much difficulty putting your relationship out there for everyone to see."

Gorman merely grunted. After a minute more of fuming, he threw the vehicle into gear and resumed driving into the pitch-black desert.

"And, just so you know," Nick continued, "in America men don't give a shit who knows who we're seeing. We just see what we want and we go and get it. There's none of this sneakin' around crap."

Gorman remained silent.

A couple of minutes later, Nick said, "I think that's one of the main attractions of America for most foreigners. We don't bow our heads and ask if we can please have the things we want. When we find something we want, we go out and get it. If we can't get it, we work to find a way *to* get it. There is simply nothing we consider out of our reach or unobtainable."

He became silent for a moment, but then continued, explaining, "At least, that's how it used to be. Now I think there's a whole new breed of Americans being raised that will be much more like the rest of the world. They depend far too much on the government and far too little on themselves. Hell, most of the kids in America today can best be described as being part of the entitlement generation, depending entirely on their parents or the government – or both – for everything. They have no clue how to think for themselves or how to do for themselves. Instead, they're busy smoking pot or out volunteering in whatever cause their favorite band or actress has started up."

He shook his head. "So, I guess I really have no right to offer advice to anyone since my own people can't even manage to get their shit straight." He looked over at Gorman and said, "Sorry."

Gorman slammed on the brakes again, nodding with a big grin on his face and saying, "No worries."

Nick nodded back and then frowned, wondering why the other man was just sitting there staring back at him. Then, from the corner of his eye, Nick caught movement in the dim headlights and turned just in time to see the two young Aborigines who'd met with them earlier in the day. The two were approaching the vehicle with what had to be a walking piece of black leather close behind them.

Nick blinked and looked closer. It turned out the walking piece of leather was actually a very old man caked in several different shades of dirt, or mud, or clay of some sort. Bright-colored intricate designs had been drawn with the stuff all over the old man's leathery skin and the closer he got, the older he appeared to be. Nick wondered if the man was over a hundred as he took in various wrinkles and gray sprinkles in the old man's hair.

Gorman cleared his throat and opened the driver's side door. Nick quickly followed suit.

The four younger men nodded to one another as the group assembled in front of the truck in its headlight beams. The decrepit old man said nothing as he joined them.

Nick looked around for a second, wondering if there was some sort of special protocol one had to follow when talking with a tribal elder. Then the strangest thing happened. The old geezer silently approached Nick and started poking him all over. He would softly jab him here with his index finger or poke him there with the stick he carried. He didn't say anything, but just kept circling Nick and poking at him.

After another round of this, Nick was getting quite annoyed and was wondering if he would be breaking some tribal law if he poked back at the old man, when suddenly, the poking stopped. The old man hurled a litany of commands at the two young natives. Then, without even a glance in Nick's direction, the leathery old man turned and walked off. He disappeared instantly into the pitch-black surroundings.

"Wait!" Nick shouted after him. But the old man was already gone. He had already been swallowed whole by the night and Nick turned confused eyes on the two young natives still standing before the truck's headlights.

Oddly, the two were looking at him as if they didn't quite know what to make of him.

"What did he say?" Nick asked. "Can he tell us

where the girl was taken or who took her?"

"Nah," the shorter of the two said. "He didn't mention the girl." Silence followed.

"Well, what did he say, then?" Gorman asked in frustration.

"He said this one need to come to ceremony tomorrow night so he can find his way home," the shorter man said, motioning toward Nick.

"What the bloody hell does *that* mean?" Gorman demanded.

The shorter man shrugged and said, "Guess he best go t' ceremony t' find out."

Gorman threw a look of utter helplessness over at Nick.

"Well," Nick sighed, "when and where is this ceremony?" He had no idea what the younger man meant when he said Nick needed to attend in order to be able to find his way home. But after he had learned the information regarding the hair strand they found at the missing girl's flat, Nick was more certain than ever that this case was directly related to the Baker case. He had nothing more to go on at this point and, since he refused to do a half-assed job with anything, he was determined to discover whatever he could about the two disappearances – however he had to do it. If that meant he had to do what some crazy old witch doctor told him to do, then that's what he would do.

The "talkative" young man gave the name of a nearby point he said they should meet at tomorrow around sunset. "It's a long way," he said, "but we should be able to make it in time from there."

Nick threw a questioning look to Gorman to see if that would work for him. Gorman nodded. "I know the place. We'll be there at sunset, then." All he got in response was a nod and a slight wave as the two dark men turned and, like the old man, disappeared almost immediately into the light brush surrounding the area.

Nick and Gorman were quiet all the way back to town, each one lost in his own private thoughts. Gorman was wrapped up in thoughts of guilt. This yank came in here and "bam", just set him straight about what he needed to do as a man. Gorman knew he was right, but he didn't have to admit it to the guy.

The sooner this American was gone, the better Gorman would feel. This case had not been his favorite from the get-go, but to have to put up with someone who saw and understood as much as this Nick Sharapov did, well it was too much for Gorman's tastes.

As for Nick, he believed whatever he was going to discover at the ceremony the next night would either be the thing to put this whole story over the edge or it would turn out to be some sort of spiritual mumbo-jumbo that led to nothing and he would be no closer to understanding what was going on than he had been before. Either way, he felt a sense of relief simply because he knew he would be going home afterward.

The next evening, Nick gripped the safety handle just above the window of the passenger side door of the vehicle as Inspector Gorman shifted gears once again. Had he not been so terrified, he might have laughed as the memory of how his college friends had always called it the "Oh Shit" handle back in the day.

It had been about an hour since the two men left Barrow Creek and the road here was very rough. To call it a road was the farthest stretch of the imagination possible and it was difficult enough traversing this terrain in full daylight. In the waning light of sunset, however, it was damned near impossible. Nick tightened his grip on the handle yet again as the vehicle lurched once more.

Gorman glanced over at his companion and chuckled loudly at the sight of the yank illuminated by the vivid colors on the horizon. The young man looked as if he was about to spew chunks all over the dash and Gorman chuckled again as they hit yet another giant rut in the road. "Been unseasonably dry for this time of year," he said, expertly maneuvering the truck through the rut. "Normally, travel out these parts is a damned nuisance because of all the mud. This is more like summer, though. We're lucky."

The vehicle suddenly shifted violently to the left, nearly flipping over, and Nick gasped, "*Lucky?* In what way would you call *this* lucky?"

Gorman expertly managed to right the vehicle and dig it out of the gulch of a pothole it had been in. "Well," he explained, "you want to get to the ceremony tonight, right?" As Nick nodded, he continued, "During a normal Wet season, it would take another hour probably just to get you out there to the rendezvous point. Then you'd have to traverse on foot some pretty dangerous territory prone to flash flooding. We end up with several drowning deaths each year out here, you know?"

Nick hadn't known that. In fact, now that he thought about it, the idea of traipsing off into the Australian outback under the cover of dark night on foot with only two young Aborigines to guide him sounded like a pretty crazy idea. Anything could happen and he would have no way of finding his way back on his own.

After all, he could stray into a swamp area and get eaten by a crocodile, or he could be walking along and get bitten by one of the numerous venomous snakes housed within Australia's borders. He could fall and be injured and, when no one came to help him, end up being eaten by dingoes or, worse yet, by one of those giant bird-eating spiders. He shivered as just the *thought* of coming across one of *those* things sent chills racing down his spine.

Gorman shifted gears again and maneuvered the SUV onto what he hoped would be a much smoother section of the track. He noticed his companion had become oddly quiet. Sometimes Gorman forgot that outsiders often had a somewhat distorted view of the Territory, what with all the skewed media coverage over the years. He decided it was time to turn things back to business here and he cleared his throat saying, "Listen, I think we oughtta discuss what you can expect from this ceremony tonight and what you'll want to avoid."

Nick nervously licked his lips and then suggested, "Well, why don't we both go and you can help me gather information?"

Gorman merely shook his head apologetically, explaining, "Nah, mate. I wasn't invited. Them elders are pretty strict about not allowin' outsiders into their ceremonies. Normally, only natives are allowed to attend. Frankly, I was shocked that old feller invited you in the first place." When he realized he wasn't exactly helping the younger man feel better about the night ahead, he said, "Listen, these blokes wouldn't'a invited you out to their get-together if they didn't plan on taking care of you. I guarantee you, you'll be safe as houses with the two native boys. That old feller would have their heads if they let anything happen to you and you can bet they know it, too!"

Nick merely nodded.

"Anyway," Gorman continued, "I've 'eard they mostly tell old tribe stories and do a lot o' dancin' 'round the fire at these things. If that old feller invited you out, then that means there'll be somethin' said about Miss Murdoch during the ceremony. Best to pay attention to the story tellin'. But I would offer a word of caution. Don't do or say anything without bein' instructed to by one o' them. The elders don't have any problem with just disappearin' on those they think have offended their people. Then you *will* be in a world of trouble, *believe* me."

"Well *that* makes me feel reassured," Nick said.

"Sorry, mate," Gorman said, cracking a broad sideways smile at his companion. "I just thought I should warn you." As he said this last, he suddenly stomped on the brakes. "Oh, shit," he exclaimed as the SUV came to a sliding halt.

There in the headlights were the two young natives waiting to take Nick on his cross-country jaunt to this super-secret ceremony. Nick wasn't sure if he was ready for it. They were out in the middle of nowhere in the middle of the night and the two Aborigines simply stood still in the light from the headlights' beams, unmoving as they waited, as if this was the most normal thing in the world.

"Well," Gorman said, "I'm gonna head on over to Dongara Station while you're away. I'll be back in about five hours. I'm hoping that should be enough time. If not,

I'll wait the night for you, 'right?"

Nick swallowed a giant lump suddenly blocking his throat, but then took a deep breath for courage and thanked the inspector before getting out of the vehicle. He carried his camera case and a backpack over to where the two young men waited, and looked expectantly from one to the other. Without a word, the two turned and started off into the bush, no lights or anything to help them see where they were going. After a moment's stunned hesitation, Nick had to run to catch up.

Gorman watched through the windshield as the three men suddenly disappeared into the black night. A chill raced down his spine and he softly said to no one in particular, "Good luck, mate."

***

Manning arrived at the dig site late afternoon the day after leaving Sydney. If his luck held out, he would have another good hour of sunlight to work with. After that, there would be no point in sticking around the grounds. He would have to go back to his motel room and work from there. This device appeared to be exactly the same as the others in that it was perfectly circular in shape, made of a silver-colored metal not previously found on Earth – in other words, not any metal on the periodic chart of the elements, and it emitted a high amount of radiation. Also, it had been discovered just beneath the surface of the ground, with about three inches of dirt covering it at its shallowest point. Apparently, some of the migrant kids had been digging in the dirt and had come across it. Of course, the kids had all suffered the consequences of having touched the thing. Two had already died.

Everything about the device looked the same as at the other sites, so Manning wasn't all that interested in it. What did interest him were the body parts the team had discovered on the surrounding grounds. He planned to examine these supposed humanoid body parts for himself. He also planned to walk the surrounding territory to determine whether or not other things, like the deadly hair strands, might have been missed by his team. After all, a jungle floor contained many hiding places for an object such as that, even with the strands being as thick as they were.

He started walking.

At first, he didn't find much of anything. There were a lot of footprints in the little clearing, adult and child-sized alike, so there probably wouldn't be any use trying to figure out anything having to do with those. As he continued his ever-widening circular examination of the jungle floor, however, he suddenly came across what looked to be a dried patch of blood-soaked earth. He caught the attention of one of the junior team members and instructed him to cordon off the area and to take samples. He then noticed what appeared to be dried flecks of a dark-colored mud that didn't match any of the earth in the surrounding area. From what he knew of this part of the world, he didn't think such dirt could even be found on this continent.

How had it come to be in this little patch of jungle? Again, a team member was instructed to take samples. Manning was thinking to himself how relieved he was that he had gotten here when he had or the team may well have missed these things when Nisrahali finally caught up with him.

"Bullying our new intern?" the Israeli asked with a little grin. When Manning merely frowned at the young man who was busying himself with collecting samples of the things they had just discovered, Nisrahali continued, saying, "We were hoping you would return before we were finished processing the site."

"Hmm," was Manning's only response, as he continued with his search of the jungle floor.

Nisrahali took no offense. He liked the fact that the American was so focused on the job at hand. It meant he would find answers – answers they needed. "We got the results from the lab on the fingertips and earlobe we found here," he quietly informed the Yank.

That brought the American's attention around. "And?" he asked.

Nisrahali laughed a little. "Funny thing," he said.

"The official report describes the items as being humanoid, but not exactly human."

Manning frowned. He had wondered about that.

"The truly odd thing is that the report also gave a carbon-dating on the objects and the findings were, um, not what one would expect." When Manning merely continued looking at him expectantly, the man explained, saying, "The body parts were dated to eight hundred thousand years of age."

"How is that possible?" Manning demanded incredulously.

Nisrahali shook his head in wonder. "I have absolutely no idea," he said. "I simply know this case keeps getting more difficult to understand or to anticipate the further we go."

Manning frowned and pursed his lips at the man's statement. He had hit the nail right on the head with his words, accented though the statement had been. Manning liked that about this fellow. He and the Israeli thought a lot alike and he respected the man all the more for it. He wished he had a dozen more like him on the team, no matter where they came from. Instead of mentioning this, he frowned again as he watched the new intern gathering samples of the blood-stained dirt and odd-colored mud flakes. The young man was managing to touch all manner of things and Manning was almost certain he was contaminating the samples. They would be lucky to get even one useful sample out of the whole bunch.

Chapter 12

Nick nearly fell again as he rushed to keep up with the two young Aboriginal guides. It was pitch dark and they were moving at a fair clip. Nick had no idea how the two knew where they were going, but he trustingly followed along behind them. *He* certainly couldn't tell where they were headed. It was a clear night, but there was no moon and even with a sky full of stars overhead, Nick could only see just a few feet in front of himself. At this point, he admitted to himself that he was so hopelessly lost he had no choice but to stick with the two young men, even if they were just leading him around in circles.

It was odd, he reflected, that there still existed people like the Aborigines who lived in two separate worlds. The young men in front of him wore watches and cut-off jeans, but their feet were bare, as were their chests, and they carried what looked to Nick in the vacuum of darkness surrounding them like bows and very long arrows. He couldn't fathom how one could reconcile working in the modern world with all its advanced technologies and scientific discoveries and then live in a world rooted in magic and folklore. It was a paradigm simply too bizarre for him to comprehend.

Suddenly, a light appeared on the horizon. It was an orange light that appeared to touch the sky with all its brilliance. The two young men were headed directly toward the light and Nick hoped that was to be their final destination. He was wearing hiking boots and sturdy jeans, but he was still aware that he was an intruder in the bush and that there were plenty of things living out here that would happily eat him with or without such protection. He just wanted this potentially perilous trek to end as soon as possible.

It took about another hour of walking before the trio arrived at the source of the orange light. It was a giant bonfire built in the center of a clearing that looked like a giant hand had reached down from the sky and carved almost an entire circle out of a big rock smack dab in the middle of nowhere. The rock face surrounding nearly the entire clearing was massive. It towered above their heads and the light from the fire sent enormous shadows scurrying across the stone walls.

There appeared to be well over one hundred Aborigine males in attendance and, as Nick glanced around, he noticed even more natives pouring into the clearing from the black night beyond. He asked one of his companions if it was always so crowded at these get-togethers, but the young man merely shook his head. It appeared tonight was a special occasion.

Nick was taken to an area toward the center of the clearing, but along the back wall, where he was instructed to sit. That way he could see all the comings and goings both to and from the clearing as the night wore on. He made himself as comfortable as he could on the hard ground and took out his gear in preparation for the ceremony. Soon, more people found places to sit and one of the two natives who'd brought him tonight informed him the ceremony would be starting in just a few minutes. More and more dark-skinned males took their seats and Nick started clicking away with his camera.

Some of the men looked like the two who had brought Nick tonight. Some others, however, were in full ceremonial regalia, including headdresses and body paints in wild designs and bright colors. Everything was so vibrant and so filled with life that Nick quickly became enamored of all he was seeing.

So obsessed was he with how the attendees were dressed that he was suddenly shocked when the strange sounds of the ilpirra and the bimli began emitting what at first sounded like a haphazard cacophony of noises, but which soon became a finely executed musical piece. The deep sounds of the long ilpirras, commonly known as the didgeridoo, were broken only by the clacking of the bimli, or clacking sticks. The melody echoed around and around the walls of the clearing, allowing the strange sounds to overlap and then bounce back upon themselves. The effect was eloquent and entrancing. Even though the music was completely foreign to him, Nick found himself moving to its rhythm. It was almost hypnotic.

There were men who rose at random throughout the music to begin dancing in odd gyrating motions around the giant fire. Others would join in, but still others remained seated in order to carry on conversations with their peers. At least an hour of this went by and Nick was beginning to wonder if this whole night was going to be a complete waste of time – interesting and educating, but a complete waste of time, never-the-less.

Then everything changed.

The old man Nick had met last night came out of nowhere, leading a very thin Aborigine female over to the fire in the center of the clearing. She was an older woman with wild graying hair, but her face looked somewhat familiar and Nick wondered where on Earth he could have seen her before. The old man, along with several others of the group of assembled tribal elders, was painting symbols all over the woman as he chanted a strange but continuous litany. The men put flowers in the woman's hair and gave her various items, which she then proceeded to pack away in a cloth satchel she carried.

The chanting suddenly stopped and every male in the clearing, excepting Nick, whooped loudly all at once.

Nick started at the noise. He wanted to ask what was going on, but that was when the old woman turned and looked him directly in the eyes and Nick suddenly knew. This was Lisa Murdoch's mother! He had seen pictures of the two women and one of the older woman alone in a frame that read "Mum" back at the girl's flat.

What on Earth was *she* doing here? Had she had a hand in Lisa's disappearance? Did she know where Lisa was? Did she know what the strange "hair" found at her daughter's flat was from? Nick wanted answers to these questions and he was determined not to leave tonight's ceremony before getting a chance to speak with the old woman.

Fate had other plans, however, as the woman slowly nodded once at him and then, taking one step to her right, simply disappeared. She hadn't walked away, she hadn't lowered herself down to the ground and crawled off, she hadn't suddenly hidden behind anything. She had simply taken one step to her right and vanished.

Nick was stunned!

He sat there staring open-mouthed at the spot where the painted woman had been, wondering what he had just witnessed. His mind was at a complete loss. The crowd began thinning as men left the clearing to return to their other lives in the modern world. It appeared the party was over, and still... Nick just sat there. The ceremony was done, the music over, the fire was dying down. The two natives who had brought him tonight now stood beside him with their bows and long arrows. They just looked at him, silent and unmoving as they had been earlier that evening at the start of this journey.

Apparently, that was all the information Nick was supposed to get tonight and now it was time to go home. As he rose from his spot on the hard earth, he realized the old man who had invited him to tonight's ceremony was standing nearby off to the left, watching him. Nick had so many questions. But the old man nodded once, turned and promptly disappeared again without a word into the black night.

"Wait!" Jarba barked, interrupting the Jess once more. "You are saying these hybrids knew of the rifts to the other dimension before anyone else?"

The Jess merely stared back in silence. The rifts were the key to everything, yet there was still so much more the Samarean must learn before they could truly understand their predicament.

When it became clear the creature would supply no answer, the interrogator shook her head in dismissal of the question. The Jess was anything if not consistent and Jarba knew when to be quiet.

She motioned for the being to continue with its tale.

"I must now switch to another continent on the other side of the human world..."

Chapter 13

Nisrahali stood silently beside the American as he read the report the forensics team had sent over. It was crazy. The forensics team on this project was one of the best in the world – if not *the* best – and Nisrahali knew it, yet the test results on the samples from the Colombian dig site didn't make sense. The closest match on the mud samples had been from somewhere in Lebanon – yes, on the other side of the world! But that wasn't even the most confusing result.

The blood-soaked soil sample had come back as being from some other type of creature, similar to humans, but not quite human. In fact, the forensics team had found that the blood sample was of such purity, longevity and resilience that they believed it would resist most diseases and even aging. In other words, whatever this thing was, the creature from which the blood had come, appeared to have a nearly immortal quality to it.

Manning slapped the report against his thigh as he turned to the Israeli. "Are we supposed to believe this crap?" he asked in disgust. He felt as if someone was playing a practical joke on him and his team and he didn't like it one bit!

Nisrahali shrugged and suggested, "Perhaps we should attempt to keep an open mind about this. I believe myself to be a reasonably intelligent person. However, I have found that there are far too many things in this world that I do not know for me to dismiss anything without at least acknowledging that there could be a valid explanation out there somewhere for them."

Manning sighed, frowning as he wondered how the man could justify believing the insane findings in the latest report from their forensics team. Just then, the satellite phone he carried buzzed and he answered, barking into it, "What?"

"Manning?" the Secretary asked, his tone a bit irritated at having been spoken to in such a disrespectful manner.

Manning's eyes closed as he attempted to calm

himself. "Mister Secretary," he said more calmly.

The older man was somewhat mollified at the underling's change of tone and he asked, "Did you get the forensics team's report?"

"Yes, sir."

"Well? What's your take on it?"

What Manning wanted to say was "I believe everyone on the team must be smoking crack because this report is shit!" However, what he actually said was: "We're not able to draw any conclusions yet, sir. There's just too little evidence to support any valid theories at this point."

"Yes. Well," the Secretary said. "I just read through it and found the results, ah, not quite what I had expected."

"No, sir."

After an awkward moment of silence, the older man said, "Yes. Well, we've already lined up the next site for your team to examine. It's not too far from your current position, but from what I've learned of it, it's likely that it's related to this last one."

"In what way, sir?" Manning asked.

"Body parts, possible radiation poisoning and some kind of illness that appears to be killing people by eating them from the inside out," the man stated grimly.

The American's heart rate kicked up a notch and he turned to look at Nisrahali before saying, "How many have died, so far?"

"Seven."

After a moment, Manning's steely voice said, "We're on it, sir."

"Von – be careful out there, son." The other end of the line went dead and Manning returned the black phone to its case attached to his utility belt.

"What is it?" Nisrahali asked when Manning remained silent.

"New site," he finally told his friend.

Nisrahali merely nodded. He knew there was more to this next site that the American was not telling him, but he would not press for more information. He knew Manning would tell him when he felt he needed to know it, so the

Israeli turned without a word to go pack his few belongings.

Manning looked at the ridiculous report he still held in his hand. This mission was turning out to be far more dangerous than he had ever thought possible. A part of him was growing concerned for what the future held – if there was to be a future!

***

Nick dropped his bag in the entryway of his uptown apartment as he shut the door. His keys were the next to go, dropping with a loud clang into the decorative bowl on the expensive yet tasteful little runner table along the entryway wall. He was exhausted. All he wanted to do was to crawl into his big comfortable bed and sleep away the next few days. But he couldn't do that. He had just enough time for a shower and shave before he had to catch the red-eye to Boston he had booked earlier.

He made his way back to the bedroom and gathered some underwear from a drawer before proceeding to the bathroom. His thoughts turned to the last 24 hours. After the old man disappeared into the night after the ceremony, the two young native men had led Nick directly back to where Gorman was waiting for him.

The two Aborigines had said not a word, neither on the way to where Gorman waited, nor before they left him there with the inspector. Nick watched them with an odd sense of awe as they walked off into the black night, disappearing the moment they reached the limit of the SUV's headlights. He held a new-found respect for the Aboriginal culture, to be certain.

How they managed to visit the modern world, to even be able to adapt to it enough to fit in so they could live and work there, getting along with those not of their culture, while at the same time remembering and practicing and teaching the knowledge of their ancestors, which *so* did not gel with the modern world, was far beyond Nick's ken.

Gorman had driven Nick back to Barrow Creek where he collected his few belongings, but neither one of them had been much for conversation on the drive. Their good-byes had been short and business-like and Nick had soon been on the road back to the car rental station at the little airport in Alice Springs.

His flights back to the States had been uneventful, no brainless cheerleaders or flatulent businessmen this time, and Nick had found plenty of time to reflect on the spectacle he had witnessed at the ceremony. How had the old man made the woman disappear? Where had she gone? Were they trying to tell him Lisa Murdoch, herself, had "disappeared" like that?

As the flight from Sydney to New York wore on, Nick suddenly had an epiphany. Years ago, when he had first been getting his feet wet in the business, he had done a piece about a physicist who decided there were many more dimensions than just the few the majority of the populace recognized. The physicist in question had even gone so far as to postulate that people might someday create the technology to travel from one dimension to another, although this was pure theory and conjecture, since humans were supposedly in their infancy as far as physics and the other sciences were concerned.

The man had also proposed that there may already exist holes or natural passageways between some dimensions, and that humans might someday devise a method of detecting those natural passageways so that they could travel from one dimension to another. Nick remembered that in particular because the guy had joked that his theory might actually explain things like the disappearances of planes and ships in places like the Bermuda Triangle.

Most of the scientific community had laughed at the physicist, but Nick believed this was as good a theory as any for what he had witnessed out in the bush, especially considering that there had been evidence revealed during recent years to suggest the Nazi regime working under Hitler's command had even experimented with trans-dimensional travel.

As soon as he stepped off the last plane in New York, Nick had made call after call to anyone he knew who might be able to tell him who was currently the leading authority on dimension work. Oddly enough, he hadn't gotten the usual television mavens' names thrown at him. Instead, almost all of his contacts had come up with the same answer – a 19-year-old grad student named Seth Green, who could currently be found in one of the super-secure physics labs at the famed Massachusetts Institute of Technology. Apparently, the kid was some kind of idiot savant in physics and he basically *lived* in the physics lab there.

Nick didn't care how old the kid was. He just wanted to know if inter-dimensional travel was actually possible. And if so, was the technology for man to be able to do it in existence today? If the kid could get Nick to wherever the old woman had gone, Nick would have the story of a lifetime and he knew it.

The difficulty, Nick thought, was going to be getting the kid to believe his story about the old woman. Nick hadn't recorded the incident because he had been so stymied by everything that had been going on during the ceremony that he had simply not remembered to use his video recorder. So, this Seth Green was likely going to laugh Nick off the campus. But Nick *had* to convince him the story was real. Two – no, *three* – ladies' lives now depended on it and Nick would stop at nothing to get them back to safety.

After his shower, as he dressed and shaved for his trip, he listened to the world news. There were still massive protests taking place in North Dallas where Sarah Baker had lived and now there were groups arranging similar protests in other cities across America as well. One report even linked the protests with an incident in London where the bodies of nine Saudi nationals had been found in an underground parking garage. All nine men had been decapitated and a burned pile of copies of the Qur'an had been found at the scene. This, of course, had prompted a whole barrage of protests and riots across London and in multiple Muslim-majority cities around the globe.

The reporter on the piece said officials suspected radical followers of the Baker woman's blog to be to blame for the gruesome murders, though it was speculated that other evidence at the scene had suggested the incident might actually have been a botched terror attempt that had been stopped by an anonymous group of avengers. Apparently, however, the entire Islamic community was up in arms about the incident.

Nick hurried with his shaving. He spared only a minute to call his editor to leave him a message explaining where he was going and the purpose of the trip before grabbing his wallet and keys and rushing out the door. He had to convince the kid to help him so he could find Sarah Baker and break the story that would end all of this. He only hoped it wasn't already too late.

***

The last movement the older man's body made was a sharp jerk as his oxygen-starved brain made one last-ditch effort to rob the rest of the body before giving up. With a practiced hand, the man wearing the black leather gloves unwound the garrote line and deftly removed it from around the now-bloodied neck of this, his latest mark.

He had been otherwise engaged while that last call had come in and so he hadn't gotten a chance to hear the whole message. Now, however, as he cleaned his line and returned it to its hiding place within the special watch he always wore, the man made his way over to the answering machine situated on the other end of the massive mahogany desk. It took a moment to figure out the ancient machine, but soon he was skipping through message after message until he found the last one left.

"Hey, Frank. It's Nick. I know you're expecting me to be in the office tomorrow morning with the story, but I've got one more lead to follow up on before I can complete it. I am back in the States and you're not gonna *believe* what I've got for you. I just need to get this one last piece of information from a guy up in Boston. I should be back no later than tomorrow night with everything, so I'll talk to you then."

The machine beeped and switched off.

Nick. The man wondered if that was the same Nick he had been sent to New York to find. Nick Sharapov was his guy's name and, although the editor hadn't said a word about where Mr. Sharapov could be found – had even chosen to die instead of giving up the information – it appeared now he had a solid lead on the man. Well, that was okay. He had at least been able to have some fun before getting back to work.

Chapter 14

Another jungle, this one in Nicaragua, and the stench was incredible. Rotting vegetation and a jungle floor so completely blocked from sunlight by the thick canopy of trees high above that the team had to carry flashlights out to the site. The native guides hadn't wanted to go out there because they believed it was inhabited by evil spirits. It had taken more than a whole day and a lot of palms being greased to convince them to lead the team to it.

Now, as Manning and Nisrahali took their time looking around the small clearing, the Israeli called out, "Here!"

Manning raced over to where the man stood pointing toward a few long strands of what looked like thin white worms that writhed on the ground before them. Nisrahali bent to pick one up and Manning grabbed the guy by the wrist, yanking his hand away from the evil moving tendrils just in time.

"What are you doing?" Nisrahali demanded, extricating himself from the American's hold and looking at him like he was nuts.

"You can't touch those things," Manning said.

"Why? What are they?"

He sighed and filled the man in on the incidents in Dallas and Sydney. The Israeli's shocked expression showed that he finally understood the danger of the situation.

"So, what are we to do with these, er, dangerous hair strands?" he asked.

"Watch them," Manning instructed as he moved over to a bag he had brought out to the site. Because he had been forewarned by the Secretary that there was the possibility of the team encountering the deadly hair strands, Manning had brought along a sealed plastic tub and a professional reptile snake catcher rod he had picked up in the last city they had been in before coming to the site.

The rod was three feet long and he kept himself far from the business end of it by stretching his arm out full before squeezing the pincers together as he picked up each individual strand. There were nine strands of the deadly white hair in total, all concentrated in this one particular spot, and the plastic tub was soon jumping all over the place with the writhing things locked inside it.

"And you said these things are hair?" Nisrahali asked in disbelief. When Manning merely nodded, he asked, "From what type of creature?"

"Beats me," he answered, shaking his head. "But I know I don't want to meet up with it, whatever the hell it is."

A call off to the South of the site from one of the other team members immediately had both of them headed in that direction. What they found when they reached the younger team member had them stunned. There was a body. Its tongue had apparently been ripped out, but the rest of it remained intact.

"What do you think it is, boss?" the younger team member asked.

Manning looked the kid in the eye, shaking his head. The body was that of a female of some kind. She appeared almost to glow, even in death. She was remarkably beautiful, but definitely not human. She was too perfect to be human. Her hair was blond, but not white and not deadly, apparently, as the young guy bent and reached out to turn the creature's head just slightly so they could get a clearer look at it.

The clothing she wore was just a simple robe, though it had been ripped and one of the creature's breasts was completely exposed. There was dried blood everywhere on her and the team set to work collecting samples and processing the scene. Manning wondered if the strange creature with the deadly hair had been responsible for this creature's death, but he found no evidence indicating that.

He wondered how this creature figured into the whole mix and why it should have died, or been murdered, near where the other creature had obviously been.

"From now on," he instructed the team members, "Everyone is to wear full protective gear. Buddy up and make sure everyone takes the proper precautions, understood?"

When everyone nodded their understanding of the rules, he said, "I need time of death, people, but tread carefully. We can't afford to mess this one up."

Three hours later, under the light of several large halogen lamps, the team worked to wrap up the scene. Everything they could possibly fit into evidence bags had been bagged and tagged and readied to be shipped off to forensics. As Manning and Nisrahali stood watching the team's progress, the Israeli turned to him and quietly asked, "What the hell is happening here?"

A muscle worked in the American's jaw a few seconds before he simply said, "I wish to God I knew."

***

Nick lost his way three times before he finally found the lab he had been told was where Seth Green could be found. He knocked on the door, but there was no response from within. There was no window on the door, either, so Nick couldn't tell if there was anyone even inside or not. He decided to wait.

Almost an hour later, the door opened and a slew of students exited, giving Nick the opportunity he needed to enter. Several students were at one end of the room where they each waited to speak with a young, gangly guy whom Nick assumed was Seth Green. Supposedly, he was one of the Teaching Assistants for the Physics Department and this was the lab where he taught. Nick hoped he was on the right track here. He waited patiently as student after student discussed their particular issues with the kid.

Finally, when everyone else had gone, Nick approached the young man.

"Can I help you?" the kid asked, eying the newcomer suspiciously.

Nick introduced himself and identified the paper he worked for, asking if the young man was Seth Green. A look of caution immediately overcame the young man and Nick thought the kid was going to take off running.

"Hey, wait," he said. "I just want to ask you a few questions about dimensions, that's all."

Without warning, the kid *did* take off running, shooting through the door at the other end of the room faster than Nick even knew was possible. By the time Nick recovered from his shock, the young man was gone. He followed after and tried checking a few nearby hallways, but the kid was just *gone*. Nick had Mr. Green's home address already from his research, so he left the school and made his way to the townhouse just a couple of streets over from the campus. He got no answer when he knocked at the front door, but that was to be expected.

Either the kid was already inside and wasn't answering, or he wasn't home yet. Either way, Nick figured he was in for a long afternoon of more waiting. He made his way across the street to a park there and found a comfortable spot where he could watch the comings and goings at the townhouse.

Why had the kid taken off like that? Nick wondered. He hadn't turned up anything suspicious in his research on the kid, so what could have caused that kind of reaction? Had someone else indicated interest in Mr. Green's work? Had someone threatened him in some way if he talked with a reporter? That would indicate government involvement.

He made a note in the little notepad he always carried to remember to check out Mr. Green's school funding. He may be working off grants or perhaps even through some type of fellowship program that prohibited him from talking about his research without departmental approval. That would explain him not wanting to talk. But what could have caused the kid to be so frightened that he had just taken off like that?

Nick's musings were interrupted when he noticed a couple of young men pulling up outside the townhouse in a dilapidated old foreign POS from the late 90's. They parked out front, cut the engine, and went inside the townhouse. Nick crossed the street and knocked again at the front door. One of the young men he had seen enter a moment ago came to the door.

"Yeah?" the kid asked, and then recognition appeared to dawn on him and he said, "Hey, dude, you're Nick

Sharapov, aren't you?"

Nick's brows narrowed as he slowly said, "Uh, yeah."

"Dude!" the young man said, extending his hand toward Nick. "Hey, man. What an honor. I loved your piece on the Attorney General's involvement in that money laundering scandal. You really got his part in it out in the open." When Nick looked completely astounded that such a grunged-out kid would be talking about such matters so knowledgeably, the kid explained, "Poli-Sci major." He stepped back and said, "Come on in. I'm Alex." He led Nick into a somewhat clean sitting room and asked, "So what brings you to the Geek-Dome?"

Nick asked, "The Geek-Dome?"

"Yeah," Alex explained. "That's what we call the place, 'cause everybody who lives here is either a geek or a nerd."

Nick nodded in understanding. "Well, actually," he said. "I'm looking for one of your roommates – Seth Green. I needed to ask him some questions about something for a story I'm doing. I tried talking with him earlier at the school, but I think he thought I was someone else because he got all freaked out and took off."

"Huh," Alex said.

"Yeah. He was gone before I could even explain that I wasn't there for anything other than research," Nick explained.

"Huh," Alex repeated. He considered Nick for a moment, frowning and chewing on the inside of one corner of his mouth. Then he sighed and said, "All right. Seth's over at McCarty's bar on Massachusetts."

"McCarty's, on Massachusetts?" Nick repeated.

Alex nodded. "Yeah. He met us there just as we were leaving. He was actin' all squirrelly, but I guess that's because of his encounter with you."

Nick nodded. "Look," he said, "I really am just looking to do a little research here. I promise I'm not trying to get him in trouble, or anything."

"Hey, I believe you, man," Alex said. "Seth's been actin' kind of weird for a few weeks now – and for him to be actin' weird is really weird, you know?"

Nick chuckled and then offered Alex his hand again. "Well, thanks," he said as they shook hands.

Alex didn't immediately let go and when Nick looked questioningly at him, the kid said, "I really don't want to see Seth get in trouble. I mean, the guy's a physics nerd, but he's my friend."

Nick nodded his understanding. "I don't know how the piece I'm working on could possibly affect him in any way, but I give you my word to protect him against any harm, okay?"

"Thanks." Alex closed the door behind Nick as he left.

Nick's gut was telling him there was more to Seth Green than he had anticipated. Something was obviously going on with the kid for his friend to have noticed he was acting weird lately. Nick just hoped it didn't have anything to do with what *he* was working on. He was already neck-deep in intrigue and he didn't know how much deeper he could go without drowning.

Chapter 15

The Humvee flew into the air as it bounded over the crest of the hill. It hung suspended in the air for a couple of seconds before bouncing back down hard onto the sand track, half sliding as the man driving fought for control to get it around a sudden turn in the road. Manning gripped the "Oh, shit" handle, holding on for dear life, as he screamed, "Nisrahali, I think the plan is to actually make it to the site, not to die before we can get there!"

Nisrahali flashed a wicked grin the man's way and then rammed his foot harder down onto the accelerator, flying around the next corner on only two wheels, the hummer rearing up on the American's side and then crashing back down as it straightened out once more. "We are in a hurry, yes?" he called back to his frightened partner as he rounded another corner at full speed.

Manning couldn't argue with that. The Secretary had made no bones about the fact that they were to get there as fast as possible, no matter what they had to do to accomplish it. What the older man hadn't mentioned, however, was the fact that there would be all kinds of Mexican laws that would have to be broken for that to happen!

They already had the Federales on their tail and Nisrahali's stunt work would only garner more attention, Manning was certain. He just wanted to be sure they would actually make it to the coordinates they had been given. He certainly didn't feel like spending eternity in Mexico, even dead!

The Israeli braked slightly as he crossed a giant pothole in the track and then rammed his foot back down onto the accelerator all while shifting into third gear from first. The Humvee shot up another hill, flying over the top and then crashing back down on the other side. Manning's entire body was jarred so abruptly upon the landing he knew he would be sore tonight in parts of his anatomy he hadn't even realized he could be sore in. He was on the verge of yelling at the guy again when he suddenly caught sight of something about a mile ahead in the distance that caught the sun's light.

"Go, man!" he suddenly yelled, forgetting about caution and pointing to the area where he had seen the flash of light. From this distance, he couldn't tell if there were any signs of life near the area or not. He simply knew the thing they were looking for had been there now for some time and there was no telling how much longer it would remain. With the spot in sight, both he and Nisrahali were suddenly focused strictly on that one area and no longer concerned with the growing number of law enforcement officials following behind them.

The sand track suddenly veered off to the right, heading away from the area where the object supposedly rested, and Manning pointed toward the spot where they needed to go, yelling, "Off-road it! Get us over there!"

No further encouragement was necessary as Nisrahali threw a lopsided grin over to him and then took to the bush, throwing the vehicle into overdrive and bouncing all the way over to where the object should be. The hummer slid to a halt some fifty feet from the spot where Manning had seen the shining object and the two jumped out at a full-on run, headed for it. A brusque wind kicked up suddenly from out of nowhere and then a slight whirring noise sounded. Manning's arms were fully extended as he pointed his weapon at the vague outline of a ship, though he knew he wouldn't shoot.

Without warning, the thing shot up, going straight up into the sky at an unbelievable speed that within seconds had even its outline completely out of sight. The calming breeze and sand settling around them were the only evidence the thing had even been there. Nisrahali and he stood there staring at each other in utter disbelief at what they had just witnessed.

Manning's eyes narrowed instantly as he thought he caught sight of something moving about thirty feet away in the brush. Nisrahali had heard something that alerted him and he turned and stared toward the same area where his partner was looking. The brush in that area remained still.

Both men wanted to go and explore on the off chance there could actually be something that had been left behind. But as the older model vehicles driven by the Federales finally roared onto the scene with their sirens blaring, the two were forced to abandon their intentions. Complete chaos ensued, along with an unbelievable amount of flying sand and dust.

Twenty hours later, when the two were finally released and allowed to cross back over the border at the very southern tip of Western Texas, Manning's cell phone rang and he said in a tired voice, "Mr. Secretary?"

"Manning. I see you two made it back to the States," the older man stated matter-of-factly.

The younger man sighed. "Just now," he finally said.

"Good to hear it," he said. "Get a good night's sleep, son, and then you and that Israeli head on up to New York."

"New York, sir?"

"Yes. I've got a dead newspaper editor and no perp. It appears no one knows anything about it. So I need the two of you to take over for the team up there."

"Yes, sir," Manning said.

"I'll send you the files to catch you up to speed." The line went dead then and he looked over at Nisrahali.

"So, we are headed to New York?" the man asked.

Manning merely nodded.

***

Demetrius woke with a start as a loud clank sounded somewhere nearby. The room he was in was completely dark. But as soon as he moved, the lights came on. He was on the floor by a wall and a door. The rest of the room was filled with several rows of metal tables, much like the one the aliens had put him onto when they had first taken Tyson and him.

Tyson! Demetrius still had to find Tyson.

He stilled and listened for any sounds. All he heard was his own breathing and the rapid thumping of his heartbeats. As he inched toward the door, he hoped there would be no aliens on the other side of it. It whisked open, making the little swishing sound the doors of this place always made when they opened. Poking his head around the corner, he checked for aliens. There were several on the other side of the room before him.

He quickly ducked back into the room he had slept in and moved away from the door. As predicted, it smoothly slid shut again, leaving him once more alone. A noise at the other end of the room sounded and Demetrius inched his way over toward it. There was a door there and it opened as he drew near. Inside the room the floor appeared to be missing. Bright sunlight reflected up off the sandy, rocky ground three meters below. As Demetrius blinked to adjust to the light, he realized there was a floor to the room but that it was clear like glass. He detected seams in the flooring where tiles lay and there was even an opening in it a few steps away. What looked like landing gear protruded on huge see-through beams down from the ceiling and on through the opening in the floor to the ground below.

Demetrius took a step into the room. The flooring was solid enough, but it felt kind of strange standing on what looked like thin air so far above the actual ground. He cautiously drew closer to the opening in the floor and then squatted down to lean over until his head was poking out of the hole. He was just one sharp fall from the ground below. All he had to do was jump and he'd be free. The ground beneath the ship was covered in sand and rock and there were a few mangy bushes here and there, but it didn't look like some alien planet. It looked like Earth. He was home.

But what about Tyson? If Demetrius left the ship, he might never get the chance to rescue Tyson.

Suddenly, the door at the far end of the room opened and two aliens walked in. Demetrius didn't even think about what he was doing. Instead, his mind was overwhelmed with the fear of being recaptured and he quickly lay flat onto his belly and scooched his lower half out through the hole in the floor. He hung for a moment from the inside of the ship as he looked around at the ground below before releasing his grip and falling the rest of the way down.

He tumbled as he hit the hard ground below, scraping his knees, arms and back before coming to a stop. Righting himself as quickly as he could, he looked up frantically as visions of the angry aliens coming after him filled his mind's eye. All he saw was clear blue sky. A vague outline of the ship appeared to his consciousness. But had he not known the thing was there, he was certain it would have been completely invisible to him.

But could the aliens in the room see him?

There didn't appear to be anyone following him out of the ship, but Demetrius wasn't going to stick around to wait for them to discover that he had escaped. He took off running away from the ship. He knew neither where he was nor where he was going. All he knew was that he had to get away from the ship. He would go to the military and tell them everything he knew so they could go get his brother. Hell, he and his momma would go all the way to the President of the United States if they had to. But right now, he had to get away.

A sound behind him had him increasing his speed as he lumbered through thick sand and climbed jagged rocks. The bushes scraped against his shins, cutting him with their sticky limbs. He didn't care. He just ran and climbed, hiding every now and again as best he could behind whatever was large enough to conceal him. He halted behind a larger bush as he heard the approach of a truck.

It was a Hummer that skidded to a halt as soon as it got close to where the ship sat. He both felt and heard the ship take off mere seconds after the truck stopped. Demetrius remained hidden behind the bush as he watched the slight outline of the ship disappear up into the brightly-lit blue sky. Once it was completely gone from sight, he turned his attention back to the Hummer still stopped below. Two men had jumped out of the truck just as the ship took off. They stood there staring up at the sky, their weapons still held at the ready and aimed upward.

Sirens from other cars and trucks sounded off in the distance and the two men turned toward the noise. Demetrius didn't know who these two men were, but he knew better than to ever trust the police. He turned and made his way as quietly as he could farther up the hill away from the site. He stumbled once and stopped, crouching low behind a boulder, afraid the two men had heard. But no one came looking for him. After a few heart-wrenching moments of dread and fear, he finally worked up the courage to pick himself up and move on.

Once he was on the other side of the hill, he realized he was in the middle of a desert. But the fact that there were people here meant he couldn't be too far from civilization. If only he knew which way led home. He stood looking around for a few minutes, wondering which way to choose. All he saw were mountains and desert off to one side and flat desert off to the other. He couldn't go back toward where the two men and the cops were, so he decided he had best head toward the mountains.

Oddly enough, Demetrius asked himself what Tyson would do if he were here and that's how he arrived at his decision. Tyson loved the mountains. He was always drawing pictures of mountains and Demetrius knew that would be his brother's choice. Holding on tight to the crazy belief that by going in this direction he would somehow be seeing Tyson sooner, Demetrius turned and started walking.

It looked like the sun was just getting started going up in the sky, which meant this was going to be one long day of walking. Of course, he might encounter someone out here in the desert. But from the looks of things, he may as well have been a million miles from nowhere because there was absolutely nothing as far as the eye could see.

Again, Demetrius thought of Tyson. His younger brother was still up in that ship having God-only-knew-what being done to him. He couldn't give up. He had to find someone who could help. Before long, his legs were screaming from exertion and Demetrius was hot and tired and starving. But he had to go on, if for no other reason than that he had to get help for Tyson.

The hot sun continued to beat down onto the boy as he slowly traversed the barren land.

Chapter 16

Nick made his way into McCarty's and looked around. There were several large-screen televisions placed strategically throughout the bar so no one ever had to miss a moment of whatever sports match was showing. For the moment, it looked as if a sports news broadcast was on up at the bar itself, and not too many of those sitting there were paying much attention to it.

There were people everywhere, even though it was still not quite 5:00 PM. Nick always thought it was odd that bars tended to do so well during rough times. For some reason, people couldn't pay their rent or their other bills, but they could find the money to go drown their sorrows. Nick made his way through the dark, crowded room as he continued his search for young Mr. Green. He finally spotted his quarry toward the back of the bar, near the back exit.

Seth Green was sitting alone at a half table, half booth along the back wall that faced the largest flat-screen in the joint. He had his cell phone out and appeared to be dividing his attention between whatever was showing on the flat screen before him and texting when he spotted Nick watching him. He quickly finished typing and sent his text. He dropped the little rectangular device uncaring onto the table and picked up his beer. Nick chose that moment to go in for the kill, so to speak.

"Hi there," he said jovially as he approached. He looked down at the empty chair sitting before the boy and asked, "Do you mind?"

Seth swallowed a big gulp of beer and then nodded cautiously, slowly replacing his half-empty glass onto the table. He didn't say a word, but he looked like he would bolt again at any moment. Nick took the seat and then turned to see what had captured the boy's attention on the television. Nick wouldn't have pegged a science nerd as a jock fan. But when he saw what the boy was watching, he realized his mistake.

There was a news piece about one of the two boys

who had disappeared a while back from their home in Los Angeles. The youngest of the two boys had suddenly been found alive by two cops at a beach. The boys' mom had been awaiting trial for the kids' murder, although no bodies had ever been recovered. However, apparently it was discovered that now she had disappeared.

A human-interest story, and one showing the seedier side of human society – that was what had pulled in the kid's attention, Nick figured. But he didn't have time for discussing the psyche of some whack job on the other side of the country. Nick needed answers and he needed them quickly.

Turning back to the boy, he cleared his throat. "I think I didn't explain this well earlier, but I'm a journalist doing some research for a story I'm working on," Nick told him as quickly as he could. "I'm just looking to get some information about dimensions from you. Everyone says you're the man to talk to about dimensions, so here I am."

Seth stared hard at Nick for a moment and then quickly looked around. "Look," he said in a low, conspiratorial voice as he continued scanning the faces of everyone else in the bar. "I don't know where Sarah Baker is, so you can just go away!"

Nick's breath caught in his chest. Seth had just blown the lid off this whole thing with that one statement. Now Nick understood why the kid was so edgy. Who else knew the kid had information? Had someone already threatened him in some way if he talked?

Nick quickly looked around the room. Even *he* was getting nervous now, but he was also excited. He hadn't even thought of the idea of finding anything leading directly to Sarah Baker. He had only thought the kid would be able to help him find information on how the old woman had disappeared from sight the other night. Now it was a whole new ball game.

He returned his gaze to the kid. "Seth," he said, "I need you to listen to me. I know you're in danger because of what you've discovered and I can help protect you, I promise. But you're going to have to trust me because I'm trying to save at least two, if not three, innocent people." Nick stood and stared down at the kid. "I'm sorry to put you on the spot like this, but if others already know you've discovered something, then you're already on their radar. I won't be able to help you if you're not with me." He held out his hand to the kid. "Come with me?"

Seth stared up at Nick, weighing his options. Nick could tell the kid was scared. He didn't blame him. There was apparently a lot to be scared about.

"You think Sarah and the other one who found her are in danger?" Seth suddenly asked.

Nick stared hard at the young man. Seth meant Lisa Murdoch and Nick *knew* it. How had he found out about her? Nick and Gorman were the only ones who had any information showing a connection between the two incidents. There was no time to discuss this now, though. "Yes," Nick said, "but it isn't safe to talk here. Are you with me?"

Seth looked around the crowded room and then back at the flat screen. Someone had already switched it back to a sports station and the boy sighed as he nodded.

"Good," Nick said. "Then let's go."

Seth rose and the two left McCarty's bar. Neither one of them noticed the five-person team observing them from several strategic locations, both within the bar and outside it. Nick and the kid got into Nick's rental and took off.

"Where are we going?" Seth asked.

"I've got a friend who has a place just a little way from here. I've used it as a safe house before. I think we might be able to talk safely there."

"Can we stop at my lab first?"

Nick threw a concerned look at the kid. "Is it absolutely necessary?" he asked.

Seth nodded.

Nick sighed in frustration, but whipped across two lanes of traffic all of a sudden in order to hop onto the off-ramp so he could get back over to the campus. As they pulled into the University parking lot the kid directed him to, he parked where Seth told him in the closest place to the lab, not bothering with the fact that the car didn't have a proper parking sticker on it to be able to park there. The two made their way into a back entrance to the physics building and Seth went directly to the computer there to log on.

"Um, what's going on?" Seth quietly asked after just a moment of typing on the keyboard.

"What do you mean?" Nick asked as he left the guard position he had taken by the door. He approached the computer where Seth was staring at the monitor. When he looked at the screen, Nick didn't see anything out of the ordinary. There was a blank welcome screen with a plain background.

"My files are all gone," Seth said.

"What do you mean?" Nick asked again. "Like they've been erased?"

Seth nodded. "Everything's gone," he said. "I don't understand. It was all here this afternoon before *you* showed up."

Nick looked back at the door. "We need to get out of here," he suddenly said, grabbing a tight hold on Seth's t-shirt and pulling him toward the exit. The kid pulled back a moment and took something from a hole in the wall hidden behind a dry-erase board. Nick finally managed to get the kid out of the building and into the car and then the two of them whizzed off campus at record speed. He didn't know what demon possessed him to do it, but he drove south, and that's when he realized they had picked up a tail. "Are you strapped in tight?" he asked the kid. When Seth nodded, he said, "Good, 'cause things are about to get dicey."

Nick pulled a similar maneuver to the one he had done earlier, swinging the car from one lane all the way across *four* other lanes of traffic this time to an off-ramp. The car following them crashed sideways into the guard rail as it raced to keep up with them. They didn't stick around to see if the car was still able to follow or not. Instead, Nick jammed his foot down on the accelerator and roared onto the service road. He took the first road he came to. A few streets down, he turned again, uncaring of where they were headed, just so long as they got lost and, therefore, lost their tail.

It was close to dawn when Nick finally turned onto a

road he knew would lead back to the main road headed north. The kid was on their radar, but there was still a chance Nick hadn't made their list yet. Hopefully, the car hadn't been tagged with a tracking device while they had been inside the lab. He had made the kid throw out his cell phone just after they had started their cat-and-mouse game and he had stopped for gas at a store where he was able to pick up a burner for himself. That was also where he had gotten rid of his own phone after pulling all the numbers he needed from it.

It was another couple of hours before Nick pulled up in front of his friend's cabin by Lake Winnipesaukee. He woke the kid and gathered their gear. The key was where his friend always hid it and he showed Seth into the place. After checking to make sure the place was stocked and everything they needed was there, he sat down at the simple wooden table in the little dining area and went to work on Seth. "So you found out something about Sarah Baker and someone found out about it, right?"

Seth said, "Um..."

"Look, kid," Nick said. "This is no time for 'Um.' We're both in danger here and you're gonna have to trust me. Otherwise, you may as well go back to your campus and let them come for you."

Seth thought over the situation for a moment. Then he said, "Okay. So, you want to know about Sarah Baker? Um, I've kind of been following her blog for a while and there are others who have, too."

"You mean you followed it while she was maintaining it, before she disappeared?" Nick clarified.

"No," Seth said, then he stopped and shook his head. "I mean, yes." He grimaced and then explained, saying "I mean, I've been following it for the past couple of years, you know? She makes a lot of sense with the interpretations she puts on her visions. And she's a science geek, so I kinda like following it. Now that she's started it back up again, I've been running traces on her entries like she said her loyal followers were supposed to do. And I think I may have found at least one of the origination points for the transmissions."

Nick stared at him, frowning. It was clear he didn't understand what the *hell* the kid was talking about.

"Okay," Seth said, clearly seeing that the guy didn't understand. He tried explaining, "When somebody sends something like an email or posts something like a blog entry online, there are a few ways to track down the location where the entry came from – not just what computer sent it, but where that computer is located at the time of transmission. You sometimes have to kind of catch them in the act for this to work, but, um, I guess I did. So, at first I was able to figure out the general area the signal was coming from and then I deciphered the exact coordinates of the computer being used to update Sarah's blog."

"And that's why everyone's after you?" Nick asked. "Because you know where Sarah Baker was the last time she updated her blog?"

"I didn't say Sarah was the one doing it, but I do know where the transmission originated from when her site was updated last time."

Nick thought for a moment. "Did you try contacting Sarah?" he asked.

Seth shook his head and said, "It wouldn't have done any good."

"Why?"

"Because there's nothing there – at the origination point, I mean. I checked it out. It's a park bench at Niagara Falls. I think she or someone else must have just gone there to write and post the blog entry."

Nick put his head in his hands and sighed.

"The weird thing is," Seth continued, "I pulled up a live feed of the location one of the times when I caught someone updating the blog from that origination point, but there was nobody there. It was just an empty park bench."

"Do you think your coordinates could be off?" Nick asked.

Seth shook his head. "They're correct and precise. I mean, I've found several different origination points, but each different one is correct – or was at the time when the site was being updated."

"So what you're saying," Nick hesitantly proposed, "is that, even though no one and nothing is there, a transmission is coming through from a park bench at Niagara Falls, and no matter that you can see that there's nobody there, you still think that's where the signal's originating from?"

Seth nodded. "Someone *was* updating the site from there while I watched, but there was just no one there. Weird, huh?"

Nick ran a hand down his face. "Not really," he said on a heavy sigh.

He then explained to Seth about what he had witnessed in Australia with the old woman just disappearing into thin air. Afterward, the boy sat silent, presumably stunned by what Nick had told him. Nick put a kettle of water on to boil. He definitely needed some coffee.

"For, um, the past two years," Seth finally said, "I've been working on a certain project at school. I don't know who it's for and I only have the Dean's name on my timecard copies, but rumor has it the NSA is funding the whole thing."

Nick whistled. "And you never asked?"

Seth shook his head. "I like the work and they leave me alone." He shrugged. "'Cept, maybe now I'm thinkin' I should've been a little more curious."

"It's okay," Nick said as he handed a fresh cup of instant coffee to Seth. "I've found that most uber-geniuses tend to be a little less curious about the mundane than most."

Seth nodded and sipped his coffee. "Wow," he said, his eyes opening wide. "That's some strong stuff."

"Yeah," Nick said, taking a big gulp of his own. "The stronger the better, I always say." After a moment, Nick asked, "I guess they got what they wanted from you, huh?"

"Yeah," Seth replied calmly. "If I didn't have a back-up of just about everything, I'd be real upset by now."

"What?" Nick exclaimed. "You have a back-up?"

Seth pulled out a thin thumb drive device and held it up, explaining, "All but this morning's research is on here. That's why I needed to go back to the lab, so I could save what I had done onto this, since I didn't get the chance to do it before I left this afternoon." He twirled the little stick device between his fingers. "I was being kind of lazy this morning before classes started though, so I don't think there's much missing from here, information-wise that is."

"Are the transmission coordinates on there?" Nick asked.

Seth nodded.

"Then we still have the exact location of the place you think will lead us through to wherever Sarah Baker can be found, right?"

Seth nodded again.

Nick thought about the situation as he drank his coffee. The fact that the government now possibly had Seth's data from his research changed things. If they deciphered the kid's information, things could get dicey. Nick would have to plan this whole thing out before making another move. As bad as things had become in the political arena these days, one never knew who to trust and just one wrong move could ensure a person disappeared – sometimes for good.

He had to get to that transmission site.

"You said the transmission had come from a park bench at Niagara Falls, right?"

"Yeah," Seth confirmed.

"Do you think you would be able to recognize or point me to exactly where it was if we go there?"

"Wh-What?" Seth asked nervously. "I can't-I can't go to Niagara Falls. I can't cross over into some other dimension. I mean, I don't even know if my data are correct. I could've made a mistake in my calculations, or something."

"Did you?" Nick immediately demanded.

"Well, n-no, but I *could* have," Seth stammered.

Nick grabbed Seth's sleeve and pulled the kid up out of his chair. "Listen, boy," he said right in Seth's ear. "You're gonna help me get to that transmission site so I can see if I can somehow get over to wherever Sarah Baker and Lisa Murdoch were taken, do you hear? They could be in God knows whatever kind of danger and you're gonna help me find them, even if I have to drag your ass out there with me to do it!"

***

It was a shock being in New York City. So many people and so much noise after spending so much time in South America had both men experiencing a bit of culture shock. But they had both showered and shaved and were now waiting patiently for the elevator doors to open as it ascended to the floor of the building where the editor who had recently been murdered had lived.

The doors smoothly slid open and the two men made their way down the quiet, well-lit corridor of the posh apartment building. An agent stood guard outside the apartment and he checked their credentials before allowing them entry. The editor's body had been removed already, but there were plenty of signs of a struggle and Manning was sure they would find some clue as to who had done this, if not why.

A forensics team had already worked the scene without finding anything definitive to go on. But their evidence had now been turned over to Manning's team and he was sure something would turn up. In the meantime, he wanted to go over the area just to make sure nothing had been missed.

A voice caught his attention and he turned toward Nisrahali. The man had pushed a button to play the messages on an ancient-looking answering machine on a table near what Manning believed had been the editor's desk. The voice of a man named Nick explained that he had just gotten back, but that he was going to follow up on a lead in Boston before he could meet the editor, named "Frank".

"I have the name Nick Sharapov here as an associate of this Frank," Nisrahali said. "You said that was the person you discovered had been in Australia researching the missing girl's case there, yes?" At Manning's nod, Nisrahali said, "If you would not mind, I would like to go to Boston to see if I can find this person to discover what he knows."

Manning nodded. "Keep me informed, but be careful."

The Israeli nodded and left.

Manning spent the next couple of hours scouring the apartment for any clue as to the identity of the editor's murderer. He also checked with building management for all security footage and he interviewed the doorman. All of this had been gone over and done before he and Nisrahali had come on the scene, but it appeared several things had been missed or overlooked.

The doorman had described a man with a rounded ponytail and impeccable suit as having entered the building just before the editor's supposed time of death. Manning had spotted the man on the security footage and had the local authorities put out a BOLO for anyone matching the man's description. He also found several strands of hair in the elevator that he sent over to his team for analysis. He called in to report his findings to the Secretary and was then ordered to head up to Boston to assist Nisrahali with locating Nick Sharapov.

That was fine by Manning. Twice now Nick Sharapov's name had come up. The fact that the man was still alive meant he probably hadn't come into contact with the hair sample that had been found in Australia and that made him even more dangerous. Manning wanted anyone with any knowledge of the deadly hair to be under U.S. control to ensure the safety of the American public, first of all. Second, he wanted to know exactly what and how much Sharapov knew about it. He had to know something to still be on the hunt for it for this long. And that made him Manning's new best friend, so to speak.

Within an hour, Manning was seated on a puddle-jumper to Boston. By the time he reached Logan International, his team had results for him on the evidence retrieved from the apartment. But it wasn't what he wanted to hear. The only fingerprints found on anything were the editor's.

The mystery man was still just that. His face hadn't matched anyone in any of the databases they had tried and the hair strands had all come back without matching anyone who hadn't been identified as living in the editor's building. Hell! At this point, Manning wasn't even certain the mystery man was even human. All he knew was that the guy didn't appear to be in anybody's system.

The one good lead they had was a snapshot of him from a security camera near the campus of MIT from yesterday morning. Nisrahali had caught that while researching the apparent disappearance of a young grad student named Seth Green. Manning listened to the Israeli's explanation of how he had been following a lead on Nick Sharapov when he had discovered Mr. Green had been reported missing by his roommates.

On a hunch, Nisrahali had requested security footage near the physics lab where the boy had worked and that's when he had discovered both Nick Sharapov and the mystery man had gone to the location. And it appeared the kid had left willingly with Sharapov, judging from the footage he had seen. It also appeared the mystery man had a whole team of people working with him and that they were looking for Mr. Green for some purpose of their own, seeing as how they had been seen taking the young man's research from the computer in the lab.

Manning studied the data, both from his team and from the report Nisrahali had given him. He had to give his partner one thing; the man was thorough. He had covered all the bases. But something was still missing. Manning went over everything again.

Nikolai Sharapov had been staying at the flat of the botanist in London who had received the hair samples from Diego Montoya. Checking the timeline, Manning discovered the reporter had actually travelled to Dallas at about that time for some reason – probably to check out the Sarah Baker scene. He most likely hadn't had any hair samples with him in Dallas, because there had been no reports of anything unusual since Manning and his team had left.

Sharapov had then jetted off to Australia to investigate the disappearance of one Lisa Murdoch, at whose flat another of the lethal hair strands had been discovered. Manning had no idea what the man had done while in

Australia, but upon his return from there he had left a voicemail with his editor informing him he would be contacting him with a story after he followed up with one last lead. Now the editor was dead and it appeared Sharapov and the grad student were being tailed by the editor's murderer.

The only conclusions Manning could make from all of the evidence presented him were that 1) Sharapov possibly knew more about the origin of the deadly hair strands than anyone else and 2) he and the grad student with him were now in grave danger.

How was Seth Green involved? Why had mystery man's team stolen the kid's research? Manning needed the answers to these two questions and he had to find Sharapov and the kid before the hit man and his team found them.

"Get on the horn to everybody," he instructed Nisrahali. "We have to find them before our mystery guest does." He pulled out his black phone and started dialing. The few contacts he had were rather specialized and he would have to call in every favor he had ever done for anyone. He just hoped it would be enough. Nisrahali did the same, he noticed, as the man spoke in his native tongue to people overseas whose reach extended far onto U.S. soil.

Chapter 17

Tobin watched the fire, wondering if Ana was upset with him. After their conversation a few minutes ago, she had gone to the tent she shared with Bianca and he had let her go. He felt a bit useless to her for the moment because there really was nothing more he could do. He did not know why the pick-up team had left this morning without even affording him the opportunity to ask if Bianca and Ana could stay, and the only way Tobin could discover answers was for him to contact them again.

He should have done that this morning. But when he had seen the ship take off, a part of him rejoiced and he had felt almost free for the first time in his life. This thought gave him pause. He had never felt enslaved, but he did feel as if his choices had been limited each and every day of his life.

The Samarean – who were his off-world relatives, *and* who were one of the nine factions of Watchers dedicated to the preservation of Earth's human population – were the ones who dictated what he was to do, along with when and where and how he was to do it. Instead of being allowed to live a life of his choosing, he had been created to live the life they carved out for him. It wasn't a terrible life, but was it one he would have chosen for himself? He did not know.

Because of his genetic make-up, he traditionally could not truly be part of regular human society without eventually running the risk of being discovered. Now, however, there were many ways he could make a life for himself within human society without ever having to worry his secret might be revealed. And with Ana's help, he believed it would be even simpler to fit into a large community somewhere where they could live quite happily until Bianca was grown. Then, as is generally acceptable, Bianca's parents could simply move to a new state or even a new country.

If Tobin stopped using the Geres patches supplied by his off-world relatives, which were what sustained him and allowed him to function without eating anything produced on

Earth, might he age as humans did? The idea of growing old with Ana appealed to him somewhat and he smiled to himself. What would that be like?

A sound off to his right captured his attention and all thoughts of his current dilemma flew from his mind. This area was prone to coyotes and other nocturnal carnivorous creatures and Tobin would not wish to endanger Ana or Bianca. Squinting his eyes, he thought he saw a figure moving in the brush. *What is that?* he silently asked himself. As the figure came closer to the small campfire, Tobin wondered if what he was seeing was a boy.

Sure enough, a second later a boy stepped into the small circle of light cast out by the fire. Tobin figured he had to be around ten or eleven years old, but there was something wrong with him. The kid looked like he had been put through the wringer and that he would collapse at the slightest touch. He also looked like he was starving, judging from the hungry look he was giving the remnants of the jackrabbit Ana had caught, cleaned and cooked for Bianca and her earlier.

"Hóla, amigo," Tobin cautiously said.

The boy started, but then frowned, giving Tobin a wary eye. "I-I'm sorry," he stammered weakly, backing up a step or two. "I don't speak... um... that language..." His words trailed off as his gaze returned to the small amount of rabbit remaining on the spit.

"Please, come sit by the fire," Tobin invited in English. Although the heat of day in this part of the country could be stifling, the nights were usually quite cool. The only piece of clothing the boy wore was a short gown-like piece of fabric that somewhat reminded Tobin of the Paie robes he and his classmates had worn when he had been off-world.

Tobin quickly shook off such a fanciful notion. Why on earth that memory had popped into his mind, he did not know. Perhaps, because of the bent his thoughts had taken earlier.

The boy moving closer to the fire brought his attention back to the present and Tobin motioned toward a spot not far from him where the boy could sit and relax in its warmth. As soon as the kid was comfortably seated, Tobin asked, "Would you like some supper?"

With a sigh of relief, the boy politely said, "Yes, please."

Tobin obliged and soon handed him a paper plate loaded with the remains of the rabbit. It had cooled enough that it was safe to touch and the boy dug in. Tobin studied him as he ate. Now that he was closer and in the full light of the fire, the gown the boy wore was quite visible and something within Tobin tensed as he realized it *was* a Paie robe. That's also when he saw the puncture wounds dotted all over the boy's limbs and upper chest.

The robe meant the boy had been with the Watchers. The puncture wounds were also telling because Tobin knew that that many wounds meant they had wanted a lot of his blood. That could mean only one thing – this boy was a pure-bred human!

But that didn't make any sense. The Watchers would never release a pure-bred human back onto the world. That would defeat the whole purpose of them being here. No. Something terrible had happened and it was now sitting at the same campfire with Tobin and his wards, eating the same food they ate and endangering all of them. As he thought on the matter, he was almost certain this boy had to have had something to do with why the pick-up team had left this morning without waiting for Tobin's arrival.

An ache started behind his left eye and then Tobin thought he heard Ana's voice within his mind calling him. Frowning, he turned toward the tent to ensure all was quiet there. But instead of seeing just the closed flap of the tent, he saw Ana standing before the opened flap as she regarded him inquisitively. Her gaze flew to the newcomer and then back to Tobin before she slowly approached the little circle around the campfire where they had eaten earlier.

Who is he? Ana's voice asked in Tobin's mind.

Tobin had been looking her directly in the face when he heard her question and, although her mouth had been closed the whole time, every word had been clear. His mouth agape, Tobin stared in utter confusion as she approached.

The sudden sound of an approaching vehicle pulled everyone's attention toward it. Headlights bounced up and down as the vehicle made its way over the rocky terrain and then slid to a stop ten feet from the three gathered around the fire. The vehicle was too far from the flames for Tobin to see inside it, but he quickly heard doors opening and the crunch of multiple pairs of shoes stepping out onto the ground.

There was a shout from one of the newcomers, "D!"

The boy sitting near Tobin jerked to attention, standing as he shouted, "Ty?!"

Tobin stood as well as a much younger and smaller boy similar in coloring to the one standing near Tobin came running forward and into the outstretched arms of the older boy.

"Tyson!" the older boy cried as he hugged the young boy close. "I can't believe it! You're here!"

The one named Tyson pulled back from the embrace and said, "I knew you would be here. I just knew it." He turned to three other people who had also emerged from the vehicle and said, "See? I told you my brother would be here."

His companions all nodded and then all three pairs of eyes focused on the older boy. "Are you Demetrius Bradley?" the female of the trio asked.

The older boy spared her a glance as he said, "Yes, ma'am." But then his attention returned to his younger brother and he asked, "Ty, how'd you 'scape?"

"They let me go," Tyson simply said. "How'd you 'scape?"

Demetrius thought for a moment. He couldn't tell Tyson about all the horrible things the aliens had done to him. Hell, he didn't want to even think about it himself! Instead, he said, "I-I just did." He looked toward the trio of newcomers and then asked, "Where's momma? Was she mad when you got back?"

Tyson shook his head, explaining, "I ain't been home an' she ain't there anyway. They took her, D. The police 'rested her 'cause they think she killed us... you, I mean."

"What?" Demetrius demanded. This didn't make any sense to him. "Wait," he said, his baffled mind working to sort out this new mess. "Whatchya mean?"

The lady who had spoken before stepped forward into the fire's light and cleared her throat for attention. "Um, Demetrius?" she asked, smiling at him. "Hi there. I'm Stacy." She turned and pointed at her two male companions and continued, "This is my husband, Matt, and our friend Lonnie. I know this is all very confusing and that you probably have like a zillion questions. Believe me when I say that we can help you and Tyson find the answers. But I think it would be better if we could all sit down somewhere and talk first."

As Stacy spoke with Demetrius, Tyson frowned and looked around. Within his mind, he heard another female voice – a soft one he had never heard before, but which was very appealing to his mind's ear.

Who are you? it asked.

Tyson focused on the woman now standing with the man Demetrius had been sitting with at the fire before they arrived. She looked nice, but scared. The voice in his mind hadn't sounded scared at all and he didn't think it belonged to this woman. Anyway, she appeared too old to be the voice's owner.

I'm Tyson, he silently responded. *Who're you?*

The reply was immediate. *I'm Bianca.*

That's when Tyson noticed the tent in the background. He suddenly felt a pull toward that tent and he knew without a doubt that that was where this Bianca person was. He started toward the tent, intent on meeting her face-to-face. Immediately, the man and woman who were standing off to the side moved to block his way, a strange fear coloring their faces. This sudden movement halted Stacy's conversation with Demetrius and everyone's attention turned to what was happening with Tyson.

Demetrius pulled up behind Tyson and rested a protective hand upon his younger brother's shoulder. "Ty? What's goin' on?" he asked.

At that moment, the most beautiful little girl any of

the newcomers had ever seen emerged from the little tent behind the couple standing guard. She had a great big smile just beaming across her face as she walked around the couple and straight on over to Tyson, where she took his hand with her own without speaking a single word.

As if that hadn't been odd enough, the moment the two touched hands their eyes actually began to glow!

Demetrius, who could only see the glowing eyes of the girl, pulled on Tyson's shoulder to get him away from what he assumed was another alien. Tyson turned as he shook Demetrius' hand off him and that's when Demetrius saw that Tyson's eyes were glowing as well. He screamed as he backed away from his younger brother, his heart beating a mile a minute as he shook his head back and forth. This couldn't be happening! It just couldn't be happening! It had to be some kind of nightmare the aliens had put into his head.

All Demetrius could think was that the aliens had done something to change his little brother into one of them and it was all Demetrius' fault. He was supposed to protect Tyson and now the aliens had turned him into an alien, too. Tears flowed freely down his face as he realized his brother was gone. He was too wrapped up in his own misery to notice the couple standing directly behind the little girl alien. But Stacy, Matt and Lonnie noticed.

They had been fascinated with the two children whose eyes had begun glowing, but that was nothing compared to what happened next. The trio watched as if mesmerized as the older couple practically transformed right before their eyes into some new type of creatures. The hair on each one's head grew at least two feet and their eyes began to glow as well. What was really cool, though, was when their hair started moving all on its own, as if each head of hair was a mass of new limbs.

Stacy and Matt had immediately pulled out cell phones to record everything going on while Lonnie focused more on what he heard going on inside the minds of the creatures before them, for their minds were not quiet in the least and he could hear all of it.

None of them knew what was happening. The two

young ones were simply happy to be together, as if they had been waiting the entirety of their short lives to be united. But the older couple, who went by the names of Tobin and Ana, were clearly frightened – both by the changes they had witnessed in the two young ones *and* by the changes they themselves were now experiencing.

"Oh, my God," Lonnie softly said in fascination.

Stacy and Matt looked away from the scene they were recording and simultaneously asked, "What?"

"He's a Star child and she's a human," he said. "They mated and the girl is their daughter."

A couple of moments passed in silence as the three adult humans watched the others in fascination.

"Why are they changing like that?" Stacy finally whispered, as she tore her gaze from the scene before them. "What's happening to them?"

Lonnie simply shook his head and said, "I don't know… and neither do they."

Ana was not happy that their safe little world had been intruded upon by these strangers and she was going to put a stop to it. First the boy, and now a whole foursome of strangers? Who did they think they were, just appearing out of nowhere to… what? It sounded like this Demetrius kid had been taken by someone but had somehow managed to escape. It also sounded like the younger brother, Tyson, had been taken by the same people but later returned, but why?

She didn't care. She just wanted them all to leave before they woke up Bianca – or worse, before they discovered that Bianca and Tobin were only part-human. Before she could make a move to stop this insanity, however, the younger boy, Tyson, began walking toward her as if he planned on going to the tent to wake up Bianca. A sharp pain lanced through her head and she heard Tobin's voice within her mind shouting, *Stop him!*

Without hesitation, both she and Tobin moved in unison to block the boy's path. Ana didn't know why she was suddenly able to hear Tobin's thoughts, but she had no time to think on the matter now as her mission to protect their daughter surged to the forefront. When Bianca suddenly appeared by her side, Ana was too stunned to stop her from continuing on to where Tyson stood. With stupefied fascination, Ana and Tobin watched as their beautiful little girl reached out and touched Tyson and then... Bianca became someone else.

Two very different thoughts flashed through Ana's and Tobin's minds upon seeing the change within their daughter. Tobin first felt fascination at what had happened. Then he feared the Watchers would discover Bianca had somehow had a reaction to a human and that they would then come to take her from Ana and him. Curiously, he himself caught fear coming from within Ana's mind. As he examined it, he realized she was afraid Bianca was changing into an alien and that Tobin would now take their daughter to live in space without her. He turned to her to reassure her that he would never allow anyone or anything to come between them. And that's when it happened.

The moment he touched her hand, an incredible burst of energy poured through Tobin's entire body and he felt like he was on fire inside. He gasped at the feeling and tightly grabbed Ana's hand to keep himself from falling. To his surprise, he felt another burst of energy shooting up his arm from their clasped palms and he shot a glance to her face to discover if she was feeling the same thing. What he saw was even more shocking as he witnessed the most wondrous sight in his entire life. Ana, his Ana, was transforming from the human form of a chrysalis to the form she must always have been meant to be. It was not a butterfly's form her body became, but the most beautiful creature with long, dark hair and softly-glowing eyes.

Her thoughts came to him then and he realized his own form must have transformed as well, for she was fascinated by his long waving hair and his softly-glowing eyes as he stared back at her. But her fear was still there and she silently begged to know what was happening. The only problem was that Tobin didn't know the answer. He heard the man named Lonnie talking to his companions and he wanted to scream at the intruders to just go away. But how could he do that?

Tobin turned to face Bianca and Tyson, who were standing together, hands clasped, as they happily watched Tobin and Ana transform. A lock of long hair moved up and out toward the children, startling Tobin, and he knocked it away, as if it was a serpent he had to protect them from. That's when he realized the lock of hair belonged to him. He turned back to Ana, his eyes crazed and desperate. Her hair was moving around at the ends and he stared in terror as it now reached out for him.

The loud sound of another vehicle fast approaching caught everyone's attention and fear ran rampant throughout the entire assemblage. There was no time for escape and the whole group simply watched with dread as an old beat-up extended-cab pick-up truck came to a halt twenty feet from where Tobin and Ana stood. An older man with gray hair stepped out of the truck. He carried a shotgun in one hand and a brightly-shining flashlight in another.

"Quien estan ustedes?" he demanded. When no one answered, he raised his rifle and shone the flashlight directly onto Tobin's face. There he stopped. Because of the flashlight, no one within the group could see the stranger's face. But there were several within the group who suddenly heard within their minds a silent inquiry spoken in an alien tongue, but clearly asking who they were and why they had come to this place.

"Oh, my God," Lonnie said again as he picked up on the newcomer's thoughts.

Stacy and Matt turned and asked again, "What?"

Lonnie nodded toward the newcomer and said, "He's one of them."

Chapter 18

The dilapidated old pick-up truck bounced along the dirt road with Lonnie's over-sized SUV following close behind. The pick-up truck's driver was a man named Juan de los Santos and he owned this land. That was all the information he had given the group before inviting them up to the main house on the ranch. "It is not safe for you here," he had said.

Clearly, the man knew more than he was letting on so Tobin and Ana and the rest had decided it would be best to go with him to find out what he knew about their situation. Tobin, Ana, Tyson and Bianca had climbed into the truck with Santos, while everyone else had piled into the SUV. Now, as the main house came into view, a shiver ran up Ana's spine. She had no idea what might be waiting inside that house. Another shiver raced up her spine as a lock of Tobin's hair caressed her cheek.

She supposed Tobin had picked up on her fears somehow and his hair had touched her in an effort to comfort her. Although the idea of him trying to comfort her was nice, the very act itself had only served to freak her out and she was now even more uncomfortable than she had been just from wondering if they were about to walk into the lion's den, or something worse.

Tobin caught the drift of her thoughts and he quickly gathered up his hair and stuffed it inside the neck of his shirt. He hoped it would stay there. Controlling the damned hair strands was definitely beyond him and he hoped this Santos guy could shed some light on what was happening to them.

Santos parked the truck near the house's front door and they all climbed out. The SUV was quickly parked and its passengers disembarked as well. The whole horde stood for a moment just looking at the house. It was a single-story ranch house with several lights shining from the inside. There was smoke coming up from the chimney and no one else appeared to be around.

"Come," Santos said as he headed for the door.

Before anyone could move a muscle, the door opened and an older gray-haired woman stepped out onto the front porch. She put her arm around Santos' waist as he drew up next to her. He did the same and the couple turned to look expectantly at the group.

"I am Carmen de los Santos," the older woman said in a thick accent. "Welcome to our home." As those within the group hesitantly nodded and approached the door, several of them heard Carmen's silent message in that other language. *Do not fear us*, it said. *You are safe here.*

Lonnie stared long and hard at both her and Santos as he crossed the threshold into the house, but he said not a word. The rest of the crew followed him. The four who had recently changed took a seat on one side of the small living room, while the others sat on the other side staring at them. Santos stood in the center of the room studying each individual. Finally, he turned to Tobin and stopped. "Why are you here?" he asked, his own words heavily accented.

Tobin balked at the idea of having to speak in front of so many – even though most of them had witnessed what happened earlier. He was tense from the situation, freaked out about the changes he and the three others had experienced and he was unsure as to who knew what about Bianca, Ana and him. "We... were waiting to meet someone," he said nervously. It was the best he could think of with such short notice. His hair slowly swished back and forth at the ends within the confines of his shirt.

Santos grunted, turning and pointing toward Demetrius and asked, "And that one? Why is he wearing a Paie robe?"

Tobin swallowed hard, but said nothing. He simply didn't know what to say.

"I will tell you why," Santos spat. He looked the older boy up and down and then said, "He is pure bred. Just look at the marks on him." The moment the words left his mouth, everyone in the group turned to stare at Demetrius. They all saw the marks on his arms and legs and most within the group wondered what the significance of the marks was, along with what Santos had meant when he had said

Demetrius was pure bred. "He is the one they have been talking about all day," Santos continued. "And here he sits... with you and your *Jess*."

He moved to stand directly in front of Ana. "What did you think would happen? You would take the boy as a bargaining chip?"

Ana immediately shook her head. "We-we didn't take him," she said, her eyes and voice full of fear.

"What does that mean, '*Jess*'?" Tobin asked, interrupting the two as curiosity won out over his inner fears.

Santos whipped around toward him and pointed back at Ana, explaining, "This one. She is your *Jess*, just as you are her *Joss*."

At the blank look on Tobin's face, Carmen de los Santos moved forward. "Santos, mi amor," she said as she gently took hold of his arm. Her voice was full of wonder as she continued, "They do not know."

Santos looked down at her like she was crazy before he stepped over to where Tyson and Bianca sat. Pointing at the young couple, he said, "And I suppose you do not know about these *Jus*."

Tobin frowned, totally confused now, and asked, "*Jus*?"

"Yes," Santos said, rather gruffly. "If one is Joss, he is a Ju. If one is Jess, she is a Ju. *Joss* and *Jess* are *Jus*." He pointed to Tyson and Bianca, saying, "These are *Jus*." He then pointed to Tobin and Ana and said, "You are *Jus*. All four of you are *Juish*."

Just then, Stacy interrupted, asking, "Excuse me, but you're telling us they changed because they're Jewish?" The look of disgust she got from Santos made her want to crawl into a hole in the ground to hide from him.

"*Juish*," Santos explained. "Not Jewish!" He turned back to Tobin and asked, "You always travel with hybrids?"

"Hybrids?" Stacy asked.

At the same time, Matt demanded, "Who are you callin' a hybrid?"

Lonnie remained quiet. He was too busy listening to everything – that which was spoken aloud *and* that which was spoken silently.

Tobin held up a hand to silence everyone. He rose and stood directly before Santos, saying, "I am afraid we do not understand any of this."

Carmen approached Santos again, taking his hand in hers this time, as she asked Tobin, "You were what humans call Star child, yes? Half human and half something else?"

Tobin nodded, as he responded. "I *am* a Star child, half Samarean and half human."

"No," Santos said. "You *were* Star child. Now you are a Ju – you are *Joss*."

"But what does that mean?" Ana asked, desperate to understand.

"Means you are more than Star child," Carmen explained to Tobin. "You are more than Samarean or human. You," and here she gestured toward Ana, "and your *Jess* are now *Juish*, as are the scion and its *Joss*, which makes danger for you."

As Tobin made to protest again, Lonnie stepped forward. "Hey, man," he interrupted, directing his words to Tobin. "I think what they're trying to tell you is that you and... uh, Ana right?" he asked, looking at Ana.

"Yes," Ana answered.

"Right. You and Ana, as well as Tyson and the little girl here, have all changed... evolved, if you will. You get it?"

"Yes," Santos agreed, nodding. "Evolved is word. And because you have evolved, you have much danger."

Tobin thought for a moment, frowning, before saying, "Earlier, you said 'He is the one they have been talking about all day.' You meant Demetrius, right?" At Santos' nod, he asked, "Who are 'they'?"

Santos threw a hesitant look Carmen's way, as if asking permission, before finally explaining, "I referred to Samarean and others – Grigori."

Realization dawned on Tobin as he recognized the ancient word for Watchers and he said, "You have found a way of monitoring them."

Lonnie interjected again, announcing, "He *is* one of

them – a Watcher, I mean."

Santos threw him a look of such disdain Lonnie blanched and immediately clammed up. He could hear this Santos and Carmen communicating with each other within their thoughts and he knew the two were much more powerful than they were letting on.

Finally, on a heavy sigh, Santos said, "Carmen and I… we are Toti." As Carmen once more grasped his hand in hers and smiled up at him, he continued, saying, "We were sent here to monitor the Star children of this region."

Matt stepped forward and asked, "Monitor them for what?"

"For changes," Santos explained.

"Changes?" Tobin asked.

Nervously, Santos nodded.

"What kind of changes?" Ana asked as she sidled up next to Tobin, gripping his hand with her own.

Carmen looked her directly in the eye and said, "The kind we see in you."

At that moment, Tyson stood and stepped forward, his hand still clasped tightly with Bianca's, and he looked at the older couple and said, "You said you were Toti." He looked them up and down. "You don't look like Toti. My teacher on the moon was Toti and you don't look anything like her."

Although Stacy and Matt gaped at Tyson at his mention of the moon, Carmen and Santos ignored them and exchanged another serious look with each other before Carmen explained, "We were made to look more like hybrids."

"You keep using this word 'hybrids,'" Stacy said. "What do you mean by that?"

"You," Santos said, pointing at her and the two men beside her.

All three shook their heads and said in unison, "We're humans."

Santos rewarded them with a shake of his head, explaining, "No, you are not. You are hybrids." He turned and pointed toward Demetrius, saying, "That one is the only true human here."

Demetrius had had enough! He couldn't listen to another word. He wanted out of this crazy dream and he was getting out right now! "Look," he said as he went to stand by Tyson. "I don't know what you people have been smokin', but me an' my brother are gittin' outta here right now to go find my momma." He tugged on Tyson's arm to get him to move, but Tyson pulled back.

"We can't, D," Tyson said, his chin wobbling a little.

"Whatchya mean?" Demetrius asked.

"The po-lice took momma."

"So? If they took her to jail, we can go find her an' get her out."

Tyson slowly shook his head. "I 'on't think so," he said, tears forming in his eyes. "I 'on't know where they took 'er. To some f'cility, I think." He turned and pointed to Lonnie and said, "I think Lonnie knows where they have 'er now."

As all eyes turned to regard Lonnie, he nodded, saying, "Yeah. I think she's at a government research facility in Las Cruces."

The looks on Carmen's and Santos' faces spoke volumes and an ominous feeling descended upon five of the adults in the room. Carmen turned to Tyson and Demetrius, saying, "My dear children, su madre is gone."

Demetrius was floored. With tears in his eyes, he asked in disbelief, "Wh-What?"

Lonnie asked Santos, "You know this place?"

Both Toti nodded and Santos explained, "It is a very bad place."

"Well, we have to go get my mom, then," Demetrius screeched in desperation. "We have to save her."

"Child, you would not like what you found," Carmen cautioned him.

"I don't care!" Demetrius shouted, already heading for the door. "If she's there, we have to go save her!"

Tyson soon followed after his elder brother, with Bianca dutifully in tow. Ana wasn't about to let Bianca out of her sight and she quickly tugged on Tobin's arm to follow the children. Stacy and Matt were already following along right behind the three kids when Lonnie asked Santos, "So, can you tell me how to get to this place from here or give me an address or any information about it?"

After thinking hard on the matter for a few tense seconds, Santos sighed heavily and said, "You will need more than directions. That place is difficult to get into and even more difficult to escape. You will require protection and... a different kind of help."

"What do you mean?" Lonnie asked, growing more than a little nervous now.

"Santos!" Carmen gasped, gripping his arm as if to stop him.

The elderly man turned to her and gently extricated himself from her grasp. "Mi amor," he softly said. "They are *Juish*. We must help them any way we can."

"But...," she pled, shaking her head.

Santos pulled her close in an almost tender embrace, whispering, "I know." Then he pulled back and looked her directly in the eyes, asking, "But what have we been doing here all this time, mi mariposa, if not hoping for this? If this is really happening, do you expect me to remain quiet and not help?"

Staring right back up at him, Carmen's eyes lit with a tiny spark of hope and she said, "Then I come, too."

Chapter 19

It was a tight fit as the six aliens piled into Santos' truck, with Santos and Carmen in the front seat and Tobin and Ana in the back and the two kids sitting on the floor boards. No one had said anything, but the others didn't feel exactly comfortable with the idea of sitting cooped up in a car with confirmed extraterrestrials – regardless of the fact that Santos believed all of them to be some type of hybrid beings, themselves. Even Demetrius couldn't gather enough courage to go with Tyson.

Santos led the way in his pick-up, taking the group on a less direct route out of Mexico than the one they had taken in. The road they were on supposedly led to an unmanned and unblocked path across the border on a small stretch of farm land. It would take longer, but that way they would not encounter any Border Patrol into the U.S. For the most part, it was a boring journey and eventually Tyson and Bianca ended up sleeping the remainder of the trip.

Lonnie followed behind Santos and turned wherever the old truck turned. For some reason, his mind remained connected with everyone in the old pick-up truck, the two Toti, Tobin, Ana, Bianca and Tyson. It felt strange hearing all their thoughts, and Lonnie wondered if he shouldn't say something to let everyone other than Tyson know he could hear them. But Tyson hadn't said anything about Lonnie's ability before he had nodded off and no one else appeared to have noticed, so Lonnie remained quiet. The constant excited chatter between Matt and Stacy was mere white noise for as much attention as he paid it.

What had started out as a trip to reunite a boy with his mother had turned into what was perhaps the greatest adventure of Lonnie's life. He felt he needed to know what this meant, what his part in everything was, how it was going to turn out, and why the hell he could suddenly read other people's minds!

It was getting on toward early evening when the troupe finally pulled into a local diner's parking lot in an unassuming section of Las Cruces, New Mexico. Lonnie had been monitoring Santos' thoughts throughout the trip and he knew the creature had a plan in mind for breaking into the place where the boys' mother was supposedly being held, but he didn't know many details or how well it was going to be received by everyone else.

From what Lonnie could tell from the two Totis' minds, he believed anyone who went into the research facility would be lucky to get out alive. The few things the two knew about the place were terrifying and Lonnie could only hope there was a chance the boys' mother still lived. He himself was determined to do whatever he could to help get her back, *if* she was still alive.

The group got out of the vehicles without much ado and went into the diner. They were seated at one of the larger curved booths and a waitress approached and took orders. When she turned to Tobin, Carmen and Santos for their orders, she was waived off by each. As soon as she had left the area to go put in the others' orders, Stacy asked the three, "Aren't you going to eat?"

While all three looked nervously from one to the other, Tyson chimed in innocently, explaining, "They don't need to eat. They wear Geres patches."

The waitress returned with their drinks and then left the area again. Stacy and Matt were immediately brimming with curiosity, asking what Geres patches were and how they worked.

"My friend on the moon told me all about them," Tyson said. Stacy and Matt both looked like they were dying to ask about what he had meant about the moon, but Tyson continued as he drank the chocolate milk he had ordered. "They're patches with food that's 'sorbed right into the body. Right, Tobin?"

Tobin wore a small smile as he nodded to the boy. "That is true. They contain the essential nutrients, vitamins, amino acids and proteins required to live."

"And you're wearing one right now?" Matt asked, eager to catch a glimpse of this miracle patch.

Tobin nodded.

"Can we see?" Matt and Stacy asked in unison.

Hesitantly, Tobin turned to Ana. After a moment, he released her hand and slowly raised his left arm, using his other hand to raise the bottom of his shirt on that side up to his left armpit. He then pointed to the nearly invisible patch affixed to his skin just beneath his armpit.

"May I touch it?" Stacy asked. At Tobin's shrug, she reached out and ran her fingers over it. "It feels like skin – like there's nothing even there," she told Matt. As Tobin lowered his shirt and arm once more, she asked, "How is the stuff absorbed? And how long does it last?" At Tobin's look of extreme discomfort, she apologized. "I'm just curious," she explained, looking around the busy diner. She carefully chose her words when she said, "I mean, I've never met... um, foreigners like you before."

The waitress appeared with their food and everyone was quiet as she placed loaded plates of steaming hot food before those who had ordered. When she was gone again, Tobin said, "I understand your curiosity and I will answer your questions to the best of my ability. I ask only one thing in return."

"Anything," Matt and Stacy declared in unison.

Tobin was dead serious as he said, "I ask only that you do not betray our secret to anyone."

Stacy and Matt looked around at the expectant and hopeful eyes of all those seated around the table. They had spent the last five years working together to get the truth about UFOs and Aliens out in the open to show everyone that the world's governments were hiding the truth from the public – and probably had been for decades. To not reveal Tobin's presence on Earth, nor his story, ran against every instinct they had, save one.

Over the past couple of days, they had come to care for little Tyson. He had been through so much and had only just been reunited with his brother. Now he had experienced some kind of heretofore unheard-of physiological change that would lead to God only knew what kind of dangers ahead. It took but a second for each to decide that they would rather keep Tobin's existence secret so that they could continue this journey with Tyson than to expose the alien. Slowly, they both nodded their agreement.

As those with food all ate, Tobin explained that the patch, as well as its adhesive, were actually an amalgamation of a full 24 hours' worth of all the essential life-sustaining nutrients. It was absorbed through the skin throughout the day and then directly into the bloodstream where everything was distributed throughout the body as needed.

Afterward, the entire group was silent as each individual digested this information. The very idea of never eating stymied most within the group.

Matt was the first to speak, asking incredulously, "Don't you miss food?"

Tobin thought for a moment and then said, "I have not eaten since I was five years old and so I truly do not remember how food tasted. I do not recall the texture or what it was like to eat."

"That's so sad," Stacy whispered.

"Yeah," Lonnie chimed in. "But look at the upside to it – especially with his lifestyle. He doesn't have to worry about finding sustenance or where to store it or where to dispose of his waste. I bet that really helps out if you're havin' to travel a lot, huh?"

Tobin nodded agreement. "It does eliminate the necessity of voiding one's bowels or emptying the bladder."

"Ever?" Matt asked, gaping.

Tobin thought for a moment and then said, "There may be the occasional build-up, but those moments come maybe once a year." He shrugged. "The main advantages of the patch are, of course, the extension of life expectancy and improved health of the body."

"You mean you don't age?" Stacy asked, growing more interested in this patch idea by the minute.

"No, no. One does age, just not as quickly or to the debilitating degree to which creatures that eat do."

"How old are you?" Lonnie bluntly asked.

"How old would you think I am?" Tobin asked.

Everyone within the group studied his face and form, working to determine just how old he looked and yet how old he might be from the use of the patch.

Lonnie finally shook his head and answered, "Well, you look like you could be either in your late twenties or early to mid-thirties. But I'm guessin', since you said you hadn't eaten anything since you were five, you're probably older than that. I guess I'll say you're closer to 50."

A small smile lifted the corners of Tobin's mouth as he threw a quick glance over to Ana and squeezed her hand. When he again lifted his gaze to Lonnie, he said, "I actually do not know my exact age. I know I was born in the springtime because I once asked my bearer. But I do know I have lived on this planet for more than 200 of your years."

All but the Toti gaped as they looked him up and down again.

"Wow," Stacy said, shaking her head in disbelief.

"You could be a billionaire overnight, if you sold those patches online," Matt said.

Santos immediately tensed, demanding, "Geres patches are *not* for sale to hybrids!"

"You keep saying that," Stacy noted, her irritation with the Toti male obvious to everyone. "Why do you keep calling us hybrids?"

Santos shrugged and said merely, "Because you are."

Stacy fixed him with a glare of ridicule and demanded as she pointed at Demetrius, "So out of all the people in this restaurant, he's the only true human?"

Santos looked around the joint. There were about 30 customers in the room seated at the various tables and then there was the wait staff of three and two cooks in the back who could be seen through an opening in the wall. He paused on a couple of tables and on one of the servers, but then he returned his gaze to Stacy and informed her, "There is the possibility of three or four more humans here, but the only one I know for certain is this boy."

"Who are the ones who might be?" Lonnie asked.

Santos turned and rudely pointed at one older man sitting alone at a table and a younger couple sitting at a booth. Finally, he pointed at a young waitress who was pouring coffee at another table. All four of the individuals were black.

"So, you're saying only African Americans are humans?" Stacy asked.

"The country of origin is of no importance," Santos gruffly explained. "It is genetic lineage that makes the difference."

"But what about Tyson?" Stacy demanded. "He's Demetrius' *brother*."

Santos frowned as he turned to study the boy. He then shrugged again and said, "He is *Joss*." The statement was made as if that explained everything.

"I still don't know what that means," Stacy said, completely unsatisfied with the Toti's answer.

Santos nervously shrugged off her request for information. As she pressed for an answer, he became frustrated and barked, "Is not important! You are hybrid and you do not need to know what is *Joss* or who is *Joss*."

"Are you *Joss*?" Lonnie suddenly asked.

A dance of fear skittered across the two Toti faces. Carmen inched closer to Santos and he quickly wrapped an arm around her as he studied the man. After a tense moment of this silent scrutiny, Santos moved to stand, helping Carmen up as he tersely stated, "Is time to go."

There appeared to be nothing left to say – especially not in the ever-increasing crowd within the diner. The group headed for the door as Matt took care of the bill. Once they were gathered at the two vehicles, Stacy asked no one in particular, "So what's the plan? I mean, we didn't discuss this yet. Are we just supposed to break into the place and hope we can find Tameka Bradley and then hope we can somehow break her out?"

"No," was Santos' immediate answer. "Carmen and I will take the boy *Ju* to the facility to locate the woman."

Matt frowned. "You mean Tyson?"

At Santos' nod, Demetrius and Stacy moved to stand before Tyson. "You can't take my bro' to that place!" Demetrius declared.

"If we are to rescue the woman, then yes. I can and I will."

Tobin suddenly experienced the strangest sensation. He could actually feel fear emanating from his daughter. Ana had obviously picked up on the same thing, for she pulled up beside Tobin and then pulled Bianca close to her side. When Bianca looked up at the two with desperation in her eyes, Tobin pulled away and said, "I will go instead of Tyson."

Santos shook his head. "You will stay here," he said.

"But the boy...," Tobin began, before Santos cut him off.

"One *Ju* is enough! I will not be responsible for two... You will stay here."

"But, I...," Again, Tobin was cut off – this time by Carmen.

"You do not understand," she said. "You are too new." She clasped his arm for a brief moment as she said, "This is the best way." She dropped her hold on Tobin's arm and then held her hand out for Tyson.

The boy *Joss* gave Bianca one meaningful glance before taking the Toti's hand and walking with her over to where Santos stood waiting. "It's okay," he said to his brother and all the other worried faces surrounding him. "I ain't 'fraid."

Stacy, who was growing more and more attached to Tyson with each passing hour, didn't like this plan one bit and she demanded, "So what are the rest of us supposed to do – just sit and wait and hope you're able to get in and out without being caught?"

"No," Santos said. He pointed at Lonnie. "This one is coming, too."

Stacy immediately reacted. "Wait. Lonnie? Why?"

For a tense moment, no one spoke. Then, as realization dawned on Matt, he explained, "Because he's a hacker."

Lonnie's sigh of relief went unnoticed as Matt continued.

"He's the only one who can get past the security measures."

"Okay," Stacy said before reiterating her previous

concerns. "But what about the rest of us? Do we just wait here?"

Carmen and Santos exchanged a tense look and then Santos nodded to her. Again, Carmen addressed Tobin, asking, "Do you remember the lessons you learned when you were five and you were taken off-world?"

Tobin frowned as he thought back, recalling everything he had been taught during his time off-world. He had enjoyed his studies and believed he could fully recall everything he had learned. He didn't know what any of that had to do with this situation, but he nodded.

"If anything happens and we do not return," Carmen continued, "find the Mahdii."

Tobin's frown deepened. The Mahdii? All he remembered about the Mahdii was that they had once been the rulers of the universe. Well, he did also recall an old Toti legend about them having been seen once on Earth many thousands of years ago. He turned to Santos for an explanation, but the older male merely nodded and reiterated Carmen's words. "Find the Mahdii. It is your only hope, if we do not return."

Dumbfounded, Tobin and the others watched as the four climbed into the Totis' truck and drove off.

Chapter 20

Not even an hour later, Manning and Nisrahali were on the road headed north. A good solid lead had come in from both fronts regarding a site near Lake Winnipesauke where a long-time acquaintance of Sharapov's owned a log cabin. Manning wasn't anticipating actually finding the reporter or the kid there, but he at least wanted to check it out in the hope there would be some clue there as to where the two were headed.

The property was pretty secluded and appeared empty when they arrived. By the time Manning located the spare key under a flower pot, Nisrahali had picked the lock to the front door. Throwing a sardonic glance the Israeli's way, Manning opened the door. The first thing both men noticed was the smell of strong coffee.

As Manning had suspected, the place was empty. But the coffee smell and the dishes still drying on a cloth on the counter to the side of the sink indicated they hadn't missed their targets by much. Other than that, the place was barren of clues. Whatever gear – if any – they had brought with them to the cabin had been taken with them when they had left.

Instead of accepting the predicament as a dead end, the two men jumped on their phones again to obtain whatever surveillance footage they could of all roads leading away from the area. Within an hour, they had a good fix on Sharapov and the kid as well as on the mystery man's team chasing them. They hopped into their rental and took off. Manning willingly allowed Nisrahali to take the wheel for this trip. Time was of the essence and, if anything, the Israeli had proven he was a demon behind the wheel.

As they traveled west along I-90, Manning was on the phone with his team. For the first time in his life, he was thankful for the internet as his team managed to keep track of the targets for him in close-to real time using social media and by hacking into local municipal traffic systems. The chase team was not far behind Sharapov and Green, but

Nisrahali and Manning were still more than an hour behind. They would have to do some fast maneuvering to catch up.

There was a gleam in Nisrahali's eye accompanying a wicked grin when Manning asked if the Israeli could speed things up. Before long, they were within 30 minutes of the lead team. It appeared the cars were headed toward Buffalo, NY. Manning made arrangements with his team for back-up to be in the area and on alert, should he need them. He had a bad feeling about this whole situation and something told him things might get dicey when the teams all reached their final destination.

It was nearly midnight by the time Nisrahali turned into the entrance to Niagara Falls. He cut the lights and cautiously proceeded toward Parking Lot Number Two (2) on Goat Island, near the Nikola Tesla monument. Brief flashes of light up ahead caught the two men's attention. Nisrahali already had his weapon drawn as he stopped the car and leapt from behind the wheel out onto the parking lot at a dead run. Manning was hot on his heels as both men surveyed the scene. Behind the closest car were two figures. It was Sharapov and Green, crouching in fear as what Manning could only guess was the other chase team fired round after round at their already ruined vehicle.

Manning and Nisrahali instinctively went into protective mode as they headed directly for the two unarmed men. Each had his sidearm and they fired into the darkness on the other side of the parking lot before ducking behind the bullet-hole ridden vehicle with Sharapov and Green.

"Who the fuck are you?" Sharapov demanded, gasping as he attempted to scooch as far away from the two newcomers as possible without giving up cover. The overhead parking lot lights revealed a trail of blood from the man's leg. The reporter was holding the wounded area of his right leg, but blood still seeped from it, revealing that he had been shot. His companion, Seth Green, was crouched down beside Sharapov, shaking like a leaf and gripping a laptop like it was his only protection.

"We are the cavalry," Nisrahali said as he aimed and fired once more.

The answer appeased Sharapov somewhat and he appeared to relax a bit. Another shot rang out, followed immediately by the sound of a window breaking on the vehicle and the man tensed up again as he demanded, "So who are they and what the hell do they want?"

Manning fired at the spot where the last shot had come from and then glanced at the wounded reporter. "Look," he explained, "these are dangerous people who want what you and Mr. Green have." He spotted another flash of light and fired at that exact spot. Someone in the darkness howled with pain. Manning didn't celebrate his direct hit, for he knew there were more out there. The next second proved him right, as another flash of light ushered in the next bullet hole in the cover car. Nisrahali took aim at this one and fired. Another shout of pain was heard immediately thereafter.

Manning was readying to fire again when Sharapov reached out with his bloody hand and grabbed his arm. "Listen," he pleaded through heavy gasps. "You've gotta help us."

Another shot rang out. Again, Nisrahali responded with his own fire. This time, there was no shout of pain – merely a grunt and then a thud onto the hood of a vehicle.

Manning took a moment to demand of Sharapov, "Do you have anything from Lisa Murdoch's flat?"

The reporter paled, even more than he was already, before saying, "No. It had already been sent to Sydney by the time I arrived." As Manning started his response, Sharapov interrupted, explaining, "It's at a lab there. They know what they're doing. So don't worry, it's safe. They know how dangerous the things are."

Manning thought for a moment. Then he brusquely said, "Look, I'm gonna be straight with you. More than one of the lab techs is dead. We got the one that was sent to London, but not before it killed the botanist there and we got the one from Lisa Murdoch's flat. But we have to keep these guys from getting their hands on any of them." He paused to point toward the area where the enemy was on the other side of the parking lot before continuing. "My guess is, on top of the hair strands, this welcoming party wants whatever Mr. Green has on that laptop and they don't care who they have to go through to get it."

Sharapov recoiled inside. He had dated Isabella Franconi a short while during his stay in London. Now, if what this man said was true, he was to blame for her death. He was searching for logical explanations that would make this theory untrue when the man's next words solidified it for him.

"These people already killed your editor. We have his body at the morgue in New York. Pretty messed up and painful way to die, the garrote."

Frank was dead... and it was Nick's fault. The information hit like a ton of bricks. He looked at Seth. The poor kid was scared half to death. He had trusted Nick, had left everything he knew to go with him on this crazy venture and Nick had promised to keep him safe. Now look at them. They were hiding behind a car while being shot at.

And what about Sarah Baker and Lisa Murdoch? They didn't know him, but he was the only one who knew they needed help. Nick doubted the shooters on the other side of the parking lot would be too friendly, should they get through the portal to where the two women had been taken. Another shot rang out and missed the car entirely, but it helped Nick make up his mind as to what steps to take next.

"Listen," he said to Manning, "you've gotta help me get through the portal."

Manning frowned, having no clue what the man meant.

Nick turned, disregarding the pain in his still-bleeding right leg. He pointed toward an area off to the left. "Over there, just under that light, there's a park bench. You see it?"

Manning saw the thing and nodded.

"At the back of the bench, in the middle and just above the top of the back, is a portal – a-a doorway – that leads to where Sarah Baker and Lisa Murdoch are." The expression on Manning's face told Nick the man at least believed a little of what he was saying and that was all Nick needed. "Whoever kidnapped them took them there and I'm afraid they're in some serious danger. That's why you've gotta help me get through that portal."

Nisrahali, who had heard nearly all of what the reporter had said, now turned to the young Mr. Green and asked, "You have discovered a portal through to another dimension... and the information is on the laptop?"

Still hugging the laptop like it was his only protection, Seth Green finally spoke. "I-I've discovered s-several portals to where Sarah Baker is. This was just the closest one."

Nick gasped at the boy's admission. He was surprised the boy was so quick to tell the two newcomers of the portals' existence.

"You are certain of this?" the Israeli quietly demanded. At the young man's nod, Nisrahali fell strangely quiet.

It was odd, but some instinct within Manning told him this was real. Sharapov and this kid had put themselves in the line of fire for this thing and they were both the best in their fields. Well, it was certainly no crazier than hair that could kill you! He decided he would trust his instincts.

His mind made up, he said, "Right. This is what we're gonna do. Nisrahali, you lay down cover fire while Sharapov and I get over and through that portal. Then, once we're gone, you take the kid and get the hell out of here." He reached for Sharapov to help the wounded man get ready to run.

"Wait," Nisrahali called.

But Manning was already on the move, his arm supporting Sharapov as he half dragged the man across parking lot two toward the bench beneath the lamp post near the Tesla Monument. Multiple shots rang out and several glanced off the pavement and even a nearby tree before the two men reached the bench. Nisrahali's shots rang out and the two men rushed toward the center back of the bench. And then... they were gone.

A gust of breath burst from Nisrahali's lips at the sight of the two men disappearing. More shots rang out and there was no time to think about what he had just witnessed. He had to get the kid safely away from this place.

He checked how much ammunition he still had. He was down to three rounds in his last clip. They might make it on those three rounds back to the rental Nisrahali and Manning had come here in, but there was another problem. Mystery Man and his team may have witnessed what had just happened. How could Nisrahali make sure they didn't go through the portal, too?

A diversion. They had to create a diversion – something to draw the team away from the Falls until Nisrahali could dispatch them for good. Only then could he come back and go through the portal himself.

As if someone had been listening to his thoughts, their first problem was suddenly solved with the arrival of the Niagara Falls Security team from the Aquarium area.

"NFPD!" someone yelled, and then the gunfire that had been pointed at Nisrahali and the kid turned in the direction of the newcomers to the party. Nisrahali didn't waste any time. He quickly directed Mr. Green toward the back end of Parking Lot Number Two where he and Manning had parked their rental. If they could make it to the rental car, Nisrahali was certain they would be safe.

Within minutes, the two were secured behind seatbelts, with Nisrahali in the driver's seat and Seth Green in the passenger seat. The Israeli ducked as low as he dared behind the wheel as they drove past the barrier at the entry/exit to the parking lot. He had no clue as to what had befallen the officers of the Niagara Falls Police Department who had so daringly laid their own lives down to save theirs, but he was certainly thankful to God for the fact that the Almighty had sent them to distract the terrorists long enough to allow Nisrahali's and Seth Green's escape.

He drove like a demon to get away from the scene. He had no idea where they should be headed and he asked, "Where can we go?" as he continued pressing on the accelerator.

Seth Green stared in stupefied admiration at the dark young man. That was the scariest experience he had ever been through, and yet here sat the most logical and sane person he had ever met, waiting for instructions.

"Um, I'll have to check," he stammered. He opened his laptop and punched a few keys. "We have to head northeast... to Bar Harbor."

"What? Where is Bar Harbor?"

"Just head northeast!" Green bellowed. He was scared, he was tired and he was starving. But most of all, he was freaked out by the fact that what he had just witnessed had proved his theories correct. Whatever might happen to him and this strange dark man tonight, Seth Green knew without a doubt that his research had led to the discovery of a doorway to another dimension.

How did one reconcile something like that? Sure, if he had had a life, Seth would have been able to tell friends and family about his discovery – and definitely his bosses. But he had no life. He only worked and studied. He had no true friends and his family didn't understand him at the best of times, let alone when he was in full-on geek mode talking about his work.

Logically, he had all the information he needed to get the strange dark man and himself to the next portal on his list, but could they get there without getting killed? Seth hoped so. Bar Harbor wasn't all that far away – just a few hours. And then the new portal was just a little farther. But judging from what Seth had already seen – and the fact that Sharapov had already been shot – Seth figured he and the dark foreigner would be lucky to make it out of New York State alive!

He opened his laptop again. He was thankful it had survived the assault at the Falls without any damage, and he looked up the next portal location. He had gotten a strong signal from that one the last time Sarah Baker's site had been updated and he believed it would be their best bet, since the Niagara Falls location was no longer a viable option.

If they could get there without mishap, they would be home free. He had to believe there would be sanctuary on the other side, if only they could get through the portal. The bad thing was, he believed the portal at this new spot was not exactly in an ideal location. All his data pointed to something bad. From what he could tell, it wasn't going to be like it was at Niagara Falls and this worried Seth. He closed up his laptop and sat scrunched down in his seat, hugging the thin computer close as he wondered how this dark stranger would take the news once they arrived at the new location.

***

"You don't really need me to go with you to this place just to hack into their systems, do you?" Lonnie asked as the old truck made its way down the final stretch of road to the research facility where they hoped Tameka Bradley would be found. They had been on the road for nearly ten minutes and Lonnie couldn't figure out why the Toti male had demanded he accompany the group on this mission. The look Santos threw him via the rearview mirror clearly indicated how insane *that* idea was before he said, "Believe me when I tell you the security systems at the facility are immune to the meager hacking skills of any hybrid or human."

Although the Toti's statement was insulting, Lonnie chose to overlook it. Instead, he asked, "So why did you specifically want *me* to be in on this mission?"

Carmen turned in her seat to regard him, her brow raised in display of her waning patience. A sliver of fear ran down his spine at that look and Lonnie quietly asked, "How did you know?"

Another look from Carmen, this time accompanied by her voice in his mind. *You are not the only one with such abilities*, it said. *Most* Juish *couples use telepathy for communication and can easily communicate with others who are gifted with the skill.*

Lonnie had suspected that Santos at least had figured out his secret and learning that Carmen also knew was no real surprise. But the fact that they knew and were clearly capable of doing everything he could do only served to confuse him more as he wondered why they should need him along, and he asked about it now.

"As I said," Santos explained. "This place is not a good place. We will *all* be in danger once inside the gate."

"But what can *I* do to protect anyone?" Lonnie asked, even more confused now.

Without looking away from the road before them, Santos explained, "When one becomes *Ju*, certain abilities develop. Each member of a *Juish* couple will develop his or her own skills over time and they usually complement the other member's skills. My best skill is in reading other people. I can know more about a person in ten minutes just by concentrating on him than that person probably knows about himself. I do not even have to be in the same location with him, as long as I know something about him – a face, a name…, anything. Do you understand?"

Only a second passed before Lonnie quietly said, "Yeah. I get it." He wasn't happy to learn about Santos' ability, but he was glad the guy had enough honor and respect for Lonnie that he had chosen to tell him about it.

"I do know a lot about you, Mr. Lonnergan Whittaker," Santos continued. "Just as I know a bit about our young *Joss* back there named Mr. Tyson Germaine Bradley."

Tyson turned to Lonnie and smiled, saying, "That's me."

Through the rearview mirror, Lonnie saw a corner of Santos' mouth raise a fraction at Tyson's remark. But when the Toti spoke again, his voice was back to business. "You both have the specific skills we will need for this mission, and that is why you were included."

The cab was silent a couple of minutes as each individual thought of the task ahead. Finally, Lonnie asked, "So what exactly is the plan? I mean, back at the diner I understood that you wanted Tyson and me to come along. But what's the *plan*? How do you plan to get us in at the gate and then into the building and all that?"

"The plan," Santos explained, "is to drive through the front gate after the guards open it to allow us through. Then, Tyson and I shall walk through the front door where we will be met by an employee who will act as our escort while we are inside."

Lonnie frowned. "Wait," he said, confusion lending a little too much credence to the good amount of fear already dancing along his veins. "First off, who's this employee? Somebody you already have on the inside? And where are Carmen and I gonna be? And, for that matter, how do you figure we'll just be let into the place at the front gate? Do you know these people? Have you been here before?"

Carmen turned to him again, this time simply for educational purposes – *his* education. "Santos can read others. Once he does this, I enter their minds. I have several skills that allow me to… take over for them for a time. That is how we get the hybrids to do what is needed."

Lonnie thought about what she had said, and then he asked, "So what you do is like mind control?"

She turned his words over in her mind a moment before explaining, "Not so much mind control as mind removal."

"Whoa, wait," Lonnie said as he shook his head. "You lost me there."

Santos interrupted, explaining what Carmen meant, "She connects with the hybrid's mind and ensures it is occupied in one way while she uses the hybrid's body to do other things. The hybrid is never aware of its body's actions, nor can it have any memory of the actions afterward."

"Well then, why couldn't she just control Tyson's mom's body and have her escape on her own without anyone having to go in after her?" Lonnie asked.

"It is more complicated than that," Santos said cryptically.

"Why is it more complicated?"

Santos glared at Lonnie through the rearview mirror and said tersely, "Because she is currently strapped to a table and is unable to move."

Immediately, Lonnie was contrite. He had forced Santos to say aloud something that might be upsetting to Tyson. "Oh," was all he said before shutting up. Tyson didn't react at all and Lonnie wondered if he had even heard the conversation.

Carmen resumed her description of her abilities, explaining, "One problem of me entering another mind is that I can only be in one mind at a time. I cannot be in my own at the same time as I am in someone else's mind. That means someone must keep watch over my body until I can return." She paused, a slight frown marring her wizened face before she said, "It is also dangerous. If the mind linked with mine regains consciousness while we are linked, I could become trapped inside the hybrid's subconscious mind. Then, the only way out for me is when that mind leaves its host body."

"You mean the person has to die before you can escape?" The woman nodded and a shiver ran down Lonnie's spine at her description of being trapped in someone else's subconscious mind until the person died.

"That is why you are needed," Santos told him. "You must monitor her body as well as the mind she chooses to let her know when to pull back."

"How?"

Santos chuckled at the question before answering. "I can sense others with abilities similar to my own. You are capable of monitoring others when you choose. You may not realize that is what you are doing, but it is."

Lonnie thought about this. If he was honest with himself, he would admit that he could actually read people pretty well. He usually knew what kind of mood someone was in just by being around them, even when they were trying to hide it from others. "But how can I monitor someone without being there with them?"

"You have been communicating telepathically with Tyson since not long after you met, yes?" Santos asked.

"Well, yeah." He had no idea how Santos could know that, but he was right.

Santos nodded. "It is like a muscle. The more you use it, the stronger and more powerful it becomes. I will communicate to you something about the individual Carmen needs to use. You will follow her thoughts to that individual's mind. From then on, you will monitor the mind she links with to ensure it remains focused on whatever task she assigns. Should you sense the mind switching focus back to its body, you must alert Carmen so that she can pull back in time before the mind becomes fully conscious."

The weight of this responsibility settled in on

Lonnie's shoulders like a ton of bricks and he wondered how on earth he was going to do this. If he failed, Carmen would be trapped inside someone else's subconscious mind. He suddenly felt a small hand take hold of his much larger one. Tyson silently stared up at him. Lonnie knew he had to at least try. If he didn't, Tyson and Demetrius might never see their mom again.

There was no more time for thinking on the matter as the truck slowed on its approach to the gate at their final destination. "Here we go," Santos said before rolling down the window to speak with the man in the guard shack.

Lonnie took a good look at the guard who leaned out the window of the little building to speak with Santos. The guy didn't look too bright and Lonnie decided to give it a try. He closed his eyes, keeping an image of the man's face in mind. He suddenly felt Carmen's mind there with him. For a moment, he was confused because of the way it felt inside his mind. But then she just kind of moved on as she linked with the guard's mind and Lonnie was left to just watch and listen. Amazingly, he knew the exact moment when the guy's mind became focused on whatever idea Carmen had directed it to and was astonished at how easy it had been.

Before he even realized what was happening, Carmen was back in Lonnie's mind telling him it was time to leave. When he opened his eyes again, he realized he and Carmen were alone in the truck's cab. The engine was off and the truck was parked just outside a huge building made entirely of concrete. There was no sign of either Santos or Tyson.

"They are already inside," Carmen said with her eyes trained on the building's front door.

A second later, Lonnie caught a flash of a name. It was a man's name, a researcher who was listed on an employee roster on a computer screen at the front desk just inside the building. Santos was sending the name, Aaron Vreeland. Aaron Vreeland... Aaron Vreeland... Aaron – Lonnie suddenly caught images of something someone deep inside the building was seeing. He caught thoughts and he instantly knew he was inside the head of this Aaron Vreeland guy.

Once more, Carmen's distinctive presence entered his mind. She fairly brushed past him on her way to the other mind. Then she was there, linked with Aaron's mind, directing it to a problem it had to solve. Thoughts of schematics and mathematical equations became that mind's focus and Lonnie could sense that this Aaron person was fully engaged. His entire world had narrowed down to solving a single problem and nothing else mattered.

Pulling back a little allowed Lonnie to hear and see not only what this Aaron guy was thinking, but also what his physical body was doing. Carmen was there, but she was concentrating on moving the body. Looking through the body's eyes, Lonnie saw that Santos and Tyson were there, walking with the man through the building's hallways. And so, the task had begun.

***

"Sir, they got away, but we have our best people on the case. We'll find them."

The man finished re-tying the knot holding his ponytail in place, throwing a mere nod toward his second in command. He was too angry about this latest defeat to speak. It was three hours past the time of the gunfight and he was still no closer to discovering the whereabouts of Seth Green than he had been when the last Niagara Falls policeman had fallen.

This operation had been planned down to the last second, so how had they lost the kid? As he replayed the encounter in his mind, he focused in on the arrival of the two armed men. Who were they and how had they known where to find the reporter and the kid? Obviously, they had come to rescue those two from him and his team. But how had they known? Had the reporter contacted them from Winnipesaukee?

Not only was there the question of who the two newcomers to the party were, but as he examined again and again the memory of everything that had happened, he realized only two had left in the car. The one he had shot and one of the armed men had not been with the other two in the car when it had left. He was sure of it. So, what had happened to them?

He skirted the bullet-hole ridden car the reporter had driven to the falls and found a blood trail. Following it, he ended up standing just behind a park bench. That was where the blood trail simply stopped. Pony-tail turned a full 360°, but there was no trace of more blood. He stared at the few drops of red staining the ground at his feet.

"Sir," his second in command said as he approached. "We've spotted a vehicle matching our target heading east on I-90. Should I send a team to intercept them?"

Pony-tail stared hard at the red drops another few seconds before straightening. "No," he finally said. "I'll take the lead on this one, myself." He turned and headed for his own vehicle. "Keep me updated and get me an exact location," he ordered over his shoulder.

"But what are we supposed to do with the dead cops?" his assistant demanded, wondering how on earth they would cover up this mess.

"Deal with it!" was the only response to come back.

***

Nisrahali pulled into a spot by the local seafood joint at Cottage & Rodick Streets in Bar Harbor, Maine. He had driven straight through and was exhausted, but they had at least made it to Bar Harbor. Seth Green had slept for many hours and Nisrahali was glad. It had given him a chance to reach out to several of his most trusted Mossad operatives as well as his best friend, Amina. She was the closest of his contacts and she had instructed him to meet her here at 4:00 AM. As he switched off the engine, he spotted Amina walking toward him along the deserted street.

She was a beautiful young woman, apparent even in the dim light from the street lamps. She would have made an exemplary wife for his brother, and Nisrahali felt the old pain stab at his heart as he thought of how sad and alone she had been left after his brother's death. He himself had been dealing with his own demons then and could not have helped her through her grief even had he stayed. One glance over at the young Mr. Green, who still clutched his laptop like a lifeline even in his sleep, and Nisrahali knew he could not spare a minute for Amina even now.

He climbed out of the rental car and greeted her in the proper manner.

"Yaniv," she said, smiling. "You look tired. Good, but tired."

Nisrahali merely smiled in response.

Amina searched his eyes for only a moment before getting down to business. "Well," she said, "I have news. We believe you are being tracked, so you must take my car." She handed him a set of keys as she spoke. "I will dispose of your vehicle." She then handed him another key, separate from the others, explaining, "This is for a room I rented last night at a hotel not far from here. You should go there and rest before anything else."

She gave him the name of the hotel and directions to it. Then she paused and put her hand on his arm, assuring him, "You will be safe there, if you stay inside – at least for a few days."

Nisrahali pocketed the hotel key and stood staring down at her a moment, his mind searching for a way to express how sorry he was that he had left, that he had turned his back on everyone who had known him before his brother's death. But nothing could convey the depths of his sorrow for his behavior, nor could he explain to her why he had needed to go.

Instead, he thanked her and then woke Seth. The two men cleaned out their few belongings from the car and followed Amina to her rental. She gave directions to the hotel and, after handing over the keys to the other car, Nisrahali thanked her once more before he once again left her alone. He didn't look in the rearview mirror as he drove away.

***

The group came to an elevator and entered when the doors slid open. Aaron Vreeland removed a key from his pants pocket and inserted it into a slot on the button control panel. Then he pressed an unmarked button. A small metal door slid open and Aaron waved his wrist before the opening. This, Lonnie realized as he watched from his vantage point in the vehicle, was a chip reader. Aaron apparently had a chip implant in his wrist and this was one of the security markers.

A computerized voice requested identification and Aaron said, "2917." The doors slid closed and the car automatically began its descent. Ding, ding, ding…. On and on it went and Lonnie could sense the noise intruding on Aaron's consciousness. He called out mentally to Carmen, hoping she could hear his warning. A second later, he felt her energies again. In Lonnie's mind, he felt Aaron Vreeland's absolute belief that he really needed to solve the problem he had thought of earlier. It would guarantee him the promotion he had been after and then he would be able to afford that new computer system he wanted.

Amazingly, Aaron was laser focused again on a particular part of a giant and complex math equation and Lonnie felt Carmen's energies calming as she did whatever she could to relax while camping out in Aaron's body. She was moving it and making it do and say whatever Santos needed it to for them to get to the place where Tameka Bradley was being held.

The dings stopped and Lonnie allowed his mind to see and hear both worlds again. Aaron's body was walking with Santos and Tyson again, this time through a well-lit concrete tunnel. At the end of the tunnel was what looked like a subway train. The trio boarded the train and it took off, whizzing through another tunnel. It traveled for some time. When it stopped, the three exited the train and went through a doorway just off the platform.

The room they entered was a crowded lab area. There were tables with sinks and all manner of chemicals in flasks and beakers. Some of the work stations had Bunsen burners heating things, and some had the vent hoods completely closed with the workers using built-in gloves protruding into the enclosed area to manipulate supposedly dangerous chemicals and other substances within. What struck Lonnie as he switched his focus was that not all of the workers in the lab appeared to be human!

He was amazed, and more than a little frightened, when he saw several Grays and other strange creatures working within the crowded room. But what really served to freak him out was when he spied a human head inside one of the enclosed work stations. The thing was connected to all manner of tubes and wires and appeared to be moving on its own. Lonnie looked closer and was terrified to discover the bodiless female head blinking as its eyes darted back and forth, as if it was searching for someone to come rescue it.

Concentrate! came Santos' voice in his mind and Lonnie clamped down on his emotions to once more concentrate on keeping tabs on Aaron Vreeland's thoughts. The man was still too busy with the equation to pay attention to what was actually going on with his body.

Lonnie's mind shifted to that double awareness again and he caught curious glances from others within the lab as Aaron's body passed through with his two guests. It appeared Santos was acceptable, but Tyson's presence drew a lot of attention.

Hurry.

It was more a feeling than anything, but Lonnie knew Carmen and Santos had "felt" it to each other. Another security measure – this one a retinal scanner and then a saliva DNA check. *Holy shit*, Lonnie thought. Santos hadn't been joking when he'd said this place was immune to human and hybrid hackers.

Lonnie checked himself. Aaron was still busy. His body continued leading the way through a door that opened out onto a long hallway with multiple doors on either side all the way down. Each door had a small window for viewing into the rooms beyond. It was at one of these doors that Aaron's body finally stopped. Instead of a door knob, there was another chip reader. Waving his wrist before it, the door opened and Aaron's body entered the room with Santos and Tyson close behind.

There, in the center of the room, was Tyson's mom. As Santos had said, she was strapped to an examination table. What he hadn't mentioned, however, were all the wires and tubes connected to or stuck into her. There were so many tubes that it appeared they were draining her of all of her blood. But there was no one else in the room and so Santos got to work removing everything from her. She was nude and Tyson made a valiant effort of looking anywhere but directly at her, but Lonnie could sense the boy's fear at seeing his mother so strung up like that.

Santos made quick work of it and was soon bundling the woman's body in a blanket he had miraculously found in a nearby cupboard. Aaron's body held the door as Tyson and then Santos exited, with Santos carrying Tyson's mom.

Too many workers in the lab, Lonnie thought he heard Santos say. *Must find another way out*. Lonnie himself concentrated on Aaron's mind and was quickly able to discover that there was indeed another exit at the other end of the hallway. The small group turned and headed in that direction and Lonnie realized Santos must have gathered the information from his mind. He watched closely as they hit another security marker. Once through that, it was not long before they were back at the subway. The return trip was a tense journey, but they soon exited the train. They hit another security marker before finally ending up in the room with the elevator again. They headed straight for it, and that's when their luck ran out.

The doors to the elevator slid open before they even got to it, revealing two Grays inside. Their large black eyes darted first to Aaron's body, then to Santos, who was still carrying the unconscious woman. As if that wasn't bad enough, they next spotted Tyson and that's when all Hell broke loose. It was as if they had just found the Devil himself, and they made a bee-line for him.

In that moment, an explosion of light darted outward from Tyson's eyes. His hair, which before had been shaved close to his scalp, grew a meter and a half, almost down to the floor. But it didn't stay down. Instead, it whipped up and out, striking the Grays anywhere it could reach. It appeared the creatures were impervious to pain as they lunged at the boy again and again, fighting off the dangerous hair as it sliced like razors through their skin.

A part of Lonnie realized there was very little blood coming from the creatures, even though Tyson's hair was cutting them all over. When several locks of hair wrapped around one of the creatures and ripped it in half, he understood why. These things, the Grays, were not truly living creatures. The core of the body was robotic.

Aaron's body was in the elevator and Santos hurried in with his burden. He yelled for Tyson, but there were already several other Grays entering the room. Tyson turned and gave his mother one last look before the elevator doors slid closed. There was a loud "BOOM" and then a flash as something rocked the elevator car, momentarily knocking out the light inside. When the light resumed, Tyson was there with his wicked long hair and sepia-colored glowing eyes looking as calm as could be, as if nothing spectacular had just happened.

As the elevator doors opened at the ground level, a loud alarm sounded and Santos suddenly screamed, "Carmen!"

Lonnie's mind was hit by an onslaught of confusion as Aaron Vreeland's mind became instantly conscious and aware of where he was and what he was doing. His vision of the old man carrying what looked like a body in a blanket was nothing compared to the fear that washed over him – and Lonnie – as he took in the wild-haired, glowing-eyed creature standing next to him!

In an instant, Lonnie was back in his own body in the truck. Carmen was unconscious in the front of the cab and Lonnie jumped over the middle storage compartment into the front seat, grabbing hold of her to shake her as he did everything he could think of to wake her up. He was still shaking her and screaming her name when the doors of the cab opened. Tyson climbed into the back seat while Santos shoved Tameka Bradley's unconscious body back there with him. He then climbed awkwardly into the back of the cab and wrapped his arm around Lonnie's throat, pulling him away from Carmen and over into the driver's seat of the truck.

"Drive!" Santos commanded.

Without hesitation, Lonnie turned the key in the ignition and shifted into gear. Ramming his foot down onto the accelerator, he drove like a bat out of hell out of the parking lot. He didn't even slow down at the gate, crashing through it instead as he careened at record speed out onto the two-lane blacktop outside it. Lonnie had no idea where he was headed nor even how he was able to drive because all he could think was, *Oh, God! Oh, God! Oh, God! She's trapped and it's my fault!*

Chapter 21

"Boss, we got a hit on the car," the underling said. When there was no response, he continued. "It was leaving Bar Harbor, Maine early this morning. But the strange thing is there was a woman driving and no one else was in the car."

"They've switched vehicles," was all Pony-tail said before cutting the connection. He would find them. Bar Harbor, Maine? Well, the trail had already led him to Massachusetts. He could be in Bar Harbor before nightfall. He jammed his foot down onto the accelerator. Fuck the cop who dared to pull him over when he was this close!

***

Seth Green was never so happy to see a hotel room in his life! He didn't undress, didn't check out the premises or even go to the restroom. Instead, still clutching his laptop tight against his chest, he crawled under the covers of the first bed he came to and immediately fell into what was probably the deepest sleep of his young life.

Nisrahali took a more cautious approach. He made sure the locks on the door were secured. Then he checked out the rest of the small room, looking under each bed and in the closet and bathroom to ensure they were truly alone. Amina had chosen a room closest to the stairwell, which could be useful should they need to make a quick getaway. She had come through, yet again.

As he finally doused the light and sank down onto the other bed, Nisrahali wished there was some way he could tell her how important what she was doing was. He wished he could find a way to repay her for her kindness and her blind devotion. There wasn't time now for him to do the latter. And as for the former, his last thought before sleep took his mind was that there simply were no words in existence to explain the importance of this mission – neither to her nor to anyone else.

***

Ana and Tobin sat in the Jeep simply looking at one

another, taking in the physical changes everyone could see in them and the new mental capabilities no one but they knew about. Had the Toti not had a name for what they were now, Tobin believed he would not have been able to handle the transformation so well. Ana appeared to be concerned only with Bianca's and his well-being.

From the thoughts to which he was privy from her mind, he knew she cared not one whit about any changes she herself had incurred, merely for the changes their daughter and he had taken on. The fact that she was okay gave Tobin a tremendous sense of relief and he smiled as he kissed the back of her hand. Whatever this was, whatever was happening, they would get through it.

"What's a Mahdii?" Stacy asked from the front passenger seat of the vehicle, her question breaking the spell that had enveloped the two Jus.

The group had watched the others drive off in the truck and had simply been sitting in silence in the parking lot of the diner ever since. They had waited for nearly two hours already. They had no clue how long this rescue operation was going to take or even how they would know when or if it had been accomplished. And now they were all looking for anything to talk about to help pass the time.

Tobin was sitting behind the driver's seat where Matt sat and he leaned forward toward the middle opening in the front and explained, "The Mahdii were a race of beings that once ruled the Universe."

Stacy chewed on that information for a few moments before turning toward the back and asking, "So why would Santos and Carmen tell you to find them?"

"The Toti are known for a particular legend," Tobin said on a heavy sigh. "It was one that was started long ago – thousands of years ago, in fact." At her expectant look, he looked around and saw more pairs of eyes trained on him. "As I said, it supposedly happened thousands of years ago. I have heard tell of many human legends of that time. There was a great flood and the stories were passed down throughout most Earth cultures, though only the Watchers' stories involve the Mahdii."

He could tell the others were confused and he continued, "You see, the whole planet was at war. Some of the battles were so fierce that many feared it would be the end of life here. Several groups who had built outposts here took as many humans... er, hybrids as they could and simply left to avoid being caught up in the conflict. Most never returned."

He paused and asked, "You have heard of entire peoples simply disappearing from the Earth?" At the responding nods, he explained, "That was what happened in several areas around the globe. To save an already-infiltrated population, a host species simply chose to remove the hybrids from the threat of war."

With all eyes still rapt with wonder, he continued his tale about the Mahdii. "The Toti had a small outpost here and had decided to abandon the planet as well. But before they could depart, it is said a small group of Toti encountered a Mahdii warrior just outside their outpost.

"You must understand that the Mahdii were believed to be extinct, that they had been wiped out after some Great War many eons ago. But the Toti were adamant that they had seen a Mahdii. So instead of returning to their home planet, they chose to join the small group of Watchers in hopes of finding the Mahdii."

"Why?" Matt asked, completely enthralled with the story now.

Tobin shook his head and shrugged, explaining, "I do not know. It had something to do with the current rulers of the Universe, but I was selected to return to Earth before my lessons got that far into the legend. I do know that several other species who had planned to abandon Earth at the time of the flood also chose instead to join the Watchers after learning of the sighting. So, it appears the Toti are not the only ones who believe in the importance of the legend."

Stacy adjusted her position so that most of her was sitting backward in the seat so she would have a better view of those in the back of the giant SUV. "You said you were 'selected to return to Earth'. So, you were born on Earth?"

"Yes," Tobin confirmed, nodding.

"And you're half-human?"

Again, Tobin nodded.

"Which of your parents was human? Your mom or your dad?"

Before Tobin could respond, Ana screamed and her whole body jerked away from the back of the vehicle where Bianca and Demetrius sat. Tobin turned to see what was wrong and then he, too, started and backed away. Demetrius had already scooted as far away from little Bianca as he physically could within the confines of the vehicle and Tobin reached to help the boy climb over the seat up into the middle section.

Bianca sat alone in the third-row seat. Her eyes, which had sported a dim glow earlier, now glowed quite brightly from within, and had become a bright sepia color. But that wasn't the thing that had frightened everyone so. As they watched, long strands of dark hair moved about, as if searching for something or someone. It was kind of eerie watching the tresses slowly waving around, looking for all the world like snakes searching for food.

It had just happened out of the blue, and no one inside the vehicle had an explanation.

As the five others sat wide-eyed watching this new thing, Tobin hoped the Toti would return soon.

***

Two days had passed and Seth Green shivered as he followed the dark Nisrahali out of the hotel room and down the stairs to the car the woman had given them the other morning. It was dark now and the lack of light lent an eeriness to the mission. There was no one around and the two men silently made quick work of buckling their seatbelts. Within minutes, they were heading out of Bar Harbor and down Park Loop Road. Their final destination was not too far from Bar Harbor, but it wasn't the driving part that so worried Seth. It was the last leg of their journey that had his stomach all in knots.

Nisrahali still had no clue about the task that awaited. He knew only the general location to which he had to drive.

Neither man spoke a word as they drove on through the night. One would have thought the bright moonlight would make things less spooky, but instead, it made every tree shadow appear to move and had quite the opposite effect on the two men.

As they rounded a curve to the left on the road, Seth pointed out the main parking lot on the upper right. Nisrahali parked the car and the two prepared for their hike. They crossed the road and found the stone steps that would lead them to their final destination. The sound of the waves crashing up ahead grew louder as they walked, drowning out all other sounds.

Neither man noticed the shadow following close behind them.

As they broke through the tree line, mist from the spray lashed their faces as the wind howled against the rocky façade. Twenty feet before them, the earth simply stopped. Nisrahali turned to Seth, shouting above the din of the crashing waves, "Is this where we're supposed to be?"

"What?!" Seth shouted back, unable to hear anything above the roar at the base of the cliffs.

The Israeli turned back toward the ocean, wondering what his next move should be. He figured the best thing would be to take one more look at the location on Seth's laptop. As he turned back toward the young man, a movement off to his right caught his eye. Without hesitation, he tackled Seth to the ground just in time to keep the large figure from ramming into him and an angry grunt sounded as the attacker tripped and fell a few yards away from where Nisrahali lay on top of the grad student.

He climbed to his feet, reaching down to help Seth up – all the while keeping a keen eye on the party crasher. He could just make out a dark ponytail in the bright light of the moon. The mystery man had found them. But how, Nisrahali wondered.

He allowed his gaze to stray from the still figure just for a moment, long enough to ask where they were to go next. Seth's response had him turning completely away from the newcomer, as he exclaimed, "We have to do what?!"

Heavy mist once again lashed into Seth's face as he repeated, "We have to jump!" He pointed to the center of the cliff's edge directly before where he stood. "We have to jump right there!"

Nisrahali turned, peering at the area at which Seth pointed, the still prone figure of the mystery man all but forgotten as he stared at this new nemesis. Was the young man insane? He wanted to jump off Otter Cliff? There had to be some other way. He turned back to Seth, desperate for an alternative to what must be certain suicide. But Seth wasn't looking at him. Instead, as Nisrahali followed the young man's gaze, he realized the young genius was staring down the barrel of a pistol.

Nisrahali didn't even think about what he was doing. Instinct took over and he grabbed Seth's arm, jerking him out of the way of the bullet that fired and dragging him over the cliff with him. The last thing he saw before blackness swamped his consciousness was a tunnel of blue, green, purple and gold swirls of light.

***

When Lonnie finally pulled to a stop beside the SUV in the small parking lot outside the diner where they had eaten earlier in the day, a small part of him realized he had been driving on autopilot. But the main part of his mind remained focused on one horrible fact: Carmen was lost – trapped inside Aaron Vreeland's mind until such time as the man died!

Matt and Stacy climbed out of the SUV, followed closely by Demetrius, as all three approached the truck. As soon as the driver's side door was opened, they bombarded the returning party with questions. But their questions dried on their tongues the moment they saw Carmen's unconscious form in the front passenger seat.

Tobin and Ana had by this time emerged from the SUV with little Bianca. But Bianca didn't look the same as she had when the rescuers had left. Her eyes glowed much more than they had done before and her hair, which had been about waist-long before, was now a thick black curtain that hung near to the ground. The ends of the strands lifted occasionally on their own, as if searching for some object. When the object of interest was not found, the ends would then return to hanging limply near the ground.

Lonnie, who was still facing his inward crisis, barely took notice of the changes in the girl, especially since Tyson had emerged from the facility earlier sporting similar changes to his own anatomy. Santos was too busy squirming out of the back of the cab and then retrieving Carmen from the front passenger side to notice. The group standing outside the truck could see portions of another person who was lying unmoving across the back seats of the truck's cab. Matt and Demetrius waited for Santos to clear Carmen away before leaning in to get the other unconscious person from the back. That's when they got their first glimpse of Tyson.

Demetrius, who had been so glad to see the truck pull up in the parking lot, now simply lowered his head and stepped aside. He didn't even want to look at the thing that used to be his brother.

"Uh, Stace," Matt calmly called out.

"Huh?"

"Um, you might want to, uh…," his words trailed off as he pulled back to clear a path for her to see Tyson's new look.

She started, but then she turned to regard Bianca, motioning for her to come over to the truck. Stacy, Matt and Demetrius backed away as Bianca approached. The moment her eyes connected with Tyson's, a huge grin spread across her face and she ran the rest of the way over to him. Tyson hopped down from the truck's cab and hugged her close, his newly-lengthened hair intermingling with hers into a semi-woven blanket of strands. They spoke not a word – at least, not that those standing nearby could hear.

Lonnie heard, but his mind was still consumed by the fact that Carmen was probably lost for years to come because of his inability to pay attention. In abject misery, he watched as Santos laid Carmen's unconscious form in the bed of the old pick-up truck. The Toti male was so gentle with her. It was painfully obvious how much he cared for the female and

Lonnie's misery doubled. A moment later, however, his mind was consumed with confusion as Santos backed away from Carmen and turned. He headed back up to the cab of the truck where he removed a pistol from beneath the driver's seat.

Is he gonna shoot her? Lonnie wondered incredulously.

The older Toti male rounded the truck and headed directly for the SUV. Lonnie silently followed behind him. Whatever plan Santos had in mind, Lonnie would help him. After all, this was all his fault.

"Hey!" Matt called. "Where are you two going?"

Without turning or stopping, Santos called over his shoulder, "I am going to kill the bastard!"

That's when it happened.

Suddenly, there was a noise. It sounded like a loud horn blowing. It rang out over the land, over the hills, over the plains, over everything and everywhere. The people inside the diner trickled out into the parking lot, some turning all the way around, as each person sought the source of the din. It sounded like it came from the sky, but there was no visible source no matter where one looked. The sound simply was, and it wasn't stopping.

Lonnie, who was just as confused as everyone else, noticed Santos had stopped in his preparations for the journey back to the center to kill Aaron Vreeland. The Toti male looked almost pale as he stared up at the sky. Then the creature did the strangest thing. He headed straight back over to the truck bed, where he bundled up Carmen's still-unconscious form and returned her to the front passenger seat of the truck.

"What are you doing now?" Lonnie shouted to him in an attempt to be heard over the loud noise.

As he spoke the last word, the noise stopped.

"We must head south," Santos simply said.

"What?" several of the others asked. Everyone was confused and still wondering what the hell the noise had been.

"We must head south... now!" Santos said. "It is not

safe here."

"But I thought you were going to kill somebody," Matt reminded him.

Santos threw him a dirty look, barely concealing his dislike of the man. "If we stay here," he finally managed to say, "we all die."

Despite the shock that statement sent through each member of the group, within five minutes' time the entire team had broken up again into two groups. One group consisting of Matt, Stacy, Tyson, Tobin, Demetrius and the unconscious Tameka Bradley were in the SUV and everyone else was in the old extended cab truck. Without any questions, the whole crew was on the road again with the SUV trailing close behind the old truck. They still had no clue what the noise was, nor where it had originated. Both Carmen and Tameka Bradley were still unconscious and helpless. Lonnie still felt an overwhelming sense of guilt anytime he thought of Carmen's plight. And all any of them besides Santos knew was that they were headed south.

Ten minutes after they hit the road, Lonnie's cell rang. It was Stacy requesting that they pull over.

"There is no time for this!" Santos barked in frustration as Lonnie eased over onto the side of the road.

It wasn't long before Matt and Stacy were standing beside the truck's front door on the driver's side. Lonnie rolled down the window.

"Hey," Stacy said, a little breathless. "I think we need to turn around and head back to Cali. I mean, my sister and everybody there needs to know what's going on and I can't get through to her. I don't know if it's just that there's no service out here or if something's happened or what. But I need to at least contact her to let her know there's some kind of danger coming."

Lonnie held up his cell, reminding her that she had reached him with no difficulty.

"Look, I know. I would just feel better knowing I had done whatever I could to warn her."

Santos looked her directly in the eye and said flatly, "No."

She stood in shock for a moment, just staring at the Toti male, before both she and Matt demanded to know why they couldn't spare at least enough time to go somewhere where they would be able to call from a landline.

"For what purpose?" he demanded. At their blank stares, he continued, explaining, "There is not enough time for them to leave where they are and I do not know where they could go that would be safe."

"What about where we're going?" Matt demanded. "Why couldn't they head south to wherever it is we're headed?"

"Yeah," Stacy said. She then asked, "And where exactly is it we're heading?"

Santos sat cradling Carmen's unconscious form in his arms as he debated what to say. Finally, he relented somewhat and said, "We can stop at our home before continuing south. We will need supplies anyway and there are a few items I need for the journey. There is a communicator there you may use to contact your sister. It is much more powerful than any communication device from this world and you should be able to reach her." He paused before dropping the next bombshell. "But there is nothing you can do for her," he said quietly. "I do not even know for certain that *we* will make it." He slowly shook his head, hugging Carmen closer as he said, "There is so little time remaining."

With his nearly-whispered words still hanging in the air, Matt and Stacy agreed to this new plan without argument. They returned to the SUV and remained quiet as they followed in the wake of the old pick-up. If the others within the SUV were curious as to what had been discussed on the side of the road, they kept a tight lid on their curiosity. Not a word was spoken as the two vehicles traveled on into the darkening evening.

It was sometime after 2:00 AM when they pulled up in front of the old ranch house where their journey had started. There was no way Demetrius was leaving the SUV without his mom, but everyone else got out and headed for the front door of the place. Ana volunteered to stay in the truck with Carmen so that Santos could show Stacy and Matt where his alien communication device was and how to use it. Then Santos and several of the others would gather supplies for their journey. In the meantime, everyone else would use the restroom that had rarely been used by the Toti couple.

Tyson and Bianca appeared relieved to be together again, as they immediately clasped hands and joined the rest of the group that was headed for the house's front door. Santos was the first to enter the house, followed closely by Matt and Stacy, then Tobin and Lonnie. As Santos reached for a light switch, a heavy sense of foreboding blanketed Lonnie's consciousness and he reached out to still the Toti's hand, shouting, "No! Santos, wait!"

Epilogue

Jarba started as a sound disrupted the Jess' *tale. The* Ju *was no longer speaking. Instead, she was whispering calming sounds to the Prince as he regained consciousness. Jarba's first instinct was to slap the bitch away from the ailing Prince. But she quashed the impulse as memory of the creature's dangerous hair resurfaced within her mind. In mere seconds, the Prince had opened his eyes and was asking for assistance to stand.*

The dark Jess *backed away from him, and Jarba, along with several others, rushed in to help their leader to stand. Once it was clear the Prince had sufficiently recovered to be moved to his suite of rooms, Jarba ordered the Royal Guard to see to his safe passage. She then returned her attention to the* Juish *couple still at her feet. The* Joss *was now awake, what with his* Jess *supplying him with her life-giving energies, and Jarba sensed the two planned to leave this place – something she could not allow.*

As this thought raced through her mind, Joss *Tobin's voice captured the attention of her innermost mind.* You need not fear us, *it said.* We have vowed to remain until the end of the tale, for you must be made to understand.

Jarba narrowed her gaze, wondering what new game this was and thinking that some way, somehow, she had to gain the upper hand with these creatures. It was clear each one knew more than he or she was letting on and the knowledge they carried was possibly vital to the Samarean race's survival. But what was most clear of all was the fact that the Prince would not survive without these two until he was reunited with Jarba's mother. And until that happened, Jarba would do whatever necessary to keep the Juish *couple near her beloved Prince – no matter the consequences!*

www.ingramcontent.com/pod-product-compliance
Lightning Source LLC
Chambersburg PA
CBHW031319280626
47169CB00019B/2186